RUNAWAYS

on the
Inside Passage

JOE UPTON

ALASKA NORTHWEST BOOKS®

ANCHORAGE • PORTLAND

**To my mother, Ann Upton, with deep appreciation for setting my feet
on the creative path so many years ago.**

LIBRARY OF CONGRESS CATALOGING-IN-PUBLICATION DATA

Upton, Joe, 1946-
   Runaways on the Inside Passage / Joe Upton.
      p. cm.
Summary: Abandoned in Seattle by their mother, thirteen-year-old twins join an
elderly fisherman friend on the long and dangerous voyage to Alaska in hopes of
finding their father by Christmas.
   ISBN 0-88240-564-0 — ISBN 0-88240-565-9 (pbk.)
   [1. Twins—Fiction. 2. Brothers and sisters—Fiction. 3. Fishers—Fiction.
   4. Voyages and travels—Fiction. 5. Inside Passage—Fiction. 6. Sea stories.]
   I. Title.
      PZ7.U583 Ru 2003
      Fic]—dc21
                              2002000697

Alaska Northwest Books®
An imprint of Graphic Arts Center Publishing Co.
P.O. Box 10306, Portland, OR 97296-0306
(503) 226-2402
www.gacpc.com

President: Charles M. Hopkins
Associate Publisher: Douglas A. Pfeiffer
Editorial Staff: Timothy W. Frew, Ellen Harkins Wheat, Tricia Brown,
   Jean Andrews, Kathy Matthews, Jean Bond-Slaughter
Copy Editor: Laura Carlsmith
Production Staff: Richard L. Owsiany, Susan Dupere
Design: Andrea L. Boven / Boven Design Studio, Inc.
Maps: Joe Upton

Printed in the United States of America

CONTENTS

ACKNOWLEDGMENTS

Several times, when I was a commercial fisherman in Alaska, I encountered the mysterious power of the ice. Once, in a big king crab boat, we were caught by the Copper River wind—a blast of frozen air that coated our boat with a dangerously heavy layer of ice. We "suited up" in heavy, insulated clothes and rain gear, roped up with safety lines, and cautiously began using baseball bats to break the ice off the rails and rigging. Our brand new 120-foot boat and her experienced crew were lucky to have survived this encounter.

Another time, I had gone to Petersburg in late November in my thirty-two-foot troller to get a load of lumber for our cabin in Point Baker. A hard freeze came in the night and when we left early the next morning, we found a bay skinned over with ice. Our bow cut a lane through it, with little broken pieces skittering away across the unbroken ice around us, and it was magical.

And so, when I came to write my first novel, I wanted to share with readers this powerful phenomenon.

I am especially grateful for the efforts of Tricia Brown, Ellen Wheat, and Laura Carlsmith for showing me so many valuable aspects of the novelist's craft.

I also wish to thank Foss Maritime for their kind permission to use their name.

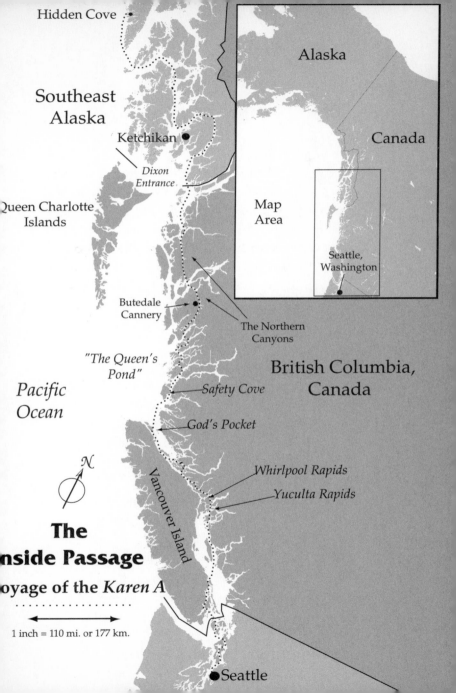

Hidden Cove

Southeast
Alaska

Ketchikan

Dixon
Entrance

Queen Charlotte
Islands

Alaska

Canada

Map
Area

Seattle,
Washington

Butedale
Cannery

The Northern
Canyons

"The Queen's
Pond"

British Columbia,
Canada

Pacific
Ocean

Safety Cove

God's Pocket

Whirlpool Rapids

Yuculta Rapids

N

The
nside Passage

oyage of the *Karen A*

1 inch = 110 mi. or 177 km.

Vancouver Island

Seattle

CHAPTER 1

Of Children and Boats

 "I dreamed of Christmas up North last night," David said slowly, looking out the bus windows at the rain-blurred streets.

The bus slowed and Annie stood up. "C'mon, David," she said. "Pull up your hood. Stay dry."

The bus driver looked at the kids, wondering again where they had come from, and why they lived in such an unfriendly part of Seattle.

Hoods up, heads down, the twins stepped the best they could around the places where there was water instead of sidewalk. The morning hadn't been rainy, unusual for November, and they hadn't worn boots.

They stopped on the narrow porch of the run-down duplex, stamped the water off their sneakers, and opened the door.

The furniture was gone.

"Annie, look," David said, startled, "everything's gone!"

She stepped wordlessly inside, crossed the small living

room, and looked into the bedrooms and tiny kitchen alcove. Except for two sleeping bags and several boxes of clothes, the house was empty. Without furniture it seemed stark, dingy, and tired.

"Close the door," Annie said quietly. "You're letting the heat out."

David stood there for a long moment. A gust of wind eddied across the little porch, and a few raindrops pittered on the floor. Finally he closed the door. It echoed, oddly loud in the empty space. He put down his bookbag and looked around.

"Maybe we're moving again," he said hopefully. "Maybe Mom got that house over by the park she kept talking about."

Annie shrugged her backpack off onto the built-in table in the eating nook, rummaged around, and pulled out a package of spaghetti. She rinsed a dirty pot in the sink, filled it with water, and put it on the stove with the resigned air of a thirteen-year-old who had made many such meals.

"At least the electricity is still on," she said.

David slumped his thin body onto the bench, elbows on the table, shivered involuntarily, and peered through the window at the rainy world outside. The streetlight on the corner shone on shuttered buildings and abandoned cars.

Headlights appeared in the distance and David straightened up, studying them as they came closer. But it was only a truck headed for the warehouse complex at the end of the street.

"What'd she say to you last night?" Annie asked. "Did she mention anything about moving? She didn't even talk to me."

David sighed. "She was bummed. She'd lost a bunch of money gambling again. I think she'd been drinking, too."

"What else?"

"She just said she'd be in real bad trouble if she didn't get the money."

The water began to boil. Annie put in the spaghetti and slumped down across from David. For a long while there was only the drip of the water outside and the soft bubbling of the spaghetti water. They didn't say much to each other at supper.

In the morning there was no heat. Their breath made white clouds in the air above them as they lay in their sleeping bags.

"They must have turned off the gas," Annie said.

"Mom?!" David cried out, hoping she had come back in the night.

But there was no answer. Annie scurried into the kitchen, turned on the electric oven, opened its door, and snuggled back into her bag until she could feel the heat seeping into the room.

"At least it's warm in school," David said as he warmed himself by the open oven. "Maybe we should tell someone there what's happening. Maybe they'll find us some furniture and get the heat turned back on."

"Don't you dare!" his sister turned on him angrily. "Do you want to be in another foster home like last time?"

"Why couldn't they just help us stay here until Mom comes back?"

"Because it doesn't work that way."

Annie made oatmeal and used the last of the bread to

make peanut butter sandwiches for their lunches.

"Dad wouldn't let this happen to us," David said.

"Dad's in Alaska, and he doesn't even care about us any-more. He hasn't written in two years."

"He writes."

Annie stopped in mid-bite. "What?"

"He still writes. I'm sure of it. Once, before we started moving so much, I saw an envelope with Dad's writing on it in the trash; it was addressed to us. I asked Mom about it, but she snatched it away and said I was mistaken. But I saw the postmark. It was from Alaska. Sitka, I think. It had to be Dad."

"Why didn't you tell me?"

"I don't know. Mom always said such bad things about Dad, and you always agreed with her."

"I only agreed with her because she got so ugly when I didn't. Of course I love Dad. But why hasn't he come to see us or tried to get us?"

"Maybe he doesn't know where we are," David said. "We've been moving so much, we hardly get mail anymore. Maybe he came down to get us and couldn't even find us."

In the afternoon, when David and Annie came back from school, the landlord's car was there and the front door was open.

"Where'd she go?" the man said brusquely when they came up the steps.

"She didn't say," Annie stammered.

"She didn't tell you anything?" He was a rough-looking man, and he gave the kids a hard look. "She left you, didn't she? Just skipped out on her kids just like she skipped out on the rent." He picked up the phone, put it to his ear, then slammed it back down. "You kids stay here until I get back. I'll find a phone that works and get someone to take care of you. Some people shouldn't be allowed to have kids." The door closed and he was gone into the cold November dusk.

"Get your stuff," Annie said. "We've got to get out of here."

"What do you mean?" David complained, turning on the oven, opening the door, and standing in front of it. "It's cold, and I'm hungry. Where would we go?"

Annie dragged a duffel bag out of the closet and started stuffing clothes into it from the boxes on the floor. "Get some plastic bags from under the sink for our sleeping bags. You know who he's going to call, don't you? The cops. And then we'll be split up and put into one of those foster homes again, and Mom'll be in real trouble again. Is that what you want?"

"I just want to get something to eat," David said.

"I got some Oreos at the store," she said over her shoulder as she fumbled under the sink for plastic bags. "We can eat them on the road. Get the money from the jar. We got to get out of here, quick!"

Fifteen minutes later the children were huddled in the shadows next to a dumpster at a truck loading dock, catching their breath and looking down the long street toward their house. As they watched, two cars turned the corner and stopped in front of the house. One was a police cruiser.

Annie drew her body back, but kept watching.

"It's that same man who took us away before," she said. "See, I told you that guy was going to call the cops."

David huddled deeper behind the dumpster. Annie

could see the men coming out of the house and looking up and down the street before leaving. One car turned the corner and disappeared out of sight, but the cruiser moved slowly as the officers peered out to the left and right.

Only after a long while did they dare emerge from their hiding place.

"What do we do now?" David said miserably, beginning to shiver. "I just want to eat and get warm again. So what if it's a foster home?"

Annie stretched to get the kinks out of her body, and dug into her bag for the Oreos. As they ate the cookies they heard the low throbbing sound of a Burlington Northern railroad switching engine nearby, and the faint toot of a ferry's whistle out in Puget Sound. Then the wind came on a little harder, bringing the first of the rain, and she knew it was no night to be on the streets.

"We'll go see old Lars Hansen," she said finally. He was one of their father's best friends. "We'll be safe there. Maybe we can stay on his boat until we figure out what to do next." She stood up, moved out of the shadows, and looked around for a moment, orienting herself. "C'mon," she said, "let's get going. Maybe we can get there before this rain gets any worse."

But the drizzle thickened into steady rain, and the wind increased. They trudged through a dark complex of warehouses, railroad tracks, and equipment yards near the waterfront. Once they saw the flicker of a smoky fire beneath a railroad overpass and approached it, staying in the darkness, and studying the homeless men around the fire. There were some opened cans steaming on a makeshift grill, and off to one side were sleeping bags or blanket rolls laid out beneath plastic. The men's faces seemed hard and unfriendly, and after a last envying look at the fire, Annie nudged David, and they picked up their bags and stepped out again into the rain.

It was almost eight o'clock when they came to Fishermen's Terminal on Lake Union. Connected to Puget Sound by locks, it was the winter home for much of the Alaska salmon fleet.

Annie's pace quickened as she recognized the dock where Lars kept his old salmon boat, but then as they got closer, she suddenly stopped.

"What's the matter now?" asked David. "This is the dock, isn't it? How come you stopped?"

"Yes, but it's full of boats. When we were here before, it was just Lars's and a few others. Now there are so many. I'm not sure exactly which one is his."

Dim in the light of a single swaying bulb were dozens of boats, large and small, rafted up three and four deep to the docks. Most were Alaska fishing boats, tied up for the long winter, their crews and owners scattered among the houses clustered on the hills that rose on all sides around the lake.

"Do you remember what Lars's boat looked like?" Annie asked.

"Just a big boat," David answered quietly, peering out among the darkened shapes for some clue.

"Hey, look," he said suddenly, "there's a TV on in that one. If it's not Lars, maybe they'll know where he is."

Annie squinted into the rain, making out just the dimmest flicker of what could be a television among the dark shapes at the end of the dock.

"Good eyes, David. Let's go!"

Soon they stood in the rain near the end of the dock. The boat with the light in the window was tied on the outside of another boat. They clambered down onto the first boat, and stood for a moment on the far side of the deck, peering at the lighted porthole on the cabin of the outside boat. It was definitely a television, the bluish light dancing behind a porthole misted over with condensation.

"R-r-recognize the b-boat?" David said, shivering all over. Now that they had stopped walking, he suddenly realized how cold and wet he was.

Annie walked closer to see the bow of the tidy, white forty-footer, trying to make out the name in the gloom.

"K-A- . . . *Karen A*! Yes, this is it! This is Lars's boat! Come on!" She walked quickly back to David, took his hand, and they stepped onto the *Karen A*, crossed the deck to the cabin, and rapped on the door.

After a long moment the pilothouse door slid to one side and a balding head peered out.

"Who is here on such a night?" the man said in a heavily accented voice. He studied the figures, his eyes adjusting to the dark. He reached behind him, and a light went on halfway up the mast, bathing the back deck in a pool of white.

Surprised, he exclaimed, "Ah, Annie and David Ross, for crying out loud!" He waved them in, stepping aside to let them pass. "Come in out of rain, children." He hugged each of them as they came inside, and then stepped back to look at them.

"Uff-da! You're soaked, both of you. Here, follow me," he said, leading them down the steep, short stairs into the cozy fo'c'sle, the forward lower part of the boat with bunks and a small cooking area, or galley. "Come down by stove, and get out of those wet clothes." Then he saw their backpacks, and the plastic-bagged sleeping rolls. "Lord, what's happening, children? Did your ma go on a tear again?"

"Oh, Lars," Annie put her face against his shoulder, shaking all over from relief and cold. Her resolve crumbled and the story all came tumbling out. "We didn't know what to do. We came home yesterday and the furniture was gone and there was no sign of Mom and then today the landlord was there. He left to call somebody, and we had to get out of there. We just can't go into a foster home again." Finally she broke down and started sobbing, "Oh, Lars, I'm so glad we found you. We didn't know where else to go."

When Annie had at last stopped shaking, Lars drew a dark blue curtain across the forward part of the fo'c'sle, and pushed her gently toward it. "You've got to get out of those wet things first, child. Pass them out, and I'll hang them by the stove."

Annie disappeared behind the curtain with her backpack, and David took off his jacket and backed up until he was almost touching the small oil stove, soaking up the wonderful, welcome heat.

"It's an awful night out there, Lars. I don't know what we would have done if you hadn't been here. There was a dry place by an overpass we found, but some homeless men were camping there." David was still shivering and his teeth were starting to chatter.

Lars rummaged in a cupboard until he found some cocoa. He spooned some powder into two cups and added hot water from the kettle on the stove.

"Have a mug-up of this, boy. It'll get chill out o' your bones. You did right, not stopping by the overpass. Them's a rough crowd that stays there. Sometimes they get to drinking that hard old wine. There's no telling what they might do when they drink so."

David sipped the hot cocoa, still shivering violently, and holding his mug with both hands so as not to spill. He was standing so close to the stove that the back of his pants was beginning to steam.

"Take them wet pants off, David. You have to get dry 'fore you get warm." Lars took David's cup and motioned at the little puddle that had begun to form on the well-worn floor of the fo'c'sle.

David looked down, surprised, as if realizing for the first time that his pants were soaked too. He shucked them off and fumbled in his backpack until he found a dry pair, and resumed his spot by the stove as he pulled them on.

"Ta-da!" Annie pulled the curtain aside and stepped into the light as if making a grand entrance. She elbowed David over a bit and stood beside him, smelling the cocoa, and soaking up the heat of the stove.

Her damp brown hair shone in the light, and she put down the cup of cocoa, took a brush, and began stroking her hair out so that it would dry quickly.

She had still been a child when he'd last seen her, Lars suddenly realized. Had it been only six months ago? In the spring, they'd both come down one day after school, to say good-bye and wish him a good season in Alaska. And now a young woman stood across from him brushing out her hair. Such a change in such a short time. He'd never had children to watch grow up and was surprised that the sight of Annie, so frail and vulnerable and strong all at once, touched him so.

"Ooooh, it just feels so good to be here, Lars," she said. "It's so warm and cozy. Dad's boat must be like this. I can barely remember it anymore, but I think it was like this." She waved around at the small space, every nook filled with cupboards, bookshelves, clothes neatly hung on hooks, a little sink, and a small table. "Like a miniature family room, bedroom, and kitchen all put together, and everything so tidy."

The old man laughed softly. "Is not always so clean. When you're on the fish, there is hardly time to eat and sleep when you get anchor down at the end of the day, and the cleaning gets put off."

"Did you see him, Lars?" David asked, quiet and serious. "I know you usually do. Did you see him this year? How was he doing and what did he say?"

"You mean Peter, '*Sea Bird* Pete'?" A smile crossed old Lars's wrinkled face. "Yah, 'course I see him. He is half the reason I go up there anymore, old and crippled as I am.

"When your dad bought his first boat, the old *Katrina*, I helped out. I showed him how to fix engine. He was just beginning, so I showed him where fish were. And now your dad is helping me. Peter always fishes near me. I fish alone, so I go in early unless the fishing is very good. Peter has crew, both of them young and strong to put in long days. But if my light is still on when they come into the anchorage, he will stop and we have nice chat or nip of rum maybe, before they anchor up."

Lars stopped talking, and there was only the rain drumming against the portholes and cabin sides and the hum of the wind in the rigging. He got up slowly, moved up the steps into the small pilothouse, flipped on the deck lights, and looked out at his docklines and the wind-whipped lake beyond. Satisfied, he returned to his seat.

"Come on worse since you got here," Lars said quietly. "Is a bad night to be without a home." Then, even quieter, "I was real sorry yer ma took you away from up there. Is not much of a place for her, to be sure. Nothing like what she was used to, what with just one store and one teacher for all them kids. I don't know what you remember, or what she told you after she brought you down away, but it was never a bad place. Kids in them places grew up strong, and boat- and woods-smart. Still important. Maybe not here," and he waved at the lights of the city, outside the rain-blurred portholes.

"But how come you left, Lars?" David said. He'd finally stopped shivering and moved a few feet from the stove to slump on one end of the lower bunk.

"I come down to tend my sister, winters," Lars said simply. "Her husband died six years ago, and she was slowing down. Her kids all moved away back East. She needed someone to look after her. She just went to her resting place last month, but we had six good winters together."

"I'm sorry," David said quietly, looking down. Then he turned to Lars. "You miss it, don't you?" he asked.

"Ah, miss what now, son?"

"The North, being up there winters. Don't you miss it when you're down here?"

The old man swiveled around to get a better look at

David. He wondered how the child, who had seen him but a few dozen times all those housebound Seattle winters, could tell, so quickly and surely, what lay in his heart.

"It pulls on a person, David," Lars said quietly. "That first winter at my sister's place here in Seattle was hard. But after that, sometimes a week goes by and I never even think about the North. Then we would get one of those clearing spells, when the wind switches 'round to northwest, like it was scraping whole sky clean, and I look out and see mountains, and Sound would shine bright, and sure, I would miss it bad. Or sometimes, I get woken up in middle of the night by some boat tooting for railroad bridge to open, and I would get up and take my binoculars and watch tug and barge, or maybe big crab boat, just leaving the locks, and I sometimes could see crew out on the back deck, putting away docklines, and getting everything ready for long trip up. And I miss it." Lars stopped, suddenly aware of the children looking at him intently.

"You could go back now, couldn't you, Lars? Your sister . . ." David's voice trailed off.

"Yah, I thought about it," Lars said. "I moved back aboard here. I even loaded up on supplies for trip." He waved at the full cupboards. "But then my hands start to act up again, and I remember how hard it was that last winter for me up North." He held up his hands in the light for the children to see. The tendons had begun to shrink, as they sometimes do in the hands of older people, and his fingers were slightly curved inward. "Is as far as I can open them. Oh sure, your dad, he helped me every day. His cabin was just down beach from mine, but is not right, taking so much from somebody like that, never being able to pay back. Is not right," he sighed. "So, I don't know. Sometimes I think I should take off and get back up North this winter. Other times, I think I should go back up to my sister's house, and just go on up in the spring like most folks do."

Lars crossed the little triangle of floor over to the stove. He lifted the lid on a heavy cast-iron pot. Steam rose up and the sweet smell of beef stew quickly filled the small room. He stirred it with a long wooden spoon, tasted it, and waved David and Annie over to the table. "Sit you both down now. Stew has been cooking all afternoon; just right for folks who been out in cold and wet." He spooned out the thick, steaming stew into three heavy china bowls and set them on the small table with a loaf of homemade bread. The twins ate greedily, cleaning their bowls.

When the supper was over, the fo'c'sle cleaned up, and Lars was in bed, the twins went for a few minutes into the small pilothouse, above and behind the fo'c'sle. Side by side they stood, looking out the five small windows that afforded almost a 270-degree view of what lay ahead and to the sides of the boat.

The walls were all dark varnished wood and the big wooden steering wheel was directly in front. The spokes were worn from decades of use. To the right, or starboard of the wheel, was the radar, a portable, TV-sized electronic apparatus that displayed on a small screen the shapes of the land, boats, and buoys around the vessel, especially useful at night or in fog. To the left, or port, was what fishermen had come to call a "paper machine," a device that displayed on a slowly advancing strip of paper both the shape and texture of the sea bottom and the presence of fish in the water beneath the boat. Above the wheel, two radios were fastened to the low ceiling. From the captain's chair, the helmsman could easily and readily view all the equipment around him, and, by swiveling slightly to port, have easy access to the chart table on top of which lay a chart of Puget Sound.

"David, look at this pencil line," Annie said. "Must be the route Lars takes down from Alaska."

David was at the back wall, his attention focused on a wide cabinet with many small drawers. The front of each drawer held a sample of what lay inside: hooks, large and small, single and triple; small swivels; spoons of the sort one might catch a trout on, but much larger. A flat rack beside the cabinet held many coils of nylon fishing leaders, each with a small clip or swivel knotted carefully on each end. And above the leaders were rows and rows of salmon plugs, in different colors, patterns, and sizes.

"Wow, look at this," David said, picking up a medium-sized plug from the wall rack. "It's one Dad made. Remember? I'm sure he made it." He turned the plug slowly in his hand, studying it in the dim light before passing it to his sister. "Look at all the scratches and cuts. I bet it's caught its share of fish."

It was clearly homemade, without the perfectly regular shape and glossy finish of many of the others. And yet, from its nicks and scars, it was obviously a popular and well-used plug.

Annie held it closer to the light, and suddenly recalled a childhood Christmas Eve from their years in Alaska. A wet snow had come in the night and blanketed the little cove with its dozen cabins. Their dad had gotten up early, stoked up the woodstove, lit the Aladdin lamp, and gone to check on the boat. Annie had awakened to the soft closing of the door, and came out of her room to stand by the woodstove and look at the tree. They'd cut it a week earlier on a nearby bluff, and they had walked back in the early twilight, the bushy Sitka spruce on their father's shoulder.

Of course there'd been only a handful of store-bought glass balls or other ornaments. There was hardly any spare money then; nor did the tiny store or once-a-week mailboat have much of a choice for those who had money. And so in the evenings, as the firewood crackled and popped in the woodstove, the twins rummaged among their dad's fishing tackle, fashioning their ornaments out of the colorful spoons, plugs, and other lures, all the graceful tools of the salmon troller's trade.

On the topmost bough had been a driftwood cedar angel their father had carved for them one evening. The angel's wings had come out a little lopsided, and she had aluminum foil for a crown.

The storm wind rattled a burst of rain against the windows of the pilothouse and startled them. Annie put down the plug and looked around, surprised, as if suddenly realizing where she was.

There had been other Christmases since the ones in the cove they'd left behind. Their mother had always tried hard to make it special for them. But working at least two jobs and moving from place to place, it seemed like each Christmas had become a little quicker and a little more disappointing for them. At the last, there'd been only a small, artificial store-bought tree on the table with a few hastily bought and wrapped gifts to be quickly opened before their mom had to go off to work somewhere.

"Maybe Lars can take us up to Dad," Annie said quietly, picking up the lure again, and holding it up to the compass light once more. "He said he was thinking about going up North, and he's already got most of the supplies for the trip. If his hands are bothering him, we could help him with whatever has to be done. What do you think?"

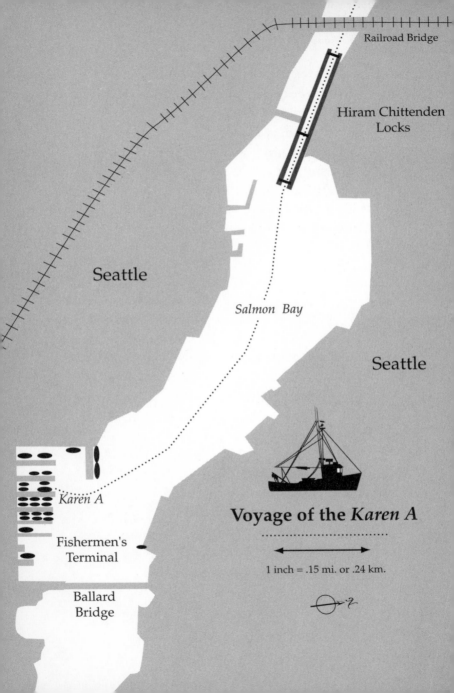

Railroad Bridge

Hiram Chittenden
Locks

Seattle

Salmon Bay

Seattle

Karen A

Fishermen's
Terminal

Ballard
Bridge

Voyage of the *Karen A*

1 inch = .15 mi. or .24 km.

CHAPTER 2

The Going Away

 By the end of two weeks aboard, Annie and David had transformed the *Karen A*. All the places where Lars's arthritic hands had been unable to reach had been cleaned, sanded, and painted. Worn rigging was replaced and a new hatch cover built.

While the twins painted and cleaned, Lars had worked on the mechanical and electronic equipment. Once they had decided to go, Lars had explained that they must hurry to get the boat ready to travel before the winter storms began.

The twins had spoken little of what had brought them to Lars. He was pleased to be going, but concerned that the twins would find the preparations tedious, the tight living quarters difficult. But if David or Annie felt those concerns, they never voiced them. Instead they seemed to jump into their new life as if the old one had never been.

Annie organized the cupboards and went through all the supplies, and Lars gave her money to shop for what they didn't already have. After decades of cooking for himself, Lars had the very distinct pleasure, the second night the twins were aboard, of sitting in his own cozy fo'c'sle, feeling the weariness of a long day's scraping and painting, and watching and smelling a meal being prepared by someone other than himself.

When he first helped Lars with the outside chores, replacing worn rigging, overhauling the anchor winch, and attending to other maintenance tasks, David worked awkwardly. Lars could see that he wasn't used to such jobs and places. And Lars worried, for he knew that on the trip ahead, on some black and windy night, with rain slashing down sideways, his own hands might be needed at the wheel and radar, and it would fall to David to feel his way up to the foredeck to set out the anchor and chain, where a slip or wrong move might mean injury or worse.

But then, as the days went by, Lars could see David's moves becoming surer, quicker. He asked Lars less and less the hows and whys of doing things, and began to clamber around with a reassuring balance and swiftness.

Lars marveled at the resilience of the twins, at their difficult transition so easily made. Sometimes, it seemed to him, whatever it was in their past that had brought them to his doorstep, sodden and distressed on that wet night, had simply ceased to exist. It seemed that for them there was now only him, the boat, the journey ahead and, somewhere in the hazy future, their father and dimly remembered Alaska home.

One evening the twins were up in the pilothouse, where the muted sounds of Lars's snoring came up from below. Annie asked softly of her brother's shape, "Are you scared?"

"I just wish there were more boats going, that's all."

"I know," Annie said. "Lars told me he's used to going with another boat, but that heading up so late and all, we'll just be traveling alone."

"You miss Mom?" David asked.

"Yeah, don't you?"

"Uh-huh. Sometimes I think about her a lot."

"I know," Annie said. "I do, too."

"Do you think we should try to find her?"

"Maybe she doesn't want to be found."

"What do you mean?" David said.

"I mean she left us with no food and no money, and not even a note. If she thought about it, she probably would have figured out that Lars's boat would be one of the places we might go, and she never came around." There was bitterness in Annie's voice.

"Maybe she got hurt or something," David said.

A big green tug and black barge stacked high with forty-foot steel containers came into sight, the biweekly Alaska freight run. The long, dark shape blotted out the lights on the far shore of the lake as it cut the corner close, heading for the locks, just a quarter-mile to the west.

Annie stared out at the dark shape of the barge before replying. "Mom had her chance, David. I guess that's what I really mean. She left Dad five years ago and brought us down here, and each year it seemed like things got worse instead of better." She sighed and rubbed her finger in the condensation on the window. "After she left us, I figured we only had three choices: go to another foster home, live on the streets, or try to get up to Alaska and find Dad, somehow. Now we've found Lars, and he's willing to take us up to Dad, so this is what we've got to do, that's all."

David came over and leaned against her, the closest he would come to hugging his sister. "Sounds like you've got it all pretty well figured out. But I just still wish Mom hadn't left. I hope she's okay."

"Well, children," Lars said at breakfast on the last day of November. "We are good and finally ready. Now you take this. Lars stretched his clawlike hand across the table and dropped a folded fifty-dollar bill before them. "Where we are going, there are no stores like here," he waved out at Seattle all around them. "So you must get things you need before you go."

Annie tried to give the money back to him. "Lars, you don't have to do that. We both had jobs before Mom left. There's still a little money left from that. You're helping us enough just by taking us up to find Dad."

"No," Lars said. "Fair is fair. Look how spiffy *Karen A* is now. All you and David. I am not sure I could go to Alaska anymore without your help."

"Why do you say that?" David asked quietly.

Lars waved his arthritic hand. "This, my eyes, my back sometimes. Sixty-one years I fished up North, living in that little cabin all those winters. In the beginning, some winters I was the only one in the cove. Too long and lonely. Now, ten, twelve families living there all winter, is better. But still, up at my sister's, it felt good to be in a house where the heat would come on without wood, and you didn't have to pump water. Hot water. Never did I have this before, hot water that is running. The first thing I did when I got down from the North, was to run a big tub of that hot water, and just soak in it. Oh, my old hands and bones, didn't they like that hot water! Oh, yes, it was so good!

"I missed the North, but still I am not sure I would have gone back, if you two did not come along. So do laundry this morning, and better take a long, hot shower, too, at the dock bathroom. Go see a movie. Where we are going, there is none of that."

The twins did all those things and, finally, in the gray afternoon dusk, stopped near the middle of the bridge that spanned the channel next to Fishermen's Terminal. They set their full backpacks down on the sidewalk to rest for a moment, and looked out at the scene spread out before them to the west. Directly below them were long rows of docks and silent boats. The docks were totally full, every slip taken, the bigger boats tied two and three deep in places.

Yet the fleet was mostly dark, the men gone home for the winter, the boats laid up until spring. Only on the *Karen A* was light pooled on the back deck, with a man, bent over and working on something. On either side, only the occasional docklights punctuated the gathering darkness. To the west, down the shining lane of water lit by the faint color in the sky, were the bright lights of the entrance to the locks, the exit from the freshwater, and the beginning of their long journey north.

And beyond, over the brows of the low house-covered hills that rose gently on either side of Fishermen's Terminal, a dully shining body of water was just visible: Puget Sound.

Seen in the thin, fading light of a chilly November afternoon, with the snowy wall of Hurricane Ridge on the Olympic Peninsula rising up steeply behind, it was a forbidding sight. A cold wind from the north eddied around the bridge and the children shivered suddenly inside their coats and flannel shirts. They took one more look out at where they were to go, at how empty and cold it was, and how warm and friendly all the lights in the houses on the hills seemed, just now winking on all around them. Finally they returned their packs to their shoulders and hurried across the bridge and out of the raw wind.

When Annie and David got back to the boat, they stopped a moment to take in what Lars had been doing while they were away. The decks were all tidy, the trash carried up to the dock, the paint cans gone to Lars's storage locker. Every wire in the rigging was straight and tight, every line neatly coiled. Set on top of the pilothouse was an odd-looking orange cylinder sporting a short antenna and set in a bolted-down metal frame. Beside it was something else they hadn't seen before, a white cylinder or canister the size of a small trash can, also set into a metal frame.

Just then two white lights on the mast and a red light on the pilothouse came on, the door opened, and Lars stepped out onto the back deck.

"Why, how long have you been standing there?" he asked them, surprised. "And how was the movie?"

"Oh, fun," Annie said. "We just got back. But what are those new things on the pilothouse? We're just trying to figure them out."

"Well now, first you look around front and say if you can

see a red and a green light on the pilothouse and two white lights on the mast."

Annie walked up to where she could see the lights. "Yep, they're all on."

"Then that's done." Lars reached inside the door and the lights went off. "Is better to be fixing these things now, than on some nasty night when we really need them."

"So what are those things? David asked, waving at the top of the house.

"Ah, the white is emergency life raft. If we hit a big log or maybe burn up, it is our ticket home. But we will never need it. It is the law to have one, is a good law."

"Well how about that weird orange thing?"

"Ah, is even better, special emergency radio beacon. If *Karen A* goes down, it floats off, sends special radio signal to satellite. Coast Guard chopper come right to raft, very good."

Lars rummaged around inside the pilothouse for a moment, then came out, carrying what looked like two small, orange duffel bags.

"Here. He set the bags on the hatch cover and motioned for the twins to come closer. "Here, you must both try putting these on."

Annie opened one of the duffels and looked over to Lars with uncertainty as a very large suit of orange foam rubber coveralls, complete with hood, unrolled on the deck. "It's huge!"

"Ah, I know. Is foolish. Still only come in one size." He waved at the ungainly suit again. "But put it on anyway. Better to practice now."

Lars helped the children find and pull down the full-length zipper on each suit, and then stood back as the twins awkwardly put their legs and arms in and managed to pull up the zippers unassisted. When they were done, all that could be seen of whoever was inside was a small circle of flesh below the hood with two sets of big eyes looking out.

"Mmmf, oofh, mmm. . . ." Annie tried to say something. Lars reached over and adjusted the fit so that her mouth was visible.

"We can hardly move in these things, and I'm starting to sweat!"

"Just one minute." Lars inspected the twin's suits carefully, making sure there were no rips or other damage. Finally he waved at them to climb out and roll them back up.

"What are those things? They look like moon suits," David said when he'd finally climbed out.

"Survival suits to keep you warm if we must go in the water or in raft. Enough now, supper is ready." He shooed them inside.

The twins marveled at all Lars had accomplished while they'd been away. The pilothouse and fo'c'sle floors were swept, with every single item and piece of clothing put away. To the right of the compass were binoculars and a small compressed-gas horn, and on the chart table was a chart: "Puget Sound–Admiralty Inlet to Seattle."

When they went into the fo'c'sle, they could see that Lars had hung a long storage hammock behind each of their bunks, a place to put their clothes other than under their sleeping bags. The tidiness and organization left the twins with a feeling of assurance. They were as ready as they would ever be. Tomorrow was the big day.

After dinner that evening, Lars turned on the television and puttered around the fo'c'sle while David investigated Lars's inventory of lures in the pilothouse. Annie had stretched out on her bunk with a mystery novel. Then the voice of the news anchor shattered their peaceful evening.

". . . and, in other news, both the Department of Human Services and the Seattle Police continue to search without success for a missing pair of thirteen-year-old twins. The boy and girl, identified as David and Annie Ross, were last seen two weeks ago."

Annie instantly rose to one elbow and listened anxiously for more information, but there was just the short announcement and nothing else.

"Lars? David?" she called out. "Did you hear? That was us they were talking about! The police are looking for us. Human Services, too! That means they want to put us in a foster home again."

David dropped down into the fo'c'sle with a look of surprise; he had missed the announcement entirely. Lars swiveled and fixed the twins with a serious look.

"Is good no one saw you today. But is also good we are leaving."

Annie put down her book when the news came on again in thirty minutes, but there was no more mention of missing twins, and she relaxed the tiniest bit and began reading again.

Lars had just put the charts away when the boat suddenly settled slightly to port and someone knocked at the door. Then it slid open and three dark-clad figures pushed their way in and down to the fo'c'sle.

"Well, now, Lars," the tallest of the three said, setting a squat bottle squarely in the middle of the table. "We must have a going-away nip." The twins had become accustomed to the sound of the old country in Lars's voice, and this man's accent was similar.

Lars stood up in the suddenly crowded space and somberly shook the three offered hands: "Ah, boys, is good you came by."

One of the men spied the children reading by their bunk lights.

"And it is a fine crew you have, Lars. Good to have such help on a long voyage."

"David, Annie," Lars turned to the twins and waved at the three rough-looking men. "These are Karmoy chums. Karmoy is small Norwegian island. Very small, just few farmers and fishermen. We all came to United States together in 1940. We were just boys, fifteen, sixteen years old. We had no money, so we spent a whole year working our way west across Canada. Work for farmer few days, stay in his barn, eat at his table, just keep going west."

"Se-at-le," one of the other men said, pronouncing Seattle in a hoarse and heavily accented voice. "All we knew was that many Karmoy men fish from place called Se-at-le, and that it was in West. We didn't know where in West, so we just keep saying 'Se-at-le' when people ask were we go. Hah, one time in Saskatchewan, Lars see skunk. We never have skunk in Karmoy and Lars think it was kitty and try to pick it up." Suddenly the four of them convulsed in laughter at what had happened so long ago.

Then the group turned from the twins and crowded around the table together. Little glasses were brought down from the cupboard and the bottle was opened.

After a while the twins got onto their bunks, and lay for a while, listening to the voices around the table, the Norwegian and the English flowing together as one.

"What happen to them fellows in that big crab boat *Clipper Bay?*" asked Rudy, the largest of the three. "They say seam in hull opened up, but that was one good boat. I have one just like it. I don't think seam could open up."

"Ah," started Torvald, the lanky one, "I think maybe they just have too many crab pots aboard. I saw that boat when they went through locks. She was loaded very high. Seven layers of pots. This time of year, is too many."

"Seven layers, too much for that boat," agreed old Erik, who was the shortest and stockiest of his companions. "Them fellows was lucky. She rolled over too quick to use radio, and they spent two days in that raft before Coast Guard found them. Very lucky."

"You think it was ice that made them roll?" Rudy asked.

"No, there was no ice," Torvald said. "Just too many pots, and she got into that big tide rip where Hecate Straits meet Alaska, roll too far once, and *boom,* over she went with no warning."

"Ice," Erik snorted. "Hah, who remember that March of '52 in Bering Sea?"

There was a murmur of assent from the others.

"I was with Harold in *Tordenskjold.* We work seven days to fill boat. Finally *Tordenskjold* is all loaded, and we are just resting, taking turns steering for long trip to Kodiak to sell, and Harold yells down into fo'c'sle, 'Everyone on deck, boys, we must chop ice.'" The man's voice was filled with awe as he remembered pulling on his clothes and climbing up the steep ladder to the deck almost forty years before. "Ice! Why, man, we come on deck, and hardly recognize our boat. Everything thick with ice. Why, anchor chain was big around as my leg, and pilothouse look like one big, white hill of ice and snow. Three days we chop that ice and when we get to Kodiak, *Tordenskjold,* she still looked like one big hill of ice."

For a bit no one spoke and there was only the sudden slash of rain against the side of the boat and the hum of rising wind in the rigging.

"Well, at least you got there," Lars finally said. "Them fellows in the *Jan and Olaf,* not so lucky."

"Ah, such a story," said big Rudy. "All them fellows jump in the raft and was never seen again, and Coast Guard find *Jan and Olaf* floating all iced up very heavy, but floating just fine."

"And unspilled cups of coffee still on the table, and all them fellows gone, ah, that was a bad one." Torvald said, and there was another long silence.

The stories went on. Sometimes the men spoke entirely in Norwegian and the twins could understand nothing. Sometimes they spoke in their heavily accented English of places that Annie and David remembered their father talking about long before: God's Pocket, Safety Cove, Yuculta Rapids, Seymour Narrows, Johnstone Strait, Grenville Channel, and others along the thousand-mile path between where they now lay, crowded in among hundreds of other boats, and the distant snowbound cove that had once been their home.

Sometimes the voices would stop entirely, and there would only be the clink of glasses, the sigh of the wind through the rigging, and the pittering of the rain against the skylight and hull.

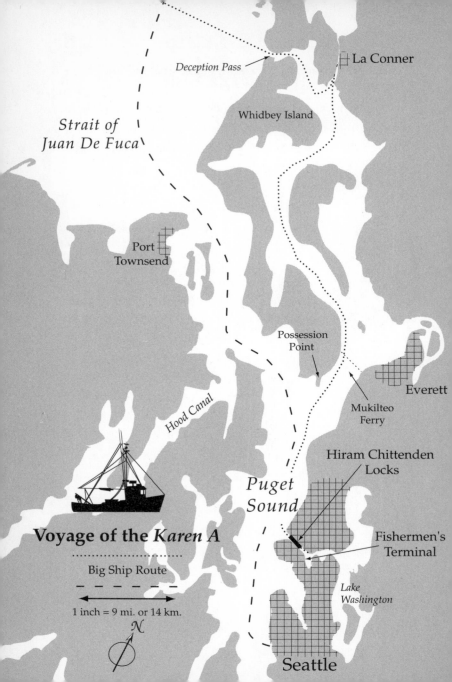

Deception Pass

La Conner

Strait of Juan De Fuca

Whidbey Island

Port Townsend

Possession Point

Everett

Mukilteo Ferry

Hood Canal

Hiram Chittenden Locks

Puget Sound

Fishermen's Terminal

Voyage of the *Karen A*

Lake Washington

.... Big Ship Route

— — — Big Ship Route

← → 1 inch = 9 mi. or 14 km.

N

Seattle

CHAPTER 3

At Sea

 The twins woke to the sound of the engine starting, the smell of hot cocoa, a voice and a hand gently nudging them. "Wake up now, sleepyheads. Now we shall see what the journey holds for us."

David looked up at the skylight over his head. It was still completely dark. He looked at his watch: quarter to six. "How come so early?" he asked. "It's still dark for another hour."

"Ah, she just be coming light when we finish with locks. Better we travel a little in the dark now than tonight when we must find a harbor."

David swung down out of his bunk and stood in front of the stove for a moment. Two hot cocoas and a plate of buttered toast were on the table. As he sipped the cocoa, Annie stumbled groggily into the light, and a radio voice came on: "Puget Sound to Juan de Fuca Strait: small craft advisory. Southeast wind fifteen to twenty-five knots this morning with higher gusts at times. A gale warning may be necessary later in the day. Mariners should tune in at regular announcement times for possible updates."

The twins could hear the hum of the wind in the rigging.

"We still going to go, Lars?"

Lars stepped down into the fo'c'sle and studied the two young, questioning faces before answering.

"Yah, sure," he said softly. "This time of year, sometimes five days out of six have 'small craft advisory.' We must stick our nose out and have a look."

"But what if it turns into a gale?

"Ah, now a gale is different. But not to worry. Down here, this first part of the trip, many good harbors all around. If gale comes, we nip into a harbor and wait for better weather." He laughed, gently and reassuringly. "We will be doing a lot of nipping into harbors and waiting for better weather on this trip." He reached in behind the engine bulkhead and patted the gray metal expansion tank of the diesel engine. "Not to worry, *Karen A* will take us safely through it all." He waved at the table and his voice turned more serious. "Eat up now, and dress warm. Is very important to get good early start each day. We must take advantage of every minute of daylight. When you are all ready, go ahead and untie lines."

But when the twins stepped outside, the black, the cold, the rain, and the wind assaulted them.

"We're going in this?" David said anxiously to Annie.

"I hope I don't get seasick," she answered. "Just the idea of going anywhere in this makes me feel queasy. Let's ask Lars. Maybe we should wait until the weather looks better. C'mon." They huddled in the doorway out of the rain, and waited for Lars to finish writing something in a little book.

"Uh, Lars?" David said hesitantly, "Have you been outside? Maybe you should have a look at it before we untie."

Lars stepped past them and out onto the deck, and tilted his head up for a moment so he could better feel the wind and the rain.

"Ah," he said gently, stepping back inside. "It always seems worse just before you start a long trip. But you must remember, if you wait for perfect weather this time of year, sometimes you never go. Go ahead now, take in the lines. We must be going."

And so with little fanfare, the twins drew in the lines and the *Karen A* moved away from the silent dock and the sleeping fleet. The first of the morning traffic was just starting to hum across the bridges as they turned west, toward the locks, the saltwater of Puget Sound, and that windy northern highway.

The Hiram Chittenden locks separated the freshwater bodies of Lake Washington, Lake Union, and Salmon Bay from the saltwater of Puget Sound. Built in 1913 along what was a muddy creek that cascaded into Puget Sound, the locks allowed logs cut all around Lake Washington to be towed easily in rafts to sawmills on the saltwater. They also provided a calm mooring area for thousands of pleasure and commercial boats. The shores east of the locks were crowded with marinas, barge terminals, shipyards, and maritime support facilities of every kind. But west, beyond the steel and concrete walls of the locks, was an untamed world. Deep, with large tides and strong currents, the saltwater of Puget Sound in winter was a place where the prudent mariner traveled carefully.

There were no other boats that early morning, and the lockkeeper waved them into a wide and long concrete-walled chamber with closed steel gates on the far end. Lars brought the boat neatly to a stop, and Annie passed the end of the stern line to a man on top of the wall. The man tied it off, then caught the bowline from David.

Then a bell started ringing, and from each side of the lock behind them a huge hinged steel gate began swinging shut, creating a strong current which swirled around the *Karen A*, pushing her heavily against the big round fenders that hung over her side.

"You must pay strict attention when water drops." Lars showed them how to pay the lines out slowly around the cleat, keeping a strain, but being careful not to let the line jam. "Tide is low outside." He waved at the big steel gate ahead of them. "Water will go down very far." As he spoke, the water level in the locks started to drop. The twins had to pay full attention to the lines that had begun to pull heavily at the cleats. Dark jets of water spurted from the place where the two steel gates behind them met in the middle, and still the level of the water dropped until they were in the bottom of a great pit surrounded by slimy dark walls.

They'd seen the locks many times before. They were one of the more exciting of Seattle's attractions, and most of all, they were free. They'd eaten their lunches on the grassy banks, and watched brightly painted yachts and fish boats pass through on sunny afternoons. They had taken class trips to watch the salmon migrating up the fish ladders to the lake beyond. It had never occurred to them that what had always looked like fun from afar could seem so ominous and threatening up close.

The dropping of the water finally stopped, and the big steel lock gates began to open. The current began to rush through the gap between the gates, pushing heavily against them as they waited for the signal to begin their journey.

It was a journey whose beginning lay revealed in the widening gap ahead: a narrow gutter of wind-darkened water, between muddy shores above which large homes rose, the first lights just winking on in a few windows. The bow-line fell in a pile onto the deck ahead of David; the stern line followed a moment later next to his sister. The engine thunked into gear, and Lars throttled up until they were moving cautiously ahead. The first puff of the outside breeze struck David, cold and damp, smelling of the sea and the low-tide shore.

The *Karen A* slid gracefully under a railroad bridge, and then lay stopped for a moment, sideways to the current and the breeze. Lars stepped out of the pilothouse door and waved to the twins and the coils of line that still lay on the decks.

"Bring in those lines. It will be wet going ahead. Everything loose must be off deck." They did as he asked and watched as Lars deftly tightened the coils and hung them securely from two cleats on the back of the pilothouse. "In small boats like this," Lars said gently, "everything has a place so when the wind blows nothing comes loose. My friend Torvald once forgot to tie up lines like this," he said as he patted the lines. "They came loose in bad weather, washed back and forth in stern. One end came loose, came out through scupper holes and tangled around propeller. Torvald very lucky; if Johnny Johnson didn't just happened to be close, he would have gone on rocks, just because line didn't get put away just right. You see, these little things, they maybe not seem like much, but are very important."

Lars slipped back inside, and the diesel exhaust purred once again from the stack as the *Karen A* swung around and headed for the open water ahead.

"Look," Annie whispered. She had come over to rest her chin on David's shoulder as they both stared ahead. They were moving toward the place where the channel opened up into an expanse of rough and white-capped water. The *Karen A* came close abreast a little point just then, where the channel passed close to the shore, and they could look into the windows of several houses. In one, David and Annie could clearly see a family sitting around a kitchen table. In a moment the scene was gone, for the current had become swifter as the channel narrowed. And yet that scene—and the yearning it stirred— was etched in the twins' minds for a long time. There was no need to speak, for the twins often read each other's thoughts. Home and family. Glimpsed for a moment and then gone. A scene like that, so unexpected and so full of all that the twins didn't have, affected them deeply.

"You'd best come in now." Lars's gentle voice broke the spell. His hand was on Annie's shoulder. "You'll get a soaking if you stay out any longer."

"Hey, look!" David pointed at a red buoy with a big brown sea lion on it. As they approached, it slithered heavily into the water. Then the bow of the *Karen A* started to rise and fall into the first of the southerly swells that was driving around the point ahead. The twins took one last look at the houses and lights of shore disappearing into the misty, windy drizzle, and slipped into the pilothouse behind Lars.

And then they were out in a mean Puget Sound late fall morning with a wet southerly blowing. The worst part was the tide and the currents that it created. Just three hours earlier, the effect of the current, then ebbing north and flowing with the wind, would have been to flatten the seas. But by the time the *Karen A* poked her nose out into it, the tide was coming in and the current was flowing against the wind, pushing the waves higher, shortening the space between each one, and causing the larger ones to break.

At first, for a few very long minutes, the *Karen A* had to run in the trough, parallel to the waves, far enough to get clear of the shore before she could turn north. For the twins, it was frightening. The waves, or seas, were pouring around the point as five- and six-footers, and the narrow and deep boat rolled heavily as each wave passed beneath her. With each roll came the clunk and clatter of things thumping around in the cupboards, and on one or two especially steep seas, the confused water seemed to assault them from all sides. Yet through it all, Lars was calm, even serene.

After what seemed like a long while, Lars picked a spot where the seas were a bit lower, worked the spoked wooden steering wheel over to the right, and suddenly the rolling stopped as they headed straight up the Sound with the wind behind them.

"Yes," Lars said gently to the twins, "we run with the wind, now—is much better." He touched a switch, and a motor and chain apparatus came to life on the floor beneath the compass. Lars waited a moment, then nudged a lever with his foot and took his hands off the steering wheel, which had begun to rotate back and forth on its own.

"Automatic pilot. We sometimes call it 'Iron Mike.' We watch for a little bit to see if she can handle this weather. Sometimes when we run before the seas, it cannot turn boat fast enough and we turn sideways. Is not good."

Lars stood at close attention behind the wheel, watching the seas outside until he was satisfied that the machine was steering the boat properly.

"You see," he said finally, smiling as the boat plowed contentedly along on its course, "going to Alaska isn't so bad. All we do now is to watch our course and keep sharp lookout for other boats."

Even as he spoke, a dark shape appeared out of the mists ahead, and resolved itself into a squat green tug approaching them a little to the west of their course. The twins watched as the two boats neared each other and finally passed a few hundred yards apart. Even though the tug was easily two or even three times the size of their boat, she was throwing sheets of white water over her pilothouse, while the *Karen A* was running without making any spray at all.

"See now, he is bucking," said Lars. "If wind was coming from north," he nodded out ahead of them, "we would be beating our way into seas like that." Only when the tug was abreast of them could they see that it was towing a barge, black and very low in the water, sometimes completely hidden by the breaking waves.

"Fuel barge," Lars said. "That is why you always must be very careful passing a tug, especially at night. Sometimes the things they tow are very far behind, and some boats, not knowing it was a tug and not seeing the lights on the barge, pass behind the tug, and *boom*! Barge come out of the black and trample them right under it.

"Come, David," Lars waved the boy into his place. "You and Annie must learn to take watch. Now I am too old to make the journey by myself. I show you both how to steer and how to watch and when to call me, and we will set up schedule. Everyone steers for just one hour, and has two hours off. Very easy schedule for young folks."

David hesitated. So much had happened so quickly— leaving in the darkness, the wind, the rain, the locks, and then entering that mean and gray sea world that seemed to have so totally swallowed up the land and all that was familiar to him. It was almost overwhelming. Lars nudged David gently into the seat.

"Ah, I always be just a few feet away. The smallest thing you do not understand, call me. Things can happen very fast on the water. Here . . . " Lars lowered the chart table, and David swiveled the chair around so he was looking directly at the map. Annie leaned forward on her elbows. "I always draw line on chart where we travel," Lars said as his finger traced the penciled track line on the chart.

"But where are we?" David asked plaintively, pointing out the windows. The shore was now totally cloaked in mist and gloom. The tug and barge had disappeared. Ahead and behind and to both sides was only restless and wind-stirred Puget Sound.

"Ah," Lars said, fiddling with the knobs on the radar unit. "This is just the thing for you."

A pattern of bright green shapes appeared on the screen.

Lars adjusted the knobs a bit more, the image seemed to shrink, and then he pointed at the chart.

"You see, they are the same. Just look now, you will see."

It took a moment for the twins to grasp that the two bright shapes that ran up and down the screen an inch and a half apart were the shores on either side of the lower Sound.

"We are always in middle of the screen." Lars pointed to a bright dot in the very center of the screen. "And the shore moves down the screen past us. See, that tug looks like this." He tapped at a bright dot halfway between the center and the bottom of the screen.

"Yes, but where's that thing he was towing?" Annie asked.

"Ah, that is very good question. You must always remember: the further away you are from something, the harder to see it, especially things low in the water like that oil barge. Sometimes if sea is choppy, the radar cannot see buoys or even other boats. Usually you can still see shore though. But you must remember: just because you cannot see something on radar does not mean is not there." Lars turned and drew a plastic-covered placard from behind the chart table and set it on the compass in front of David.

"These are 'Rules of Road.' You must study this, especially what it says about lights. When you are on watch, you both must know all these things. Here, I show you what to do to turn 'Iron Mike' off." Lars leaned over and pulled a lever on the automatic pilot, and the steering wheel stopped its back-and-forth motion. "See, when you want to change course, just push this lever, and steer the boat onto new direction, and when she is going good, just push lever in again. See, you can even do it with your foot." He pushed the lever with his foot and the steering wheel resumed its motion. "Now you try."

David pushed the lever gently with his foot, but nothing happened.

"Push, boy, you must be firm with machines!" David pushed harder, felt the lever thump out of gear, and then Lars's hands were pushing his onto the smooth and worn spokes of the wheel.

"Boat steers just like car, only harder. Turn to right, boy." Lars put his forefinger on a point of land on the radar screen. "Turn until we are pointed right at that." David turned the wheel a little more. "Good, now center the wheel up again, and you will be pointing in right direction. Just turn it back until that spoke with the fancy knot is on top, then we will be going straight, and you push in lever again. Go ahead now." David pushed the pilot into gear, and Lars stood back. "Ah, you see, you make good crew. You can do it."

David leaned back in the chair, proud that he had been able to get the boat on its course, but then, as Lars turned and prepared to go below, he turned suddenly pale.

"But . . . but . . . where are we?" he stammered.

"Ah, very good question," Lars said gently. "I will show you. Look at radar screen." At the top of the display, the channel appeared to be splitting into two directions, like a Y. Lars tapped the bottom of the point between the two arms. "This here, Possession Point," he said, and then turned David's chair so he was looking at the chart, and tapped a point on the chart. "In good weather, we go steamer route." He slid his finger to the left of the point and up the channel.

"But today we go 'inside.' It is longer, but more sheltered. The wind does not blow so hard." Lars manipulated the radar controls and a glowing circle appeared on the screen, like the target of a bull's-eye.

"See, this is one-mile ring. When ring touch this point, we are here." He pointed to the place on the chart where the course swung up into the right arm of the channel. "And you change course so we point there. Now, I just go below and make coffee, you just steer us along line marked on chart. It is not hard."

When Lars had gone down the three steps into the foc's'le, Annie came around and stood by David's shoulder, looking over at the chart. Already the place on the radar that corresponded to the cross-hatching on the chart marked "Seattle" was disappearing off the bottom of the screen.

"This was home," Annie said, tapping the bottom of the radar screen. "Better say good-bye to it."

David peered ahead into the gloom, trying to make out the headland that showed so boldly on the radar. But there was nothing, just rain-blurred windows and the gray world beyond.

"Good-bye. But you know, if Mom had showed up this morning, before we left, I'd have stayed. How about you?"

"Yeah. Me, too," Annie answered. "That was scary leaving in the dark. And then seeing that family having breakfast together made me really sad. I mean, is that too much to ask for? Just staying in the same place for a while so you can get used to things and have friends and all, like most kids?"

Annie suddenly leaned over and studied the radar. "Hey, what's this?" She tapped something at the bottom of the screen.

"Uh, that's just a buoy or something," David said, proud to show off his newly gained knowledge. "See, we're in the middle of the screen."

Annie studied the screen and the new target for a moment.

"If it was a buoy," she said, "it would be coming from in front of us, right? I mean we're traveling sort of up, looking at the screen, but whatever this thing is, it is coming from behind us, so it couldn't be a buoy. Right?"

David studied the screen with sudden alarm. Whatever it was must be moving rapidly; already it had covered half the distance from the bottom of the screen to them, and he could see that it was much larger than the buoys he had seen earlier. He swiveled his head and peered out the little rear window, but there was only the wet deck and the white-capped seas appearing out of the mists.

"Quick," he said anxiously, "get Lars." Lars was up the stairs and peering into the radar almost as soon as Annie called him.

"Ah," he said, nimbly kicking the autopilot out of gear and turning the wheel rapidly to the right. "You were right to call. It is probably big steamer. Rule is, overtaking vessel must keep clear, which means he must stay clear of us, but these big boats don't always follow rules that much."

Lars kicked the pilot back on and peered into the radar screen again. The big target that must be the ship was now off to their right. But as they watched, it still seemed to be heading directly toward them. Lars reached up and turned a knob on one of the radios and spoke into the microphone: "This is fish boat *Karen A*, northbound three miles south of

Possession Point. Very large steamer approaching rapidly please identify."

A minute passed, but there was no answer from the radio. The target on the radar screen was now very close to them. Lars picked up a funny-looking can with a horn on it, gave it to David, and pushed him out the door into the rain.

"Quick, boy, quick. Point it back and pull lever, blow horn."

David pulled the lever, wincing at the sudden sharp noise. It was answered almost at once by a deafeningly loud and deep horn blast from directly behind them and high up in the air. David blasted his horn again, felt them swing rapidly to the right again, and grabbed at the mast for support. As he did, something caught his eye behind them, and he watched in amazement and horror as a white splotch in the mist suddenly became the bow wave of a giant, dark-hulled ship. He made out the name *Nissan Prince*, glimpsed a yellow-clad figure peering down at them, and then he was holding on with both hands, crushing the air horn against his chest as the *Karen A* corkscrewed violently in the big ship's bow wave. A huge, rounded stern with an angry torrent of white water frothing underneath it appeared out of the mists, and then they were alone in the misty gray again, rolling heavily as he made his way back into the pilothouse.

Lars was speaking angrily into the radio: "*Nissan Prince, Nissan Prince*, what's the matter with you fellows? Just because you are big does not mean you don't keep good radar watch!"

He was immediately answered by a high, heavily accented voice, speaking rapidly. But between the Japanese skipper's accent and Lars's, neither could understand the other. Lars finally hung up the microphone in frustration. He gently nudged David back into the seat, and patted him on the back.

"That was good work, boy. Anything you don't understand, just call Lars."

David flushed. "It was Annie. I thought it was a buoy at first."

"Ah," Lars said, turning to Annie. "You have good eyes, girl. But lesson is for everyone. Things can happen very fast. Always you must pay attention."

"But how come that guy didn't see us?" David asked.

Lars sighed. "Maybe man on watch have too many good-bye drinks with sweetheart. Maybe radar isn't tuned in just right. Them big fellows don't always pay attention. I fished tuna in ocean many years. Sometimes you see them big fellows go by, you look with binoculars and nobody is on bridge! Either they are down below having a mug-up in galley, or maybe reading in bunk. Is not good."

They went on in silence. The weather got a little better, allowing occasional glimpses of the shore.

"Is better here," Lars said after a while. "You can see. I'll try to make coffee again." Annie snuggled in next to David when Lars had disappeared below, peering at the radar and the chart and trying to correlate it all with the shore when she could see it.

"Thanks. I think you saved our bacon," David said quietly.

"I didn't like it out there," Annie said. "Too rough, and too much traffic. Look, there's the Mukilteo ferry." A small green-and-white, double-ended ferry emerged from the gray about a mile ahead of them, crossing their course from starboard to port, or right to left. They both turned to the chart at once and found the place where the ferry was heading. Just seeing the ferry and being able to relate it to the chart and the radar was somehow reassuring.

Lars came back up with his coffee. The sea was much calmer, and the three of them crowded around the chart table as he showed the twins how to use the navigator's tools: the plastic parallel rulers and the brass dividers. He showed them how to use the radar to tell distances and how to measure those distances on the chart with the dividers, so they could tell exactly where they were. Drawing a pencil line on the chart of their course for the rest of the day, he marked it at intervals with times. Then he lightly penciled in at each hourly checkpoint the distance to the nearest shore, so they could check their position and make corrections if necessary.

"Didn't you get nervous down there, with us up here steering?" David asked.

Lars smiled. "Come," he said. "I show you secret." He led them below and sat them together on the narrow bench at the galley table. "Now look up, tell Lars what you see."

The twins gasped together. Folded down from the little skylight above the table was something they hadn't ever noticed before. A mirror, about four inches high and a foot wide, was aligned with another mirror, higher up in the skylight, so that a person sitting at the table could look up and see out ahead of the boat.

"Why, it's almost like a periscope," David said at last. "When did you do that?"

"Ah, it's been there many years now. Very handy when

I travel alone. I can sit down here and eat sandwich or make supper and still see where we are going. Look at this." Lars swiveled the bottom mirror a bit, and pointed to his bunk. "I can even see out from my bunk. When it blows in the harbor, you can see if anchor is dragging, without getting up." He laughed gently, then turned serious. "But still, is not perfect. Sometimes when things come from behind, you cannot see them. Now stay, is lunchtime. I will take watch. You eat, take a nap if you want. Lars will steer until one." He pulled a plate of toasted cheese sandwiches out of the little oven, set it on a potholder on the table, and disappeared up the stairs.

David slumped onto the bench, unaware of how hungry he was until he sat down and saw the food in front of him. And then, afterward, leaning against the inside of the hull with the stove warm on his side, and the steady thrum of the engine, all he wanted to do was sleep. He barely made it to his bunk before falling into a deep sleep.

What seemed like days later, someone was pulling gently at his arm, insistently. David came awake, looking around suddenly, trying to hold on to the last of a dream. Finally remembering where he was, he recognized Lars leaning over him.

"Oh, Lars," David said. "You were in my dream. We were all up in Alaska together, you and me, and Annie and Dad, fishing on Dad's boat. It was almost Christmas, there was snow, and it was so beautiful." He swung his feet out of the bunk, rubbed his eyes, and looked around. The light from the window over the table seemed dimmer than it had at lunch. Annie's head was sticking out of the blanket on her narrow bunk. He looked at his watch: it was three. Lars had steered for two extra hours.

"Ah, well, we will be there before too long and see if dream comes true. Now come, you must steer."

Outside was a world blurred by rain. David rubbed his eyes as Lars showed him their position on the chart, the course line following straight up a slowly narrowing channel between Whidbey Island and the mainland shore north of Seattle.

"You steer for one hour, then wake Annie. We tie up in La Conner tonight. Nice town." He tapped the chart, disappeared below, and David suddenly felt very alone. He peered ahead anxiously, hoping to get a reassuring glimpse of shore but there was only misty, rain-dappled water. But the wide and irregularly shaped channel was such that navigating by the chart and radar was easy. David spent the first few minutes comparing the two, measuring the size of a little bay with the dividers on the chart, and then studying the radar, adjusting the range rings as Lars had shown him.

After a while he developed a little routine: scan the horizon outside for crab buoys or driftwood, then study the radar for a few moments, and then look at the chart. After a half hour, he had their position memorized and could even relax, taking a minute to look at the plastic "Rules of the Road" placard.

Something in the water caught his eye, a large black object with a white patch, moving swiftly through the water. At first he thought it was a killer whale, then remembered a visit to the aquarium on a school trip: it was a Dall's porpoise, smaller than a killer whale with a much shorter dorsal fin. He made a mental note to tell Annie what he'd seen.

Toward the end of David's watch, a target appeared on

the radar, crawling slowly down from the top of the screen. As Lars had taught him to do, first he studied the chart and the radar carefully, to be sure it wasn't a buoy, and then kicked the autopilot out of gear to alter his course slightly to starboard. There were no marked traffic lanes at sea, Lars had said, but when vessels meet, going in opposite directions on a collision course, each should alter course to their starboard.

Only after a long time, when the target had come close enough on the radar screen for David to begin to feel alarm, did it appear out of the mists ahead: a small, squat green tug, towing a line that disappeared into the gray water behind it. When they were almost past it, the tug fifty yards away, he realized what the tug was towing: two rectangular rafts of logs, so low in the water that they were entirely hidden by the mist until he was almost upon them. As they approached, David studied the radar carefully, but there was no sign of the rafts. At night, they would be impossible to see, and David wondered how a person would know if they were even there at all. Something brushed against his shoulder. It was Annie.

"Mmmm," she said, brushing her hair slowly and looking out the windows. "I slept. What's that?" She nodded at the log rafts.

"Log rafts," David said. "That's how they get logs from the woods to the mills. But how would you even see something like that at night?"

"Mmmm," Annie said, still sleepy. "I don't think you would."

"You sure you're ready to watch for a while?" David asked, reluctant to give up the skipper's seat.

"Of course," she said, all sleepiness suddenly gone.

"Who saved our bacon back there with the big ship anyway?"

He moved aside, and she settled into the seat. "Okay." He waved at the chart. "We're just coming up on this point here. This line is where we're supposed to be going."

Annie studied the chart for a moment and tapped the top of it, where their course line took a sharp right turn to enter what looked like a narrow channel between breakwaters.

"What's this?"

"I don't know," David said after a moment of study.

"Well, don't you think I should wake Lars if we get there before the end of my watch? I don't know what to do there." She leaned over the chart for another long moment. After the breakwaters, the channel turned sharply again to the left and became so constricted that it was hard to even see where the pencil line went.

"Well," David said, doubtfully, "he said to just follow the pencil line and we'd be okay."

"Yeah," Annie said, "but he also said to wake him if we had any questions."

David didn't say anything, and after a while he went below and she was alone. When she looked up from the radar screen a little later, there was no horizon, no faint line between sky and water, just a seamless, featureless gray that stretched from the edge of their deck off to infinity, or so it seemed. Annie found herself looking into the radar more and more.

Once an odd, intermittent target appeared on the radar, traveling fast from the east, and she had half risen from her seat in alarm, wanting to get Lars, but afraid to leave the wheel in case she had to turn quickly. Suddenly from the gloom to the right, a flock of big Canada geese appeared. Perhaps a dozen in all, they barely gave the little boat a glance, and then were lost again in the gloom, their soft honks hanging in the air for a moment after they were gone.

At first, with only featureless gray outside the windows, Annie was anxious. But as the miles passed, she became more confident. There was something comforting about the steady drone of the engine, the ceaseless motion of the steering wheel back and forth, and her sleeping brother and skipper.

It was getting dark when the line of the breakwaters finally appeared out of the mists ahead: two long, low lines of gray rock. The closest was topped with a wooden frame-work and blinking light, and both disappeared into the mists to the east. Without warning, a white sport cruiser flashed past, close to port, arrowing toward the end of the jetties. The suddenness of it startled Annie; she'd missed its approach on radar. As she watched, it made a wide sweeping turn and entered between the breakwaters.

The breakwaters were less than a hundred yards away then. She pushed on the autopilot lever until the steering wheel stopped moving, and then pulled the throttle lever back to an idle and pulled the gearshift back into the neutral position. She waited for a moment, hoping that Lars would hear the sudden slowing of the engine and get up, come up into the pilothouse to take over or tell her what to do next. But after a long while passed without any sound or motion from below, she stepped into the fo'c'sle to rouse him.

"Lars?" First she spoke his name softly, next to his bunk, but there was no reaction. She spoke louder and louder, finally putting her hand on his sleeping shoulder and shaking harder, until at last he rolled his head and looked over at her groggily.

"Lars, we're almost at the breakwaters. It's not your watch yet, but maybe you should take over a little early." He didn't seem to understand very well, even after the third or fourth time. His face looked pale, almost gray in the dimly lit fo'c'sle, and he looked much older than before.

"Lars!" she said again, louder and more forcefully, "I think you should get up now. You need to steer us in through the breakwaters to La Conner."

His mouth started working, but at first no words came out. A weak hand pawed the air, motioning her closer. "Just stay in the middle of the channel, tie up in town." He tried to rise up and say something else, but the effort was plainly exhausting, and he slumped back onto the bed and closed his eyes.

"You mean me?" Annie stammered. His sudden sick appearance and his words were like a stone in her chest.

The boat heeled over a little just then, and there was a new sound she remembered from stormy nights tied to the dock in Seattle: the wind in the rigging. Only it didn't bring with it the cozy secure feeling of being safely tied to a dock with a wild night outside. Just the opposite—a feeling of something like terror struck Annie when she made her way up into the pilothouse and saw the very different world outside.

The featureless gray bay of just a few minutes earlier was gone, transformed into marching rows of whitecaps with rain splattering against the pilothouse windows. She dropped quickly into the fo'c'sle and shook David. "Get up, quick! Lars is sick and we're in trouble!" And then she was back up in the pilothouse again, almost all in one motion.

It was then she noticed a curious phenomenon: the waves were all breaking angry and white on the edge of the two breakwaters, but beyond, between them, the water was reassuringly calm.

David came up, rubbing his eyes, and looking around.

"David," she said, "Something's wrong with Lars—he's sick or something. I tried to wake him up. He said we'd have to take the boat into town and tie it up."

David looked around uneasily.

"Go ahead, you steer." Annie waved at the steering wheel. "You take it. I'll watch out for logs and stuff."

"Me?" David was obviously terrified at the prospect, so Annie stole a quick glance at the chart. Beyond the breakwaters to the north, where the wind was taking them, was a series of sandbars. She looked outside. It was even darker than just a few minutes earlier. If she was uncomfortable about maneuvering the boat by herself, she was genuinely frightened at the prospect of being caught out there after dark.

Annie stepped up to the wheel and pushed the gear and throttle levers forward. She swallowed hard and, with her heart pounding in her chest, swung the wheel to enter the rough water between the ends of the breakwaters. She felt her brother's hands on her shoulders, his heart pounding through his thin shirt. She wished Lars would appear and take the wheel from her anxious hands, that she could again be the learner, he the teacher.

And then they were in the tide rip. The boat lurched first

one way, then the other. The waves seemed to come from all directions, leaping in the air, and splashing alarmingly against the pilothouse walls and windows. But the *Karen A* seemed hardly to notice the commotion, needing but half a turn of the wheel one way or the other to keep her straight, and in a moment they were through and into the calmer water beyond. Annie looked out the back window at the wild scene behind them. The tide rip looked mean and threatening. Yet she marveled at how smoothly the boat had come through it, and felt a little surge of pride that she had been steering.

They traveled along in the calmer water. The breakwaters ended in a confusing maze of swampy low islands, with big log rafts tied to pilings between them, at times restricting the channel ahead. They were out of the rough seas, but the low log rafts and occasional pilings offered no place to tie up for the night, it was almost dark and they could not see La Conner.

David squeezed in close to her, the two of them peering through the rain-splattered glass.

Finally the land got closer and higher, and here and there was the welcome twinkle of lights through the trees.

"Look, houses," David said in awe, waving out at the lights in the trees, now revealing themselves as windows with people and televisions. "You did it, Annie. Good job!"

"We're not home free yet. We still have to tie up."

"Yeah, but this sure is a lot better than out there." David nodded back out toward the dark place they'd come in from.

The wind returned. All in a rush, a powerful gust hit their boat, heeling them over and rattling the pilothouse windows.

Then the rain came, hissing across the water and blotting out the shores, the comforting sight of the houses in the trees and the twinkle of the town ahead. In an instant there was nothing to steer by.

Annie, seized by fear, pulled the throttle back to an idle.

"The compass, steer by the compass," David said, trying to keep the anxiety out of his voice. "Remember how Lars showed us. It says twenty-five degrees, just steer on twenty-five."

Annie tried to shut out her fears, the frightening sounds of the wind, and the rain slashing down around them. The compass started to swing, and she got flustered, turned the wheel the wrong way, and the compass card swung even faster in the wrong direction.

Then she remembered what Lars had said, how his hands had felt on hers as he gently turned the wheel: "The compass don't move, Annie. You got to remember, the compass don't move. Imagine you're steering boat around the compass card." She turned the wheel toward the twenty-five on the card and the little white disc slowed and began crawling back the other way. After one or two swings past it, she got the hang of it, kicked the autopilot into gear, and breathed a sigh of relief as the compass steadied on twenty-five degrees.

"The radar, David. Do you remember how Lars showed us how to change it? I don't remember that part very well." She nodded up at the screen, full now with targets. "I think it's the range you have to change, but I don't know how."

David studied the machine for a moment, then cautiously reached up and turned the largest knob.

"There, oh good, David." Annie cried out in delight, "That's it, keep it there, you can see the channel again. Oh good, David."

The confusing mass of targets faded, replaced by a dark channel between the lighted targets on either side. They cruised along in silence for a while. The channel narrowed, and they could make out lights again to starboard, through the murk, and then the darkened shapes of boats, tied to floats along the shore.

"Okay," called David. "There, I think that's a marina or something. We could tie up there." David pointed at the shape of a long empty float, lit by a single light high on a piling. It was the first place to tie up that they had come to. But just when they had gotten a good glimpse at it, the rain closed in harder, blotting out the float and the shore.

"Quick, David, get a raincoat on. I want to try and get in there before I lose it again." Annie kicked the autopilot off, pulled the throttle all the way back, and turned the wheel sharply to the right, trying to peer ahead into the dark, all at the same time. As they swung around, they came up into the wind, the rain beat heavily on the glass, and a light on the dock appeared out of the murk ahead.

David stepped out into the night. Suddenly he felt the boat go into reverse and bump into something hard.

"Tie up, David, tie up! These windows are getting all steamed up. Just tie up to anything. I'm not sure I could get us in to the dock again."

The rain eased up just then, and David clambered onto the dock and managed to get them tied up securely between squalls. It was as if the storm had waited until they were tied up to reveal its true power. David was just back inside the pilothouse, taking off his rain gear, and Annie had just pulled the lever that stopped the engine when an even more powerful gust rushed down the channel from the bay outside. The boat lurched up tight against the docklines, and the rigging literally throbbed, vibrating the cabin with the power of the wind.

The twins looked out the cabin door together. Loose debris whirled down the float, and the boat heeled over at the dock. Sometimes the rain would almost stop, and they could see shore lights beyond the dock, and a moment later it would return in sheets, drumming against the front of the cabin, blotting out all light outside, and they involuntarily drew back from the doorway.

"Look," David said and nodded out astern. A set of lights had appeared in the darkness down the channel, a red and a green with three whites between them in a vertical line, and the deep throb of a big engine came to them through the night. The lights came closer and became a big tug moving slowly. Through the rain they glimpsed what looked like the pale wash of anxious faces in the pilothouse windows lit only by the dimmest light from compass and radar, peering ahead through the driving rain.

Then David poked Annie, "Look at that!"

At first she didn't see anything. But then a moment later the dimmest red light moved past them, barely visible at all through the rain, set high up on something that blotted out the faint shore lights on the other side of the channel. A sudden chill ran through her. Whatever the tug was towing was filling up almost the entire channel. The headlights of a vehicle came around the corner behind the marina just then, washing the rain-thick night for a moment and playing out on the shape of a black steel barge, almost close enough to touch. The twins got a glimpse of a flat and steeply sloping bow, high steel sides, and piles of what might have been wood chips or sawdust on top, and then the headlights swept away and all was inky black again.

"Oh, David," Annie said, suddenly shivering so violently that her teeth chattered. "What if we were still out there, trying to get in here, when that guy came by? We could have been smooshed." She slumped against the side of the cabin, totally drained by the effort of bringing the boat in.

Another gust rushed through the night around them, heeling the boat over at the dock in its fury.

"Seattle seems so far away now," Annie said when the shivering had passed.

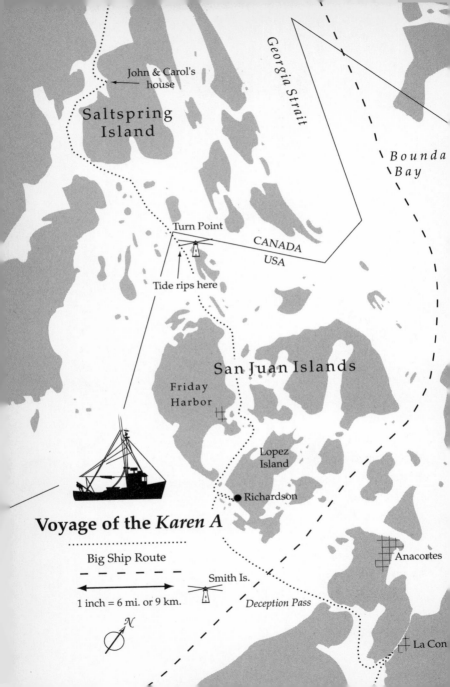

Georgia Strait

John & Carol's house

Saltspring Island

B o u n d a
Bay

Turn Point

CANADA
USA

Tide rips here

San Juan Islands

Friday Harbor

Lopez Island

● Richardson

Anacortes

Voyage of the *Karen A*

⋯⋯⋯⋯⋯⋯⋯⋯⋯⋯⋯⋯⋯

Big Ship Route

⟵⟶   Smith Is.

1 inch = 6 mi. or 9 km.

Deception Pass

✚ La Con

𝒩

CHAPTER 4

A Sick Mate

Sounds: the hiss of water in the kettle, the rattle of rain against skylight and fo'c'sle walls, the soft creaking of the docklines as the boat worked against the float. And something less comforting—the low moan of the wind through the rigging, different than it had sounded down in Seattle, more insistent, more powerful.

Annie lay for a long time listening and thinking. She remembered studying the charts down in Seattle. She hadn't understood the distances very well. She thought that they'd just start their trip, have a few rough days, and pretty soon get to Alaska and find their dad. Now, after just the first day, she knew it was not going to be easy at all.

The smell of coffee suddenly filled the little cabin. Annie sat up. Lars was sitting at his usual place at the little table.

"Lars, Annie said, "Lars, how *are* you?" She went over to sit across from him.

"Morning, Annie girl," he said in his familiar, reassuring

voice. "I see you did a fine job of tying us up. A hurricane couldn't move us with all the docklines you've put out," he gently chided her.

Then she noticed that he was drinking his coffee awkwardly with his left hand and that his right arm hung oddly limp from his shoulder. She went pale and half rose from the seat.

"Lars, what *happened?*"

"Ah, God," Lars's head sagged to his chest. "I don't want to go like this, just one piece at a time. Ah, God, these children need to go North!" Silent, choked sobs shook him.

Annie went over and put her arms around him, and after a while Lars lifted his head, sighed, and leaned back.

"We'll get a doctor," Annie said. "It'll be okay."

David got up then and came over, rubbing his eyes. "What is it, what's going on?" he asked.

"Something happened to Lars's arm. We'll get a doctor. It'll be okay," she said again, starting to put her shoes on.

"Annie, David. Just sit down one minute," Lars spoke forcefully. Annie hesitated, and he spoke again. "Please sit down and listen. Still bad weather outside. Just sit and listen." He nodded down at his arm. "Is called stroke. Something happens in brain, tiny part of brain dies, then some part of your body doesn't work. I have seen it in too many friends. Doctors don't always help. Sometimes it gets better, sometime not. We must just wait, rest a little."

Lars stopped a moment, then spoke with renewed strength. "We must go on!" He nodded his head at the wind and the rain slashing down at the boat. "When weather gets better, maybe tomorrow. You did a hard job yesterday—but you did it. See? Even if arm doesn't get better, we can do it!" His last words hung in the air for a long time, until there was only the wash of the rain and the moan of the wind.

The storm cleared after lunch and the twins walked in the slanting afternoon light along the float, up the ramp, and along a silent street into the sleepy town of La Conner. Accustomed to the noise and the press of traffic in Seattle, the stillness and peace of the place were new, yet reassuring. Houses were set back behind fences and tidy yards. The town, as they approached, revealed itself as a single street of one-story buildings beside the narrow channel through which they'd come in such difficult circumstances the evening before.

A single store was open on the water side of the street: a combination hardware, grocery, and marine supply.

"Wow," Annie stopped, pointing at the pink shape of a great snowy mountain that seemed to float above the fields and marshes at the end of the single street. As they watched, the sun's rays left the lower land that surrounded it and shone in ever-greater intensity on the slopes that flanked its almost perfect volcanic shape. They stood for a long time, transfixed. The land around grew darker, the mountain gathering the last light until it stood as a glowing beacon above the vast and empty country around it. "It's Mount Baker, I think," Annie said. "I heard someone say it was the last place the sun's rays touched in the continental U.S."

They turned and headed for the store. A tall woman was

chatting at the checkout stand when Annie came over with her single purchase, a half gallon of milk. Just as the woman picked up her bag and began to leave, two familiar faces suddenly stared out at Annie from the side of the milk carton. "HAVE YOU SEEN THESE CHILDREN?" was the heading over pictures of her and David.

Time seemed to stand still. Her head spun, her ears started to ring: "HAVE YOU SEEN THESE CHILDREN?"

"Are you all right, miss?" Annie was aware of the clerk fixing her with a concerned look. Annie nodded, stunned.

"This is it, then?"

Annie nodded again, unable to make her mouth work. The clerk reached over for the milk carton, but Annie grabbed it before she could reach it.

"Uh, miss, I need to scan the price. Are you sure everything's all right?"

"Oh, fine," Annie managed to stammer, looking over and seeing David at a display of baseball cards. "David, let's go," she said, a little too sharply.

"Hold on a moment, I might get some of these."

"No!" Annie snapped. "We have to go *now*!"

Now both David and the clerk were staring at Annie. The clerk was looking slowly back and forth between the milk carton and the two of them. "Someone's waiting for us," Annie finally managed to say, fumbling for her wallet. "We gotta go."

The clerk shrugged, made change, and put the milk in a bag. Annie swept it off the counter and headed for the door, conscious of the woman's eyes on the both of them.

"Hey, what's the deal?" David asked again. "We're not going anywhere, Lars isn't waiting for us. There were some good cards I wanted to check out."

"Keep walking," she hissed in his ear, pushing him out the door ahead of her. "Just get out of here."

"Annie, what is the *matter* with you?" David had to almost run to keep up with his sister. "You're acting so weird."

Annie looked over her shoulder. The store clerk was looking out at them. There was a telephone in her hand and she was speaking into it.

Finally the twins turned the corner, and Annie stopped beneath the next streetlight, drew the milk out of the bag, and held it up to her brother.

"That's us, David. *That's us!* Now do you see why I wanted to get out of that store?"

David stopped short and took the milk carton from his sister. "That's us," he murmured shakily.

Annie took the carton back and continued her brisk walk toward the boat.

"Do you think she recognized us?" David asked when he had caught up with her again.

"Recognized us? Not only do I think she recognized us," Annie said over her shoulder, moving as fast as she could without actually running. "Didn't you see her after we left? She was talking to someone on the phone and watching which way we went. We gotta get out of here.

"Start untying," she called out, taking the ramp down to the marina float almost at a run. "I'll tell Lars. We've got to go."

David looked out at the dark channel beyond the marina. The light was totally gone from the sky. A low mist had risen from the fields and marshes, and a chill breeze had sprung up from the north.

"Annie," he said in a frightened, almost pleading voice. "Maybe she didn't recognize us. Maybe she was just talking to a friend or somebody. Do we have to go? It was so bad out there last night."

"Do you want to go back into a foster home. Is that what you want?" Annie spun around angrily and faced him. "And how about Lars? After all he's done for us, do you want him to get into trouble, too?"

"No, I . . . " David started to talk, but she cut him off again.

"Well, that's what'll happen if we get caught. We'll never find Dad, Mom'll be in trouble, and we might even have to go to kid's prison. Just start untying those lines." She hopped nimbly over the rail and disappeared into the pilothouse.

Lars was standing inside, turning the steering wheel awkwardly back and forth with his left hand.

"Lars, look," Annie set the milk carton by the compass. "That's us in the picture. The lady in the store saw us. I think we should leave."

He fumbled in his shirt pocket, got his glasses on, and stared at the pictures before answering. "Annie girl, do you think she recognized you then?"

"Ah, Lars, I don't really know for sure," she answered in a flat, tired voice. "It seemed she was looking at us funny, and she got on the phone right after we left. I just don't want to go back and have to go into a foster home again."

He sagged back against the wheel. "Well, we must go then, but you must be my hands for a little bit. First thing every day before starting engine, you must check juices: oil, water in engine. Is easy, just take paper towel, pull off wood panel by steps, and look in for dipstick."

As soon as Annie was done checking the engine, Lars started it up, David finished untying, and then Lars turned to Annie, "You must steer. I guide but you steer. Just head down the channel where we come from."

The engine thunked into gear, and Annie took the wheel, a little uneasily but glad that Lars was beside her.

"We're going back?" David asked anxiously, when he came in from coiling the lines and saw they were turning back toward Seattle.

"No," Lars said gently. "There is another way."

"See, she called the cops," said Annie. "I was right." Thirty yards or so ahead of them on the town side of the channel, they could see the store. A police cruiser was parked in front, doors open. Inside the store, the dark-clad figure of a policeman was talking to someone.

"Turn off lights, boy, middle switch by door." Lars nodded toward a switch panel by David's elbow.

David flipped the switch and Lars pulled the throttle back and had Annie steer over to the side of the channel away from the town. They were abreast of the store just then, and the woman had come out, and was pointing in the direction the children had walked. The twins winced as the policeman turned and slowly scanned the channel. For a moment it seemed as if he was looking directly at them.

"It's all right," Lars reassured them, "with running lights off, dark night, they can't see us." Still, it seemed like a long time before the lights of town disappeared into the mists and darkness astern. Lars switched on the running lights again, throttled up, and they could relax a little.

"Oh, Lars," Annie said after they'd made the turn and could see the flash of the lights on the breakwaters ahead. "We didn't mean to get you into all this trouble. Look at what's happened—we're fugitives and you can't move your arm. You'd still be back cozy and safe in Seattle if we hadn't come along, instead of having to try to find some place to go in the darkness."

Lars fiddled with the radar controls before speaking.

"Stroke would happen here or in Seattle, no difference," he finally said, then paused again for a few moments. He nodded out at the necklace of lights around the horizon. "Now listen: old man in his boat in wintertime in Seattle—I go to store, watch a little television, talk with friends sometimes." He waved at the three of them crowded together in the pilothouse. "This is better. We are together, we are doing something, going somewhere. This is better." And then he peered out into the dark again. "This is not bad. No wind, clear night, good visibility."

Instead of turning south at the end of the breakwater, the way they had come, Lars turned north.

The radar screen showed only a dead-end bay ahead. Out the front windows, the occasional lights of vehicles could be seen along a high road, appearing and reappearing though the trees along the whole perimeter of the bay.

"We're just going to anchor?" Annie said doubtfully. "Wouldn't this be pretty close to town if they come looking for us?"

"We keep going," Lars said, nodding up at the radar

display. "There is a channel."

The twins looked doubtfully at the solid line of shore ahead of them on the screen and at the headlights moving across the darkness.

"But how can we get through?" David asked anxiously.

"Watch now," Lars said, nodding out the front windows. Just then the lights of a vehicle appeared, ahead of them and high up, illuminating what appeared to be parts of some sort of structure.

"It's a bridge!" the twins both said together in awe as the height of the structure ahead was revealed by the headlights.

"Here, David, time for you to steer. Deception Pass. Can be bad place for logs." Lars turned on the bow spotlight, and pulled the throttle back to half.

The channel, illuminated by the beam shafting out into the night, was a canyon where the tide created strong currents. On either side were the abutments and supports of a narrow and very high bridge. Although there was no wind, the water ahead seemed troubled, driven into a short, steep chop by some unseen force, and David fought with the wheel.

"Watch now, boy, current is strong!" A swirling eddy filled with debris and small logs whirled toward them out of the black.

"Ahhh, where can I go?" David cried out.

"To shore, steer close to shore," Lars said steadily and David turned the wheel hard over with difficulty against the current. The three of them peered anxiously ahead as the logs swept by close to port, and he steered out toward the middle of the channel again, the current sweeping them on with increasing speed. And in a few minutes it was done, the channel opened up, the dark, high land fell away behind them, and the twins peered ahead in amazement at the vast spaces ahead. To port, the lights of Port Townsend were spread out across the shore, perhaps eight miles distant. To starboard, the shapes of the San Juan Islands, dark, high, and mysterious, lay across the water, faintly shimmering in the dim light of the half moon. And between them lay a wide channel, stretching away into the distance as far as the eye could see.

They traveled a little farther in silence, pushed along by the tide, the twins awed by the change, so unexpected and so dramatic.

"Juan de Fuca Strait, it goes to the ocean," Lars motioned at the dark channel ahead. "Big boats go to Alaska that way. Not for little boats." Then Lars altered course slightly to starboard, toward the San Juan Islands. "We go through the islands."

Morning. The boy woke first, laying there a long while, listening, not remembering at first where he was, nor recognizing the dim gray shapes around him. Something like water lapped very close. At regular intervals, muffled and far away, came the sound of a horn, but not a city horn, deeper, somehow more mournful. Finally he remembered: deep in the night he'd dropped the anchor. Lars had said they were at Lopez Island. He got up and crept up into the pilothouse to look around.

Fog surrounded them totally, cloaking wherever they were with gray invisibility. He dozed off, then woke later. There was the smell of coffee, and then the radio was turned up.

". . . in local news, police in La Conner are investigating the sighting of a Seattle-area pair of missing children, thirteen-year-old twins, a boy and a girl, at the Harbor Market. Extensive inquiries failed to turn up any trace of the pair, and police speculate that they might have been passing through on a boat." Lars snapped the radio off. David got up on one elbow. Annie had swung her legs to sit up on her bunk.

"That's us, isn't it, Lars? What are we going to do now about groceries and stuff? They'll be on the lookout for us, and you can't carry anything with your arm."

"There is a store here." Lars nodded out at the invisible harbor around them. "Very small. I know the people. Anyway we load boat in Seattle, don't need much."

"But won't the police be looking for us? Won't they be checking boats?"

"Pah," the old man snorted. "Police plenty busy enough without chasing every runaway child. Besides what are they going to be checking boats with? No police boats up here."

They pulled the anchor and motored over to tie at a dock in front of a building with a faded sign: "Richardson Store, Lopez Island." The three of them stopped at the top of the dock and looked around at a small, austere, and windblown bay. A few tired houses were scattered here and there, but no cars moved. Across from the dock and ramshackle general store rose a high and rocky point of land, beyond which was a menacing seascape of small treeless islets and reefs surrounded by white and broken water.

"Hey, Annie, look, bikes." Behind the store was a rack with half a dozen old-fashioned Schwinns and a hand-lettered sign: "Bike rentals—inquire inside." David went over and rang the bell on one of the bicycles, running his hands wistfully over the chipped chrome of the handlebars.

"Can we, Lars? Just for an hour or so. It might be our last chance for a long time."

Lars looked at the two of them standing at the bike rack, and wondered how long it had been since they'd had what he called a regular life: a home, a neighborhood, such things as bikes and friends.

"Just tuck your hair up under that cap so you don't look so much like that picture on the milk box." He waved them off with a smile. "Yah, go ahead now. I take care of bike, grocery, too. I'm not so helpless as you think."

"Git on with you now," he waved them off again. "Is a good day for it. Lots of bad weather ahead."

"All right! C'mon, David, race you to the top of the hill!" Like two colts suddenly released, the twins rushed off, riding standing up, pumping the bikes across the parking lot, up and over the rise, and out of sight.

Annie and David passed into the shade of a little copse of trees, dropped into a dip, and then passed suddenly from the cool into the warmth of the sun again.

"Oh, David!" Annie cried out. "Don't you just love the feeling?" The rush of air against their faces and the feel of the bikes beneath them transported them to better days so long ago, to their first house after they'd moved down to the Lower 48, to their first bikes, wobbling around the little cul-de-sac where they'd waited with their friends every morning for the school bus.

Before they started moving. Before the apartment in the south end, where there were fights at the bus stop. Before they moved and moved and moved, losing a little something each time. First the box of Annie's favorite dolls, and then David's models. Before it got bad.

The island road ran by brown fields, the dew glinting brightly in the unexpected late November sun. Cattle and deer looked up, startled at the sudden appearance of the two chattering teenagers on the bikes. Into a long lane between tall, dark firs, out into the light, along a marshy beach and across a wooded isthmus, and then out suddenly into the clear again, up a hill, and finally to a stop at a gravel turnaround.

They stood for a long while, catching their breath and drinking in the view. An eagle slowly soared by, holding something big in its mouth, headed for a nest in the top of a big spruce.

"What's going to happen to us?" Annie asked quietly.

"What do you mean?"

"You know. Lars having that stroke and not being able to use his arm, and now our pictures on the milk cartons. Do you think we'll ever get up to Alaska and find Dad?"

David laid his bike down and skipped a stone off the bluff into the water below before answering.

"I know. Back in Seattle it just seemed that we'd go through the locks and a few days later we'd be seeing Dad again. I guess I never really thought about exactly how long it would take. This is nice," he said, the sweep of his arm taking in the bikes, the day around them, "but sometimes I wish we hadn't left." He turned around to face his sister. "How

come you were so down on that foster home? They treated
me okay. Harold took me to Mariners games a couple of
times. We could have gone back there."

"You were lucky," Annie said wistfully. "Harold didn't
bother you. He was all over me."

David swiveled to face his sister, a look of puzzlement on
his face. "What do you mean?"

"I mean the whole time we lived there, I had to figure out
how to avoid being alone with him. That whole business
of wanting to convert the rec room into another bedroom:
'She's almost thirteen, she needs to have her own room.' You
want to know what the *real* reason was?"

David looked at his sister, open-mouthed.

"The real reason was that he wanted to be alone with me.
I'm never going back to a foster home. Never."

When they returned the bikes, Lars was back aboard, and
the low sun disappeared into a thick cloud bank. And while
they lay snugly asleep at the dock, a snow came in the night,
sweeping down from the Canadian Okanagan country. It
blotted out the lights of Vancouver, Surrey, New Westminster,
Bellingham, and a hundred smaller towns.

"David, David!" Annie pulled on his arm and whispered hoarsely in his ear. "Snow, come see!"

He stumbled groggily across the cabin, half pulled by
Annie, up the steps, to slide the pilothouse door open a crack,
to see and reach and feel the big, softly falling flakes turn to
glistening water from the warmth of his palm.

"Snow," he spoke in awe, half turning to his sister.
"Snow. You know, I don't think we've seen real snow since that
last Christmas up North with Dad."

They stood there a long time, the two of them, staring out at that white world beyond the walls of the tiny pilot-house.

"C'mon," David said, "We gotta go out. It might melt."

Something about a good snow along that rainy coast transforms the land more so than in climates where it is common. At times Seattle may go for year without a snow that lasts overnight. And so for the twins, as they walked along the float, up the ramp, and across the white plain to the trees, the landscape was a revelation. Their rubber-booted feet paused again and again—when the boat disappeared into the whiteness behind, when the bay disappeared into the whiteness below, and then when the trees appeared, almost mysteriously, from the snowy veil before them.

The smell of coffee woke Lars, and he got up on his good elbow in his bunk, peering across at Annie working in the cone of light at the stove. She had on a brown turtleneck, and a single crystal hung on a string around her neck.

"So is coffee ye're drinking now, gal?" he said in his soft voice.

"No, I made it for you," she answered simply, her damp brown hair shining in the light. "It's snowing out there now. It's wonderful."

The old man's eyes shone, and it was all he could do just to nod at her, and think of how much better his life had become, even with the stroke, since that nasty evening when the twins had knocked on his door.

In the early afternoon they drew in the frozen lines and moved off into the snowy world. The dock, the store, the trees, and the cove had disappeared into the white. David steered first, and the three of them stood close together in the pilothouse, peering out the windows at the swirling white. Lars took a long time before they left the dock tuning the radar so that it could penetrate the snow better, but even so, there were times when the snow came on heavier, and the shapes on the radar screen that they so depended on were hidden, distorted and lost in clutter, and the twins were anxious.

"Is not so bad," Lars reassured them. "The channel is wide."

But the twins watched the radar, and a little later the snow came on even heavier and the radar picture blurred until it was impossible to determine which was the snow, the land, and the water. They could feel the tide push the boat suddenly one way, then, unexpectedly, another. Lars's voice tightened, and the steering commands to David came quicker, and David struggled to obey as he felt the strength of the current fighting him through the spokes of the wheel. David began to feel dizzy. The compass started a slow turn and he tried to chase it, disoriented and confused.

And then Lars's one good hand was on his, gently pushing the wheel the other way, and his voice sure and strong, "Just steer straight now, Davie, remember. Always steer the boat around the compass." After a bit the little spell of vertigo passed, the tide seemed to pull at them a little less hard, and he could steer straight again.

The short day died, and all was dark except for the circle of light on the compass and the dim shapes on the radar.

"Look," Annie pointed at the lights of a harbor, a town, houses seen for a moment through the snow and then gone. But Lars made no move to turn the boat.

"What was that?" Annie asked concerned. "Lars, it's dark. We're going in there, aren't we? I mean, it looks like a harbor. Shouldn't we go in for the night?"

"Ah," Lars said, "it is Friday Harbor, San Juan Islands. Good place for night, but U.S. Customs is there. Maybe they listen to radio this morning about runaway kids, now they see strange boat come in for the night. Maybe they come and ask questions." His voice trailed off.

Annie peered longingly out the window toward the town. "Well, we don't have to tie up. Couldn't we just go to one of the corners of the harbor and drop the anchor for the night? That would be okay, wouldn't it?"

"Canada border is just twenty miles. Is calm, a good night to cross," Lars said simply. "Snow, no wind, no one to see us. You see, we are supposed to go to Canada Customs, to show our papers. Maybe they have list of runaway children."

"So we're going to run all night in this?" David asked anxiously.

"Pah, we have this," Lars patted the radar display. "No wind, just snow. Watch chart, look radar, is easy. But listen— when I first started fishing in winter, we went in snow. We had no radar then, only chart. That was hard."

"Well, where are we going to end up tonight, are we going to just keep going to get clear of Customs?" Annie asked.

"Ah, no, old man like to sleep at night, too." Lars smiled and tapped a place near the top of the chart. "Special surprise for us tonight. Friend lives up here, has a nice dock, and a big house. I wrote him. We can stay with him for a few days."

"A house?" Annie brightened immediately. "You mean a house with a shower?"

"Even better," Lars smiled in the darkness, "house with bathtub!"

An hour later, the wind came. They were in Boundary Pass, where the tide swirls, boils, and rips, creating great patches of broken water even on the calmest days.

Annie was on watch then, Lars steady at her shoulder. The autopilot steered them faithfully, and as it rotated back and forth, she sat behind the wheel studying the chart and the radar in the dim light to ensure that they were traveling along the line that Lars had drawn.

Suddenly the boat lurched to the right and dropped into a hole in the water, then fetched up so hard that the windows rattled and fishing gear, a paperback, and everything loose in the pilothouse was thrown to the floor.

Annie cried out in alarm, and Lars instantly kicked the autopilot out of gear, pulled the throttle back to half, and turned the wheel with his good arm. The pilothouse door slid open with a bang, and a gust of snow and bitter wind eddied around them. Annie shrank into the corner, frightened and shivering.

"Steer, girl, right now! I cannot do it." There was anxiety in Lars's voice.

Annie hesitated. The snow and the cold swirled around the cabin. She just wanted to go below and stand close to the cozy stove.

"NOW, Annie. I cannot steer with just the one arm!"

Hesitantly, Annie approached Lars, and then suddenly he pushed her in front of the wheel, and the spokes were in her hands, fighting her like a living creature. The boat dropped heavily into another tide rip and lurched crazily to the right this time. She heard the door slide and latch shut, and then Lars was at her side again.

The great beam of the lighthouse at Turn Point suddenly shone through the snow directly at them, illuminating a confused white-capped sea beneath a tunnel of swirling white. Annie turned the wheel with all her strength, but the boat seemed hardly to respond at all.

"Lars," she called out, "help me, I can hardly turn it!"

Lars edged in close to her side and pulled on the spokes a little with his left arm, and together they turned the wheel a little further. When the beam of the light swept them again, it was from the side instead of from the front.

They dropped just then, as if the very water beneath them had disappeared, then fetched up hard, shaking the whole boat. Annie lurched forward with the impact, bumping into the wall, and biting her lip. Then the light swept them again and for a single, terrifying moment, Annie could see what looked like a vertical wall of water ahead. Suddenly the bow was lifting into it. As she watched, almost as if it were in slow motion, the water slowly came over the bow— green, solid water that pushed for a moment heavily against the window glass, then disappeared off to the sides before they started dropping once again. She braced herself for another bone-jarring impact, but the shape of the wave must have been different for they rode it a little easier. Then the beam of the light swept them again, but this time from the other side. She had steered them almost in a circle!

Nearly panic-stricken, Annie stole a quick glance at the radar screen to see if it had cleared. "Lars," she called out, "I need a course. I forgot what we were steering. Quick, give me a course to steer!" Then another sea slammed into them, and Lars was thrown against the side of the cabin.

"Just steer a little west of north," he finally said in a hoarse, pained voice. "Three hundred and thirty degrees."

She squinted at the compass, but it was spinning so rapidly that she could hardly read it in her addled state. "Steer the boat around the compass. The compass doesn't move. Just steer the boat around the compass," Annie murmured, repeating what Lars had taught her what seemed like months ago. The compass card was swinging to the left. She thought for a moment, then fought the wheel to the left, until the spinning slowed a bit. When the big decorated "N" came up, she steadied it up, and gingerly turned the wheel to the left again until the pointer was at 330 before centering it again, totally concentrating on the compass, not looking out the window at all.

"Let's go back, Lars," Annie said. "Let's go back to Friday Harbor. It's too rough out here. What if a window gets busted?"

"Tide too strong," she heard him say, in a soft and far-away voice. "We must keep going. Just steer 330, is fine."

The light at Turn Point illuminated the water around them just then, fainter now, barely penetrating the snow, obviously coming from much farther away. Annie could see that the seas were a little lower and less confused.

"What happened? Geez, your lip is bleeding—what happened, are you all right?" David suddenly appeared beside her.

"Hit my head on the wall back there." Annie didn't trust herself to let go of the steering wheel quite yet. "It was a tide rip or something. It's better now.

"Tide rip?" David said. "I thought we had hit something. You should have felt it down below. It just about threw me out of my bunk. I wonder if it loosened the lashings on that hatch cover." He started to open the door.

"Hey, what's the deal? I can't get this door open." She heard him struggle with the door until there was a grating sound, and then a cold blast of air eddied around her legs.

"Hey, it's *ice* out there!" David came in a moment later, and he spoke in an awed voice. "You can hardly stand up. It's just all ice." He turned to Lars. "That's why I couldn't open the door at first. It was frozen shut! And now I can barely close it!"

Lars moved with surprising agility over to the doorway, turned a switch and peered out.

"Ah, lord," the twins heard him say to himself. "Making ice in Boundary Pass, and not even the first of December."

Annie engaged the autopilot and joined David and Lars, looking out on the back deck.

The mast-mounted decklights shone down on a scene that she barely recognized as the boat she had lived on for more than two weeks. The big, boxlike hatch cover that dominated the middle of the back deck looked more like a lumpy white knoll of ice, and what Lars called the hayrack, the high pipe framework that held their skiff and other gear, had grown grotesquely thick and odd-looking, with thick icicles. And every time she felt the boat drop into a sea, spray would fly back over the top of the house and freeze onto the ice that was already there.

"It's pretty, isn't it, Lars?" she said in an uncertain voice, struck by the strange beauty of the ice, yet uneasy, wanting some reassurance from their experienced skipper.

"Is beautiful, yah," Lars said slowly, "But all the same, is a beauty we could live without."

"What do you mean?"

"Weight, girl. Ice is fearsome heavy, and if there's ice back there," he nodded toward the back deck, "then ice up on top and in all the rigging. You notice she feels a little bit different, the way she moves? Can you feel it?"

"It almost seems better than it was back a little ways," she said.

"Yah, that's it now, see, that's what fools you. The more ice on topsides, the slower she rolls. Feels better until *boom*, one time she takes an easy roll and just keeps going all the way over."

Annie looked out the door as the boat shuddered slightly and another sheet of spray enveloped the back deck to quickly freeze onto every exposed surface. She turned to Lars again, "You mean, that could happen to us?"

"Ten years back, two big steel crab boats, sister ships just like that *Pacific Viking* in Seattle, six guys on board each one, new, fancy boats, some of best in whole fleet, leave harbor up North to fish crab. Next day another boat sees sinking hull upside down. Other boat, they never heard from. Just gone, no survivors. Both boats had many crabpots stacked on deck. The ice made them top-heavy and *boom*!" Lars made a motion with his hand of a boat rolling over.

Neither twin said anything for a long time, remembering the big steel boat that had been behind them in Seattle. It had looked so huge there at the dock, as if surely it could go anywhere.

"But it must have been really rough when those big boats went down, right, Lars?" David asked.

"No, not rough like you think," Lars said. "Just rough enough to throw a lot of spray, and it keeps freezing and getting heavier, heavier. But not rough!"

Lars pulled the throttle back so as to slow them down and create less freezing spray.

Except for the purr of the engine, the hum of the autopilot, and the occasional soft hiss of spray hitting the windows, it was more or less quiet, almost peaceful compared to what it had been in the tide rip.

"We're okay, aren't we, Lars?" David asked after Lars had spent a particularly long time looking out the back door and studying the radar screen.

"Now make ice on radar," Lars pointed at the radar screen. "Hard to see targets." Where once the targets had been crisp and well-defined shapes, now they seemed to be getting fainter and dimmer.

"So what do we do?"

"Wait, and hope we get into shelter behind island before the ice gets too bad." Lars tried to make his voice flat, but the twins could sense the anxiety behind it.

"But what if it gets too bad, what do we do then?" David asked, a tiny tremor in his voice.

"Ah, then we have to chip ice. But not to worry, little one, we'll be okay!"

Another while passed. David stood behind the wheel and watched the compass and radar. He tried not to look at the radar, but when his eyes strayed up there, almost against his will, he could see that the targets were getting fainter.

Finally, when the radar screen had gone almost blank, Lars pulled the throttle all the way back to an idle, turned on the cabin lights, and waved over to the corner where the rain jackets, pants, and boots were kept.

"Okay, David, you must chop ice on radar. Suit up and put boots on."

"Me?" The thought of going out onto the back deck, into the black and the wind and the freezing spray, much less trying to climb on top of the cabin to the radar antenna, terrified David.

"Yah, David. I wouldn't ask if I could do it, but I can't with this arm."

"I'll do it." Annie quickly volunteered, stepping forward into the cone of light.

"No, is job for strongest. Let David do it."

David stood there for a moment, looking at the two of them, already chilled at the thought of what he had to do and wishing that they were back in Seattle again, that they had never left.

"You must do it, boy." Lars held the rain gear out to David.

Numbly, without a word, David put on his sweatshirt, boots, and rain gear. When he was done, Lars handed Annie a coil of line, telling her to tie one end firmly around David's waist and the other end around the mast.

"Safety line, boy. If you go overboard, we haul you in like fish."

Annie tied it around his waist.

"W . . . w . . . well, what if I go overboard," David

stammered, "Who's gonna pull me back aboard—Annie?"

Annie looked at him with big eyes.

"Just work carefully. You'll be fine. And hold on."

Lars slid back the door with his good arm, turned on the deck lights, and David stood for a long moment, transfixed by the sight before him.

The boat had just enough speed on for the automatic pilot to keep them pointed up into the wind and the seas. The motion of the boat was easy, and the flying spray was at a minimum. But not a single shape that lay beyond the pilothouse door was recognizable as man-made. All was reshaped by the ice into strange, white sculptures.

"Okay, boy, now listen carefully." Lars had a bag of salt and was throwing some on the icy deck as he talked. "Job is not easy, but you must do it. First chip ice off ladder rungs. Then climb up very carefully. Is very slippery on top of house, all ice. Always have one hand holding on. Always! I will stop radar, and you have to sit up, hold on to radar mast with one hand, and tap antenna gently to get ice off. Ice will come off easy. But please remember, tap gently!"

David was conscious of Annie pulling on her rain gear next to him, but mostly he stared out the door at the ice world and the black water beyond, with its long streaks of foam, now hidden, now revealed by the snow. It was as frightening a sight as he had ever beheld, and he had to go out into it.

"C'mon, David," Annie said. "Time's a-wasting. The sooner we go out, the sooner we'll get it done."

But David wouldn't move, so Annie took the mallet from his gloved hands, stepped neatly past him and, without a word, began knocking ice off the ladder. It was as Lars had said, once you tapped it, the ice really came off easily. In just a short time, she had the ladder clear as high as she could reach, and began climbing up.

"No," David put his hand firmly on her shoulder, and she stepped back. "I'll do it, but thanks."

David worked his way carefully to the top of the ladder, chipping the ice as he went. But at the top of the pilothouse, the handrails on either side were too far away to gain a grip, even if they hadn't been transformed into mere ridges in the ice. Only the cradle of the life raft canister offered any chance of a handhold, and then only if David could get half his body up onto the roof, stretch way out, and chip enough ice to create a place to grip. It looked almost impossible. He crept back down the ladder a bit to get out of the wind.

"C'mon, David. Lars says we need to get that radar going," Annie called up. He seemed to be frozen at the top of the ladder. She poked him a couple of times in the legs, and saw him nod his hooded head. Then, climbing up the rest of the rungs, he disappeared over the edge of the pilot-house until only his feet and lower legs were left, wrapped around the mast.

He felt the raw, metallic taste of fear, bordering on panic. He stretched as far as he could with his feet still on the ladder and managed to chip enough ice to grab a handhold on the raft cradle. Then the boat rolled a bit, and he froze where he was, paralyzed, unable to go forward or back, terrified of losing his tenuous grip and sliding off into the sea, lifeline and all.

"The radar, David, the *radar*. Lars says there's a rock up ahead somewhere, and he has to turn it on soon. Have you gotten the ice off it yet?" Annie was up on the ladder, yelling and poking at his legs.

He held on tighter, but the jabs in his legs came more insistently, and the voice: "The radar, David, the *radar*!"

The bow dipped into an especially steep sea, and a sheet of freezing spray enveloped them. Some of the water ran down David's neck, as if to remind him of the precariousness of his position. It was then he realized that the hammer was still tightly clenched in his hand, and that if he sat up a little higher and arched his back to keep wedged in tightly, he could maneuver his arm around and reach the radar antenna.

Though the ice was four inches thick in places, the amazing thing was how it fell cleanly away when he tapped it just right. Once he had finally gotten into position, the actual knocking off of the ice didn't take long at all.

When he was done, he picked his moment when the boat wasn't moving so badly, and slithered back along the ice and over the edge to climb down a couple of rungs, and wedge himself in between the cabin and the mast again. He needed just to hold on and get his breath back after the awful cold and wind and yawning black sea all around him. He called down, "Okay, okay, Annie, I got it, try it, try it."

A few moments passed, and then she hammered on his legs, "It works, you did it, you *did* it!" He climbed down, shivering all over.

Annie was steering in her rain gear, turning the boat sharply to port as Lars studied the radar, calling out the course in a calm and reassuring voice. After they turned, it was bad again for a little bit, and David glanced out the back door and winced at the sight, but said nothing to the others. For on their new course the spray came aboard in heavy sheets, reshaping the ice-sculpted deck almost as he watched.

But then it seemed to get a little better, the boat rolled a little less, the wind was a little less fierce, and most of all, the freezing spray dropped down.

Lars finally turned from his study of the radar screen and the chart, and slapped David on the shoulder of his wet jacket.

"Good job, David! Light on rock was out or frozen over. Without you, we might still be out there." His voice trailed off, but he didn't have to spell it out. Without knowing where to make the turn to shelter, they risked hitting the rocky shore, or if they stayed out in the exposed part of the channel, it would have been only a matter of time before the weight of the ice forming all over their little boat raised the center of gravity high enough that the *Karen A* would have simply rolled over.

David looked at the clock. Just eight o'clock. Less than an hour had passed since they'd first gotten into the tide rip by the lighthouse, yet it had seemed like all night.

Lars turned, and noticing their wet shirts, urged the twins into the fo'c'sle. "Get dry clothes on now and fix some cocoa." They quickly did as they were bid, hanging up the cold and damp rain gear on the pegs. Annie ducked behind the curtain to change, and tossed a dry sweatshirt out to David. Then the two of them stood as close to the fo'c'sle stove as they could without getting burned.

"I don't think I could have done it, you know, what you did, go up there with the ice and all," Annie said quietly. "I couldn't have done it."

"It was awful," David said in a flat voice. "If I had slipped, you two never would have been able to get me back aboard." He turned his back toward the stove and shook his head, still shivering. Annie said nothing, but leaned into her brother's shoulder while they waited for the kettle to whistle.

"If I had known it would be like this, I would never have left Seattle," David said through chattering teeth. He kept his voice low, not intending for Lars to hear. "Annie, have you studied the chart at all? This is only the beginning and this isn't even supposed to be the worst part of the trip."

The kettle boiled just then, and Annie made cocoa. She took a cup up to Lars, set it in front of him, and stood off a little ways in the darkness, studying him.

He looked older than she remembered, but he'd known exactly what to do, even if he hadn't been able to do it himself. She knew that it was a long trip, even without looking at the chart, but all they could do was take it one day at a time. But most of all she knew that whatever they were doing, it was better than going back to another foster home.

Lars turned around just then, as if noticing her for the first time, and waved her over to the chart.

"I must lie down, Annie. We have not far to go. Now we are here, and my friend's dock is here. Just stay in middle of channel." His thick finger stabbed down onto the chart. "There is no wind now, just snow. Good picture on radar. One hour and we will be there. Get me up and I will find the dock." And before she could say anything, he took his cocoa and hobbled down the stairs to the fo'c'sle.

Alone suddenly in that strange, dark world of compass,

radar, and chart, Annie tried to concentrate on the shapes on the screen and the line on the chart. It was eerie: except for a dark hole in the front middle pane where the little fan had somehow managed to melt the ice, the windows were totally opaque, iced over on the outside and frosted on the inside.

"David?" she called softly down the steps. "Come up and be with me. It's too weird up here alone."

When he was beside her, she continued, "What if something happened to the radar and it was off a little bit, and you couldn't tell until you hit something? I don't like it when you can't see anything. Especially in the snow, I'm not sure I can ever get used to steering without something to aim at."

"At least it's not rough," he finally said, "or that spray freezing onto us again. I didn't like that part."

And finally they just stood, touching shoulders, totally humbled and sobered by the dark and snowy sea world that passed unseen, just a few feet away. Now and again Annie would kick the pilot out of gear and alter course to stay in the middle of the channel, handling the wheel ever so gently, as if too great a motion would send the compass into a spin again that she might not be able to stop.

"Now I know what the sailors in the old days must have felt like," Annie said after a long wordless spell. "You know, like Columbus's crew, they were afraid they might fall off the edge of the earth."

David stood at the back door for a moment before answering, looking out the crack at the strange ice shapes, dimly seen in the thin glow from the iced-over stern running light.

"It is spooky," he admitted. "I don't like it when Lars isn't here, especially at night."

"I think that's it," Annie said after the shape of a cove had begun to crawl down from the top of the radar screen. "Go get Lars up."

David returned a minute later. "He can't get up." His voice was tight. "He's real weak. He told me we'd have to find the place ourselves, tie up, and get his friends to help him."

Annie waved David in behind the wheel and went below.

The light over Lars's bunk was on. She bent over him. His face seemed paler than before, his whiskers stuck out more prominently than she had remembered.

"Lars, Lars." She pushed his arm gently, and was relieved when his eyes opened, swam vacantly in their sockets for a moment, and finally focused on her. "Lars," she said again, "what's the matter?"

"Just tired, Annie girl. Just tired. Dock is right in middle of cove. Just go in close, put radar on lowest range, and look for it. You can do it. Johnny Jacobsen's dock, is only house there." Lars slumped back against the pillows, and his eyes closed, his face grimacing in pain.

"Okay, David," she said when she'd made the pilot-house again. "You wanna make the landing? One of us has to be outside looking for the dock, and ready to tie up, and the other has to drive." Annie spoke with more confidence than she felt.

David shrank back from the wheel. "No, go ahead. You did it before." He reluctantly began pulling on his only dry sweatshirt and the still-damp rain gear.

"Okay," she called out to her brother after ten minutes,

looking down into the radar. "I'm heading right for it. You'll have to tell me when you see it. The window's almost totally frosted over."

The target grew larger and closer and closer to the middle of the screen. She took the boat out of gear, and hollered out the back door to her brother, "I'm afraid to go any further. We must be almost on it. What do you see?"

David shivered and peered ahead into the gloom. First there was nothing but wet snowflakes hitting his cheeks. Then his eyes grew used to the dark and he saw something, first just a vague shape, but then becoming clearly rectangular.

"That's it. That's it, swing right a little bit."

Annie turned the wheel anxiously, still almost totally blind inside the pilothouse. Just then she felt the boat scrape roughly against something, and reversed, until she heard David calling out to stop. Finally she took the engine out of gear, pulled on her boots, flipped on the deck lights, and stepped gingerly outside.

The lights revealed a dock so deep in snow that David had to kick around to find something to tie up to. A long walkway led up into the darkness. The cleats on the *Karen A* were so covered with ice that David had to tie the lines around the big trolling poles. Annie stopped the engine and they stood for a moment in the silence.

"Well, I guess I should try to find somebody," David said finally, "Lars said they knew we were coming."

"No, wait," Annie said quickly. "I'll go with you." She checked to see that Lars was still sleeping, then grabbed her coat and a flashlight, and half climbed, half slid over the rail to the dock.

The snow was deep, but new and light enough that they could walk without too much trouble. Annie passed David the light, and wordlessly they began moving away from the boat toward the walkway.

"Annie, look." David pointed behind them.

Annie turned around and stopped at the sight of the boat beneath the cone of the decklights. Standing beside it or on the back deck hadn't afforded them a full view of the transformation the ice had wrought. It was frightening: the whole front of the boat had a bloated, misshapen, ghostly look, especially the wire rigging, which in places had grown as thick as a man's leg.

"Oh my gosh," Annie finally managed to find her voice. "That's us. Look at what the ice did. No wonder boats turn over; think how *heavy* it must be."

Finally the two of them moved off carefully through the snow, the beam of the flashlight penetrating barely ten feet through the steady curtain of thick flakes. The walkway led at a slight upward angle to the shore. They stopped there for a moment, uncertain, then Annie saw a glow through the snow and they moved slowly toward it.

The glow became the lighted windows of a tidy log house with a broad deck.

"Oh, they've got a fire," David said in an awestruck voice. Through the frost-rimmed glass could be seen the dancing flames in a hearth surrounded by the chairs and furnishings of a cozy room. For a moment, the twins just stood there, rooted to the spot by the sight of such a tranquil scene after all they had been through.

"Well, c'mon," Annie said at last. "Lars said they were

friends. He needs help."

In response to their knock, the porch light went on, half blinding them, and a tall, gangly man with a surprised look on his face opened the door.

"We're friends of Lars Hansen from Seattle," Annie stammered, startled by the light.

A woman with long hair and a thick sweater came to stand behind the man.

"Lars came in this?" The man seemed almost speechless that they had arrived on such a night, and finally the woman elbowed him aside.

"John," she said in a hushed voice, "they're children, and they're shivering. Come in, come in. I'm Carol; this is John. Welcome, welcome." She ushered the twins inside like a mother hen shooing her chicks away from danger.

"Where is Lars?" John said when he realized that the twins were alone.

"In his bunk," Annie answered. "He's sick, or maybe just real tired. He couldn't get up and we had to find your dock by ourselves."

The older couple exchanged glances, and without a word John pulled on boots and a coat and stepped out into the night.

The twins gravitated to the fireplace and answered Carol's gentle questions in monosyllables, amazed to have come through the ice and snow to such a place. She brought hot tea and scones and set them on a table by the fire.

After a while they heard clumping feet on the outside deck, and John came in with Lars's arm around his shoulder, the two of them with snowy hair and coats, and sat him gently down in a big chair by the fire.

"Iced up so bad you barely know it's a boat, Carol," John said in an awed voice, looking at the twins. "Lars sick in the bunk and the children found this place and brought the boat in. On a night with as heavy a snowfall as we've ever seen."

"You'll stay here awhile then," Carol said over her shoulder to the twins, setting plates of something hot and steaming on the long table near the fire.

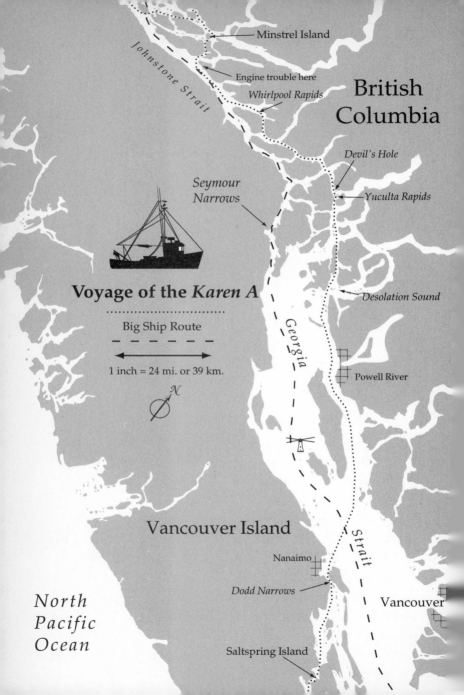

Minstrel Island

Engine trouble here

Whirlpool Rapids

Johnstone Strait

British Columbia

Devil's Hole

Seymour Narrows

Yuculta Rapids

Desolation Sound

Voyage of the *Karen A*

- - - - - - - - - -

Big Ship Route

- - - - -

1 inch = 24 mi. or 39 km.

N

Georgia

Powell River

Vancouver Island

Strait

Nanaimo

Dodd Narrows

Vancouver

North Pacific Ocean

Saltspring Island

CHAPTER 5

Engine Trouble

 Doctor Burns was a big man and he came by boat. When he tied up, he stood for a long time looking at the strange craft that lay there also. Only down by the water's edge could he see a painted surface, see the texture of the wood planks, and be sure that it was a vessel, and not some odd ice structure that had drifted in with the tide.

When he was done examining Lars, he took tea with the five of them, and stood with his back to the crackling fire to give his diagnosis. He spoke with a strong highland brogue, for he was a Scotsman.

"Awheeel now, with some people in Lars's condition, I'd say the hospital and therapy." He looked over at the twins, and thought about all they'd told him. "But sometimes it's the patient's own therapy that's best with a stroke like this. To take a man like Lars out of the place he likes best to be, and away from something he very much wants to do, well now, a doctor must be thinking of all these things. And the man's eighty-five now.

"He needs to take a blood thinner and he needs a few days in bed, to be sure. And it's to be here," he said with emphasis, looking at the twins with a twinkle. "Then, when he's ready and the weather's good, I can't see why he can't keep going north, for that's where he wants to be now, he made that very clear to me."

He drew a brown bottle of small pills from his bag, gave them to Lars along with instructions, then addressed Annie and David with a serious tone in his voice.

"There's always a chance with a stroke, that there could be another one." The doctor spoke slowly. "Sometimes they are small. Lars could live to a hundred without another one, or he could have one next week. There's no way to tell. He will need to rest often. He could get very tired quite easily." He studied the twins' faces, wondering what else he could say. "And," he finally said, "Lars will need all the help that you can give him."

Then he stood, wished the three of them good luck on their voyage, and stepped outside with John for the walk down to the dock. They stopped beside the *Karen A.*

"He's worn out, John," the doctor said after a bit, feeling the wan warmth of the sun after the storm. "And by rights, I suppose, he should be in the hospital. But he very much wants to get those children to their father in Alaska." His glance fell on the iced-up boat again. "Seeing as how you have a great deal of sea-time under your belt, I think you should spend some time with the children. Show them what they need to know in case old Lars takes a turn for the worse on the trip."

His face clouded, as if for a moment he had second thoughts about his recommendations. "And pray that they get a spell of good weather for the voyage," he said earnestly.

After lunch, when the sun shone as strong as it could that late in the year, John took the twins down to the boat and the three of them chipped ice, brushing and shoveling the pieces over the side until the *Karen A* began to look like a boat again. The oil stove was still on, and John put on the kettle, made tea, and called the twins below to warm up. He'd brought fresh scones, and when they'd eaten, he set the table with the navigator's tools: the brass dividers, parallel ruler, pencils, tide-book, *Coastal Pilot*, *Hansen Handbook*, and log.

He showed them the art of drawing a vessel's track on a chart, how to plan the day's run the evening before, and how to use the *Coastal Pilot* book for information on the best harbors. He explained the *Hansen Handbook*, a detailed list of courses and distances from Seattle to Alaska, and patiently showed them the use of the pilothouse equipment: the radio and the sounder, the radar and the autopilot. Each one turned on the machines and manipulated the controls until John was satisfied.

"But Lars'll be okay, won't he?" Annie asked when the lesson was over.

John spoke carefully. "Oh, you heard the doctor. Sometimes people live for decades after a small stroke. But it's good to know these things in any case." He studied the twins as he spoke. They'd been childless, John and Carol, and they'd gotten over the pain long ago, yet it made him ache sometimes to see children.

In the afternoon, when the early northern-latitude dusk had come and gone, Carol took Annie into the kitchen and John and David went into the shop. Carol and Annie made a pie for supper with frozen blackberries from the bushes that grew wild around the cove.

"I missed all this," Annie said, as Carol showed her how to roll out a crust. "Just being in a nice kitchen with my Mom sometimes, making bread or cooking together. It seemed like we just never had those times any more after we left Alaska."

"What happened to your mom?" Carol asked quietly.

Annie stood for a moment before answering, still having a hard time believing they they'd found such a place of peace and calm after that day out there in the snow and the ice. "Oh, it was just like after she took us out of Alaska and left Dad she could never get her feet under her again. She tried hard, she really meant well, but she could just never really get ahead. She was working so hard we didn't see her too much. It was bad." Annie's voice trailed off, and there was only the hissing of the kettle on the stove.

"It's hard for a woman, being on her own," Carol said after a bit.

"It's not like I'm angry at Mom for leaving us. I could see her getting farther and farther down." Annie looked around the kitchen again. "I just wish it had been different, that's all. Maybe it will be when we're back with Dad again."

"He must be excited you're coming."

Being with Annie in the kitchen filled Carol up in a way that she hadn't felt before, and she felt bitter that such children would have been left by their mother, while she and John had wanted children and never been able to have them. It didn't seem fair.

"I just hope he's there," Annie said. "We wrote him from Seattle, as soon as we got the address from Lars. But sometimes the mailplane can't get in there when the weather's bad, and we never heard back."

In the shop, John built a fire in the barrel stove and gave David a good pocketknife, for he had none, and showed him how to sharpen it.

"We've got a few days here, David," John said. "Did you think of anything you might like to make your dad for Christmas? Sometimes homemade is best."

David looked around the shop before answering, marveling at the tools, hanging and tidily organized by the workbench, and at the narrow shelves filled with neatly labeled containers. He stopped at a wooden model, sitting on a wooden hand-painted sea, inside a glass case. It was an older ship, with a black hull and a high deck with a tiny pilothouse forward.

"This was my first ship, the *Princess Maquinna*. I was the mate," John said when he noticed David looking at the model.

"Where did it go?" asked David.

"Ah, the old *Maquinna*, she was on the West Coast run for on to forty years, and never missed a trip in all that time."

"You mean you used to go down to California in this?" David asked, surprised.

"No, the West Coast of Vancouver Island," John smiled, waving out the shop windows at the darkness. "That land across the channel, it's a big island. The *Maquinna* used to go to all the little communities on the outside coast. There was no road; there still isn't mostly."

"Did you make this?"

"Yes. It's not that good. I made it years ago."

David looked at the model again for a few minutes.

"Do you think I could make a model of my Dad's boat for him? Do you think there'd be time? That'd be a good Christmas present, don't you think, something I could make for him?"

"Oh yeah, the best kind of present. Do you have a picture of his boat?"

"No picture," David said, "But I could draw it, easy. I'm sure I could."

"You do that," John said. "You draw, and I'll get some wood and show you how to start. We can make him a good one."

A gust of wind howled around the shop then, and the stove puffed out a bit of smoke from the cracks around the door. John put in another log and looked over at David, intently drawing.

"It was bad out there, John," David said after he had drawn a while. "Did you get ice like that on the *Princess Maquinna*?"

"Um, just once in a very great while," John reassured David. "Cold like that is a rare thing along this coast."

John picked up a thick piece of soft cedar, perhaps a foot long, started up the band saw, and deftly cut it to the shape of the boat in the drawing David had made.

"Here, David, now you use the shaper." He clamped the

wood to the table, and held out a long flattened tool to David. "The wood's soft. Use this to get the shape you want."

David found it awkward at first, the tool catching in the wood on his first strokes. But then when the top edges had been rounded, the tool cut more smoothly, and David worked steadily, pleased at his progress, at the shape the little craft took as he worked.

On the second day, when the hull had been all shaped and smoothed and sanded, and the tiny pilothouse nailed on, Lars got up for the first time and sat with them in the evening around the fire. His face was pale and he didn't speak much. The twins tried not to think about whether or not he would get his strength back.

Carol had started Annie on a wool sweater for her dad, thick and dark green, and the two of them worked together, talking and knitting at one end of the long table, while David carefully painted the model's hull at the other. John sat by Lars, close by the side of the fire, and rambled on in a soft monologue about his first days on the *Princess Maquinna* on the West Coast run.

Sometimes the voices would trail off into nothing, and there would only be the pop of the fire, the click of the knitting needles, the slow ticking of the clock on the mantle, and now and again the soft moan of a wind outside the windows.

"David?" Annie whispered across to the other loft bunk that overlooked the low flames of the dying fire. "David, did you see the sweater? It's going to be so beautiful. Dad'll love it. I can't believe Carol's giving me all that wool."

"Yeah, that was real nice of her. And John's got some great ideas about how the model should be rigged. I never could have figured out how to do all that stuff. But what do you think about Lars, didn't he seem better today?"

"He's better," Annie said cautiously. "He still can't move his arm much, but he said he just needed a few more days. He said he really wanted to get there by Christmas."

"We could just stay here, too."

"What d'ya mean?"

"I mean just stay here the winter. They'd love to have us. Just stay the winter and go in the spring when the weather's better. It was terrible out there. We could have died, easy."

"David, we can't just be their kids for the winter. Carol told me all that about wanting to have children. First of all, we'd be illegal. And then what if Lars died during the winter, we'd never be able to get up North and find Dad."

David studied the fire for a long time before answering.

"I just wish it was easier," he finally said.

"Forecast for Georgia Strait, Johnstone Strait, and Queen Charlotte Sound: light southerlies five to fifteen knots tomorrow, with a chance of light snow by evening." John snapped off the radio and sat down.

"It's a good chance then, as good as you'll get this time of year." He kept his voice neutral, looking at the graceful small model and the thick sweater at the end of the table. It had been a gift, having Lars and the twins with them, and he didn't want it to end.

"We can get there by Christmas, can't we?" asked Annie.

"Yeah, sure," John said. "You have over two weeks. Even

with two or three layovers for weather, there's plenty of time. Just remember, the tides are very big this month. There will be a lot of logs and driftwood in the water. You must always keep an extra-sharp watch, and don't travel after dark if you can help it."

"I lit the oil stove," Annie said. "I went down there this afternoon and decided to clean it up real well, and light the stove. It'll be real cozy. We can sleep on board and get an early start."

"Sleep on board?" David was surprised. "What would we want to do that for? It's so nice here. We can just go down in the morning."

"Girl is right," Lars said after no one else spoke. "Better to sleep aboard tonight. Easier to get early start in morning."

And later, when they'd all come aboard and John and Carol were below, having a glass of rum with Lars, David went out on deck for a moment. The hunter's moon was halfway up the sky, making Sansum Narrows to the south shine like a glowing canyon between ghostly white hills. On the north side of the boat, John and Carol's cottage sat in the snow with the plume of smoke from the chimney rising straight up, like a white column into the still air.

They hugged and said their good-byes on the snowy dock, and Lars and the twins went to bed. But for David, sleep came hard and he could think only of how difficult the trip had been so far.

In the morning, they got underway in the darkness with David on duty for the first watch. The autopilot steered and he tried to watch for logs ahead in the beam of the spotlight, but the air was very cold and the water vapor rose like steam, or sea smoke, as mariners call it. At times he could barely see the anchor, the vapor was so thick, and he grew anxious, remembering what John had told them about logs.

"Is okay," Lars said, seeing David craning his neck to try to see. "We only go half speed until we see better."

"Aren't there a lot of logs? Wouldn't it be better to wait until daylight to go?"

"Better, yes. But not very much daylight this time of year. Remember shortest day is just eleven days away. If we travel only daylight hours, it will be a very long trip, maybe we have Christmas aboard."

Only slowly did the darkness give way to the palest sort of daylight. Sometimes through the sea smoke, they'd see a dock or a float along the water's edge or a cabin in the trees, with the smoke rising perfectly straight into the still air of the new day.

At a quarter after eight, Lars pulled the throttle back to an idle and put the engine into neutral, startling the twins.

"We are a little early on tide. We'll drift here and eat."

The twins looked confused, and Lars showed them a place on the chart where the channel narrowed almost to nothing. "Dodd Narrows. When channel gets very narrow, the tide runs very hard trying to get through. We must wait until slack water, when tide changes." He explained in his halting way how the moon's gravity pulls the water of the earth toward it and creates the tides as it circles, and how at the top of the high water and at the bottom of the low there was always a time, slack water, when the water had to pause, sometimes only for a few minutes, before turning and running the other way. It was at these moments that it was possible to pass safely through some of the narrowest and most constricted passages that lay ahead.

"But how do you know when?" David said slowly when Lars was done explaining, still a little confused and awed at the thought of the currents turning totally around, even though John also had explained the tide book to them.

"Ah, another book," Lars drew a book from the tightly packed bookcase above the chart table and set it before David. "In the evening, when you plan next day, you must always think about narrows and rapids, and check this current book—make sure you get there at slack water."

"Rapids?" Annie asked in an uncertain voice. "There are rapids on the salt water?"

"Ah, it is not like river rapids with rocks. But still it can make big whirlpools. Bad for boats. He laughed and tapped the book again. "Just check current book carefully, and won't be a problem."

The twins went below and Annie made oatmeal and toast for the three of them.

"Can you believe we're actually going to have Christmas up North in our own cabin with Dad?" she said, stirring the oatmeal. "I'm sure there'll be snow up there. We never had a Christmas without snow when we were there before. It'll look like this," she waved at the white world outside. "But it'll be our own home again. Won't it be great?"

"I know," David said. "I can't wait. But did you know there were going to be rapids on the trip?"

Annie's face clouded. "Nope. When John showed us how to use the radar and everything, I remember him showing us the tide book, and how to find slack water. But he never said anything about rapids. I'm not sure I could do rapids."

The twins ate first and when they were done, they went up into the pilothouse and Lars went down to eat. Outside were powerful swirls and eddies in the water coming from around the point ahead. Part of a tree appeared, with branches, and birds sitting on it, moving swiftly.

Ten minutes passed and then Lars came up, peering out carefully to see where they had drifted.

"Dodd Narrows," he said. "It's an easy place, short, no rocks, no rapids. He pushed the gear lever and the engine thunked into forward. "Here, David steer out toward the middle of channel, and we will check current."

As soon as they entered the current, David could feel it through the wheel, pushing the boat first one way then the other, and he struggled to keep them straight.

"Okay, boy, we are a little early but we'll go anyway. Just stay in the middle of the channel." Lars advanced the throttle and the narrows came into sight around a bend ahead. It was just a gap in the trees; a wider bay was clearly visible beyond it, but the tide was pouring through against them with the force of a river. David could clearly see a V in the water, like current running through the deepest part of a rapids.

"Is this slack water?" David asked in an uncertain voice.

For an answer, Lars speeded the engine up and looked out carefully at their progress past the trees along the narrowing gap before speaking. "We are a little early, yah. Just keep boat in the middle of the channel."

Annie squeezed in next to David to peer out ahead. "Check it out, David!" she said after a moment. "We're going uphill and look over there: eagles!"

David caught a glimpse of something big flying close to the trees, but was busy looking out ahead and trying to anticipate which way the current was going to push them. Annie was right: the water ahead looked as if it were pouring downhill through the gap toward them.

He aimed the boat right up into the middle of the current V, fighting the wheel, amazed to see that power lines were strung across the channel at the narrowest spot—the gap was that tight.

It seemed to him that they were literally shouldering the current aside and climbing up and out of a hole as they entered the gap itself, perhaps fifty yards between the trees.

And then they were through, out of the gap and into the wider bay. He could feel the pressure against the steering wheel relax, and finally could turn his head and look behind. The channel turned just behind the narrows itself, and seen from where they were, it looked as if the current was pouring into a hole in the snowy forest wall.

"Whoo-hooooo!" David howled in relief and excitement. "That was fun! Are they all like that, Lars?"

A smile cracked Lars's whiskered face. "Glad you have fun, boy. Dodd Narrows is easy. The next one is harder."

The bay widened, a broad cove opened to port, and gaps in the sea smoke revealed the great boxy buildings and tall smokestacks of the big mill at Nanaimo, with acres of floating log rafts along the shore.

And then they entered a great cloud of the smoking vapor. The mill, the shore, and the logs were all lost to them, for a big, cold, arctic high-pressure area had settled over the lower British Columbia coast after the storm. The water was so much warmer than the air that it seemed to smoke. It was this sea smoke that David had so much trouble seeing through.

The targets fell away behind them on the radar, no new ones filled in from ahead, and they entered the Strait of Georgia—the first of the big bodies of water they had to cross.

But the wind gods were kind that short day, and the big waters were still, and in the afternoon they were in the narrow channels again. The sea smoke had disappeared by noon, and they passed the big pulp mill at Powell River and entered Desolation Sound.

With the very last of the color in the sky, Lars picked out a snowy dock and float from the shadows along the shore, and Annie reversed neatly as David jumped down to dig in the snow with gloved hands for the cleats.

The twins stood for a moment on deck after they'd tied up, peering out at the shore, expecting the cheery lights of a cabin, the tall column of smoke from a chimney. But there was only the untracked snow on the dock and dark shapes of what might be buildings, all with an abandoned, deserted look.

Later, after the supper dishes were done, they could hear a faraway, faint roaring, or rushing sound. The twins went out on deck and there was no light, nothing, no shape or form to the night, only that hollow roar that seemed to come from two places, and the insistent rustle of the tide around the pilings of the dock.

"Yuculta Rapids," Lars said when they came in. "Look at the chart." He unfolded one onto the table. "Every night I do this. Mark next day's travel on chart. I put a little cross and write the time on chart for when we should be places.

If I get sick, or take a nap, you and Annie can navigate." He put the dark green *Hansen Handbook* on the chart table. In places the pages were smudged and dog-eared, and each one was filled with columns of numbers and place names and drawings of particularly distinctive points or headlands.

"Book has where to steer all written down. For me it is easy, but you need to practice with book and chart." It looked like a maze of islands, with channels running every which way. Only a dark penciled line winding through from bottom to top indicated it was the route north.

"Wow." Annie's head leaned forward into the circle of light. "How did the first explorers ever find their way through?"

"Ah," said Lars, "you think this is hard, and we have radar and charts and sounding machine. Think about explorers, just in their little boats, with oars and sail, and no chart."

A thick finger thumped down onto the chart. "We are here, summer fishing resort, all closed up now. There are rapids here, and here, and here." The finger tapped different places on the chart. They all were along their route.

"Three rapids?" David slumped down. "I thought there was just one. Are they all bad?" He could still hear the roaring faintly, even in the cabin, and didn't even want to think what it would be like out there on such a totally lightless night. "And are you sure there are no rocks?"

"No rocks, just whirlpools. They are bad enough."

The twins studied the chart. "Yuculta Rapids" was the name of the place just north of where they lay. There the channel took a sharp bend to the west and was constricted between a smaller island and the shore.

"That noise comes from Yuculta Rapids here, and here, Hole in the Wall."

"Devil's Hole." David put his finger on the chart, right on the line that marked their path. "What's this Devil's Hole? That doesn't sound very good; look at what it says here too: 'Violent eddies and whirlpools form in Devil's Hole.'" He shook his head in anguish, "Oh, Lars, do we have to go through Devil's Hole? It sounds so dangerous."

"Ah, boy worry too much," Lars patted him on the back with his good hand. "Just be careful, read tide book twice, and there will not be a problem."

David picked the current book off the table. It was page after page of names and numbers in columns. He put it down again. "Is it all going to be like this, rapids all the time?" he asked. "And what if something happened to you, and you couldn't get up again, like before? Devil's Hole—we could never go through those places unless you were right there to help us." He was clearly upset.

"David, boy, always remember this," Lars reached out and pulled David gently over to his side. "Just one step at a time. If too windy, stay at the dock or at anchor, if storm comes up while we travel, go find harbor. But most important this time of year is to plan each night before." And he took the current book down again, explaining once more how to find the Yucultas, as well as the date and the times for slack water each day.

"Slack water, David and Annie, just remember, slack water. The tide, it runs very hard but has to slow down and stop every six hours. You are right about Devil's Hole. It is a bad place when current is running, but at slack water, is just narrow place between hills."

Deep in the night, David sat up, wondering what it was that had woken him. He got up quietly and slipped open the pilothouse door to go on deck, clad just in pajamas, shoes, and parka.

The roaring was gone. Outside there was nothing, neither light nor sound, no roaring of the rapids, no gurgling of the water around the pilings.

"Annie," he said, shaking his sister's shoulder. A light sleeper, she sat up at once, startled. The only light in the fo'c'sle was from the flame in the oil stove doing a slow dance behind its little window, just enough for her to see the outline of shapes in the small space, but no more.

"Annie, c'mon up and see, it's slack water, just like Lars told us about. It's amazing. All that roaring of the rapids we heard earlier, it's totally stopped. It's dead quiet."

At first she stopped just outside the pilothouse door, for what lay beyond was so totally without light or sound that it made her uneasy. She'd been away from the North Country a long time; the memory of the stillness, away from the ceaseless noise and light of the city, was almost erased. Finally she stepped outside, leaned against the back of the cabin for reassurance, and looked and listened. But there was nothing her eyes could pick out in the cloud-thick, moonless night. If it had been dark earlier, when they'd stood on deck after tying up, now what lay before her was so totally without form or shape or even hint of light that she turned her head until she could see the reassuring dim glimmer of light from below.

No bird nor animal stirred in the forest, no wind sighed

through the trees, and most of all, there was none of that far-away roaring of water rushing through the canyons that had so unsettled her as she had tried to sleep. Annie felt the cold eddying around her bare ankles, and remembered her cozy sleeping bag. She was halfway down the stairs when David's voice stopped her.

"Hey listen, I think it's starting again. Quick, come back, come back up!"

She stepped up, listened until she started shivering again and was just turning to go when she heard it: like some great creature starting to stir in the night—at first nothing, and then, something, a presence. Not exactly a sound, but not silence either. She waited a little longer until it had become a whispering, faraway, soft rushing.

"It's the moon, remember?" David said excitedly. "Lars explained it. It's all the water trying to follow the moon around the earth that makes the tides. Isn't it amazing?"

And she thought of what they had just seen—the slack water—the moment of the moon's passing either overhead or directly opposite them on the other side of the earth. And the water starting to move again. That presence, that rustling movement in the night, all caused by the moon. It truly was amazing.

In the morning, while Lars drank his coffee and they all waited up in the pilothouse for slack water, the current was like a river behind the boat, rushing past the point in oily-looking whirls. Logs would sweep past, low in the water, big, thick, and sinister-looking.

When the current slowed, Lars started up. As they backed out and away from the shore, the twins could see the size of the whirlpools for the first time. When they'd first studied the chart and seen the warnings, they had imagined a hole in the water, perhaps thirty or forty feet around, with glistening vertical sides, into which a vessel would literally fall if it got too close.

But no warnings prepared them for the sight of that vast and majestically revolving pool, hundreds of feet across. Sticks, branches, even whole trees revolved in the maelstrom, and long streaks of foam formed concentric circles. The middle of the pool was visibly lower than the edges, and there was a small hole in the very center, just a few feet across.

"Oh my gosh, look!" Annie cried out suddenly. "Over there, orcas, big ones."

They looked and ahead of them, just past the edge of the whirlpool, there was a quick puff of vapor from the water and the high black dorsal fin of a killer whale appeared. Then another, and a third, blowing and showing the big white patches on their sides, all a bit different from each other.

"Ah," Lars said. "See, they are smart, too. They are waiting for slack water, like us."

"Wow! They are so cool." Annie had the binoculars glued to her eyes. "David, don't you love them?"

"They're huge," David said, awed. "Lars, are they really waiting for slack water?"

As if in answer, the three big orcas surfaced again, close together, and headed for the narrow channel ahead past the whirlpool.

"Just follow them," Lars answered. "Maybe they are going to Alaska, too." He guided David along a narrow streak of calmer water between the edge of the whirlpool and the shore.

"Shouldn't . . . we . . . wait . . . until . . . slacker . . . water?" David struggled to get the words out, fighting the wheel and trying to stay in the narrow band of less disturbed water.

"It's almost slack now, boy. Just sneak along shore. We will get through fine."

The amazing thing, David thought later, was a little channel of water, perhaps ten or fifteen yards off the steep shore, that seemed to be moving little, and along which they made progress. He tried not to look at the churning rapids to their port or think of what might happen to them if they were swept out into it. And when they were through, he asked his sister to steer, for he was shaking, his shoulders tense, and his shirt soaked with sweat.

"Annie," David said, immensely relieved to have her take over. "That current was so strong! I could barely hold onto the wheel!" He stood for a long time, looking behind them at the rapids, even then, close to slack water, roaring and tumbling through the gap to the lower water beyond.

"Big country," Annie said, when David came up, pulling on a dry shirt. She nodded her head out at the land around them. The channel had become more of a canyon, winding along at the base of the steep, snow-covered mountains all around them. Ahead and behind, the waterway disappeared into folds in the steep hills. There were no houses, no docks, no other boats. In most places there was hardly even a beach or shore to speak of. Branches of huge trees extended right down to the water.

Half an hour later, a cove opened up to their port, with a float, long dock, and several substantial-looking buildings on the shore. Yet it was obviously in disrepair: no smoke from any chimney, a porch roof collapsed from the snow, and a generally forgotten and forlorn look.

"Thurlow, British Columbia," Lars said, his eyes sweeping the scene. "When hand loggers worked all through here, there was a railroad that was running back into hills. Very busy place. When they cut all the trees on that lease, the town died." Lars explained that hand logging was the way individuals worked the woods before the advent of the chain saw and the big logging companies with their floating camps.

"The boys loved this steep country," he said. "Two men would work a big hand saw, way up a hillside, cut down a really big one. The tree would slide all the way down into the water."

They came a little later to Greene Point Rapids at the very moment of slack water. The channel, constricted there by the shoulder of a mountain, and seen from the south, appeared to dead-end in the hills, then open again to reveal another winding canyon.

A few miles later Annie noticed the water through which they were traveling was moving with them. There were eddies off small projections of the land as they passed, and she could see that they were traveling noticeably faster.

"Tide is going," Lars said in answer to her question, waving up into the low clouds that obscured the tops of the hills. "The moon passed, now it pulls all this water with it to west, toward ocean."

They came to a place where the channel opened up to become a bay. The water grew choppier, the boat lurched from side to side, and it looked like they were in for a long and uncomfortable ride. But then Lars nudged David and had him turn the boat sharply to starboard into a narrow side channel, where the current was much swifter, pulling them with it.

"Ah," Lars said, "we'll be in big waters soon enough. Is better for little boats to stay in little channels while they can. More rapids now." He waved off ahead to where the canyon narrowed once again, and as they drew closer, they could feel the water beginning to accelerate with them. "This one is easy, Lars said, "We go with the current. Just stay in the middle."

David noted the name on the chart as "Whirlpool Rapids," and he saw ahead the V of water in the narrow gap. Instinctively he took a wide stance in front of the wheel. He knocked the automatic pilot out of gear and felt the muscles in his chest begin to tense as the current sucked them into the narrows and he struggled to keep them in the middle of the channel.

But if going against the current had been difficult, going with it was easy—the current sucked them swiftly ahead. David simply aimed for the middle of the V, and they surged down through it, swayed once or twice in the eddies beyond, and then were through and into bigger waters.

The land fell away on both sides, the constricted canyon became a bay, and the bay finally a wide strait.

The wind came, first darkening the surface, then pushing the ripples into whitecaps, until the spray lashed the pilot-house, and things began to thunk and rattle around inside the boat. The bow drove deeper into the seas and the twins hoped that Lars would tell them to turn, to head for one of the sheltered bays that opened up on the side of the channel.

But instead he just throttled back a bit, said nothing and sat beside them.

Every hour Lars would put a small tick on the line that was their course on the big chart, but when they asked him about the weather and if they should continue, he just said that they had very far to go, and that if they ducked into a harbor every time the wind blew, they'd never get there. But he seemed faraway, and if not actually in pain, then at least not very comfortable, and the twins grew anxious, missing the reassuring proximity of the shore in the narrower channels of the morning. The clouds pressed lower and lower to the water, the hills disappeared into the mists, and only shapes on the radar showed them to be in a wide strait and not the ocean itself.

Annie tried to go below, to lie in the bunk before it was her turn to steer. But the stuffiness of the cabin, the faint smell of diesel fuel, the creaking of the hull in the seaway, the sound of the water surging past just outside the thin hull were too much. She got up after only a short time, to wedge herself back into a corner of the pilothouse.

Lars thumped the chart, waving his good hand in front of his face in an awkward gesture. His mouth moved, but it was a long moment before the words came out, and Annie had a terrible flashback to the way he had looked when she had tried to wake him up that first afternoon of the trip.

His voice came then, ragged, hoarse, and scratchy, and he pointed to the clock on the bulkhead. "Tide changes at half past eleven. Steer closer to beach then, stay out of worst of current. Is all deep—just stay a little way off beach and we are fine." He paused to catch his breath; the effort of speaking seemed to tire him.

"We will stay here tonight." His clawlike hand scratched at the place the penciled line angled into the shore. "Is a good anchorage. If Lars does not get up, just snuggle up to beach and drop anchor." His voice failed him, and he coughed before waving out ahead. "Keep sharp lookout for logs." And then he was gone, stumbling awkwardly down the stairs before Annie could reach out to help him.

"He looks awful, Annie. Maybe you'd better go check on him," David said. But when Annie went below, Lars was already asleep, his pale face looking stretched and gaunt.

At eleven, on Annie's watch, the shape of the seas began to change, to shorten and become steeper. At first Annie thought the wind had changed direction, until she remembered what Lars had said about the tide change, and so she angled in closer to the shore.

There was, as Lars had said, calmer water along the shore, and they were glad to reach it. For with the change, the current was running against the wind, and just a half mile offshore from where they traveled, they could clearly see places where the waves were humped up into big patches of broken water.

The engine suddenly slowed, missed a beat, and resumed speed, though no one had touched the throttle. Annie quickly checked all the gauges, as Lars had shown her, but the needles were all where they were supposed to be.

She saw David's wide eyes looking at her, and then the engine missed again, and she flinched as if she had touched a live wire.

"Get Lars," she said, scanning the instrument panel.

But when David returned a moment later, his face was pale and frightened.

"He's, like, asleep again. He's breathing okay, but I sure couldn't wake him."

The engine missed again, throwing them slightly forward as the boat slowed. Annie looked over at the shore, hoping to see a place where they might pull in out of the wind and anchor until they could get Lars up to check the engine. She looked as quickly away, for the land angled slightly to the west there, and the wind, blowing a good hard southeasterly, was driving the seas onto the rocks. There was no shelter.

"Here, watch," she motioned David in behind the wheel, and went over to study the chart. Two miles away was a sort of channel leading off to the northeast. If they could get there, they might be able to get in out of the wind.

The engine sped up, slowed to half, tried feebly to speed up again, and suddenly stopped. The boat swung slowly sideways, and without the reassuring sound of the engine, the wind was a low droning howl in the rigging.

The twins stood for a moment, stunned. Ever since they'd left Seattle, the engine had always run perfectly. Annie tried the starter, but the diesel refused to catch, and she stopped, worried about wearing the battery down.

Then she was down the stairs in an instant, trying to shake Lars awake. At first she could get no response at all, but finally his eyelids opened and his eyes swam slowly up into hers. They were glazed and distant, and she shook him again and spoke loudly.

"Lars, Lars. Wake up, something's happened to the engine. It's totally stopped. You need to get up and fix it. We're getting close to shore. It won't start."

His mouth began to work and after what seemed a long time, the words started to come out.

"Filter, filter, could be just filter. Starboard side of engine, new one in drawer." His hand waved up in the air for a moment, and then he was gone again.

"Filter?" Annie's head spun. Was she supposed to change it? She'd barely touched a wrench in her life. She rushed up into the pilothouse. Already the wind had carried them a little closer to the shore.

"David," she said breathlessly, "Lars said it might be the filter. You have to try to change it. He said it's on the starboard side of the engine, that there's new ones in the drawer."

David took one last look at the bleak, wave-lashed shore half a mile to leeward and hustled down the steps, pulled up the side of the engine box, and tried to see what she had been talking about. His heart sank; he wished Lars had taken a little more time with him on the engine before they'd left Seattle, for there wasn't anything that really looked like a filter. For that matter, he didn't really know what a filter might look like.

"Quick, Annie, dig around in that drawer and try to find the filter. Then we might be able to figure out where it goes."

Annie rummaged through the drawers under the sink, drawing forth two plastic-bagged cylindrical objects. "Fuel," she said, handing the smaller one to David. "It's gotta be fuel, right? The big one says it's for oil."

David nodded uneasily, studying the filter and looking carefully at the array of belts, hoses, and mechanisms on the side of the engine. There were two vertical cylindrical units, and it looked as if the filter he held might fit into the smaller one.

"Uh, slide me the tool box." David rummaged for a moment, found a likely looking wrench, and tried it on the big nut at the top of the filter housing. The end almost fit over the nut. There wasn't enough room for the handle, but then he remembered how Lars had used the steel handle with the little detachable thingies—"sockets," he had called them.

"Better go up and check on our position," he said. Annie went up the stairs and David found the socket he wanted, fitted it onto the nut, and pulled, but the nut was on tight.

"Um, we're getting closer. How you coming?" Annie called down. David could hear the anxiety in her voice. He pulled harder and the nut turned, so quickly that he skinned his knuckles on the side of the hot engine, and dark blood welled up brightly through the grease on his hand. He turned the wrench again until the nut was looser. Diesel fuel began to spill onto the floor from the edges of the steel cylinder. Then it came off suddenly, thunked down sideways at the base of the engine, spilling the rest of the diesel fuel into the bilge. David picked it up, studying it. Yes! The dirty filter inside looked to be the same as the one in the plastic bag!

"Okay! Annie, this is it. How we doing up there?"

"Uh, not too good. We're getting a lot closer to the shore now."

David plucked out the old filter, ripped the plastic off the new one and fitted it into the canister: perfect! Working quickly, he fitted the filter housing back up onto the side of the engine, and tightened the nut.

"Okay!" he called up, grabbed a paper towel, and went up into the pilothouse. The shore was a lot closer. He could clearly see the spray from the waves flying downwind into the trees. There was no beach, just rocks. David fumbled for the starter, trying to remember if there was anything else Lars had done before starting each time. He pushed the button and the engine turned over, but didn't even pop. He tried it again, listening to the starter grinding away, until it started to slow, and he knew that he was wearing out the battery, so he stopped.

"How about anchoring?" Annie asked, watching the shore draw closer. There was a distinct tremor in her voice.

David tried the starter again without answering. Nothing happened, and he could feel his head starting to spin with all the decisions.

"David! We have to do something or we'll go onto the rocks!"

He looked quickly at the Fathometer, the flashing light on the dial that showed them how deep the water was. It was over a hundred feet, still too deep to anchor, and they were barely a hundred yards off the shore.

"Uh, I'll go let the anchor and rope all out. It's still too deep now, but maybe it'll hook on the bottom when it gets shallower."

He pulled on his jacket, went out the door and saw a boat, a troller, with its two tall poles down, fishing, just coming around the point ahead of them. He waved frantically, saw a yellow-clad person come out of the pilothouse, wave back, and start doing something back in the stern of the boat.

"Annie, it's another boat. They see us." He eyed the

shore again, and decided to go up to the bow and the anchor winch just in case. The shore was getting a lot closer.

A puff of smoke flew out of the other boat's exhaust pipe, and its stern settled into the water as it headed over toward them.

David banged on the window when he'd made his way up to the bow and yelled at Annie, "How deep is it now?" as he pointed down into the water.

Annie studied the machine for a moment, then yelled through the glass, "Still over a hundred!"

He looked around. They were laying sideways to the wind and the sea, rolling with each wave and angling in toward the base of a snow-blasted rocky bluff. The waves beat the rocks in an ugly welter of foam. David trembled at the thought of what would happen to them there, and loosened the brake on the anchor winch.

The other boat came around their stern just then, on the outside, and he could see the man steering from the stern with one hand and preparing a coil of line to throw with the other. The boat was coming on quick, and the man yelled across to him.

"Better catch line, first pass. Might not have time for another!" The stranger waved at the rapidly approaching shore.

David motioned that he understood and then studied the anchor winch for a moment as the other boat approached. If he missed the line on the first pass, he'd drop the anchor anyway.

The other boat drew closer, and David could see that she was little more than an old tired cabin cruiser, fitted out with trolling poles for commercial salmon fishing. The man was steering with one hand, and had a line all ready to throw with the other.

A wave pushed the boats toward each other and for a moment, it looked as if the stranger's trolling poles would crack into theirs, so close was the other boat's approach. The man pushed something with his hand, the boat surged ahead, and as his stern passed their bow, he gracefully threw the coil of line so that it unwound in the air as it came, the last two or three loops landing on the deck beside David.

He'd already practiced in his mind what to do with the line, for he knew there would be only the one chance, and quickly gathered it in, wrapped it back and forth around the cleat, winding the extra around the bottom.

David was thrown back heavily against the pilothouse as the line came tight, and the *Karen A* jerked forward. He sat for a moment looking as their bow came up into the wind, as the stranger throttled up, to get them clear of the rocks. He made his way around to the back of the pilothouse, shivering with cold and relief. It had been too close. The stranger had been right, there'd been time for only the one pass. The wind had been pushing them shoreward so quickly that if he'd missed the line, they'd have been onto the rocks before their rescuer could have gotten it coiled back again and maneuvered in for another pass.

"Way to go, David!" Annie hugged him as he came in the door. "I couldn't possibly have tied off the line that quickly!"

"That was a close one." David's teeth started to chatter and he threw his jacket on top of his boots and went down to stand by the stove, trying not to think how close the rocks had been when the stranger had gotten the line to them.

Annie made hot chocolate for him, but it was a long time before he warmed up and stopped shivering. Finally she called him up into the pilothouse to say that the stranger had stopped. When he reluctantly put down his cup and went up the three steps, he could see that they must have entered that channel he'd seen on the chart earlier. It was calmer there and the ugly white caps of the main channel were clearly visible a half mile astern. The other skipper had taken his boat out of gear and was standing in the stern cockpit, and taking in the slack of the line as the two boats drifted closer together. He was talking across to Annie, but David couldn't make out the words. Then he waved off towards the narrowing channel ahead, put his boat in gear, fed out the towline until it came tight and went back into his cabin.

"He said there's a little store around the corner at Minstrel Island. He'll take us in there. Geez, it is cold out there." Annie shoved the door closed, and went below to stand by the stove.

When she came up again, the channel had narrowed and a cold, sleety rain was falling. She pulled on another sweater and watched as the other boat angled in closer to the shore. A cove opened up, with a float and a ramp leading up to a few buildings huddled among the trees. And then the stranger slowed down, letting their momentum carry them gently into the float.

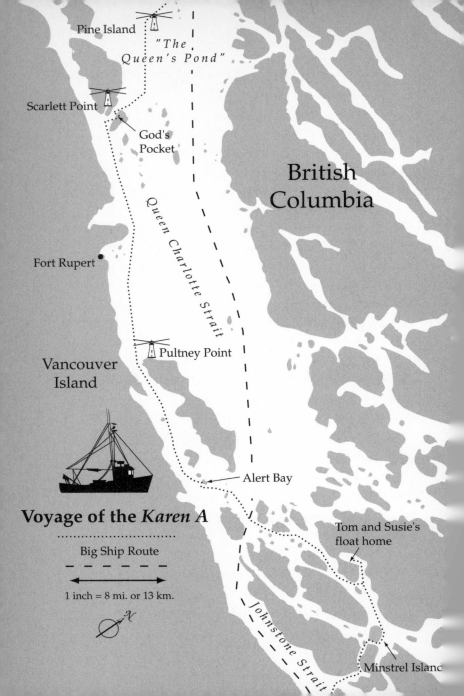

Pine Island

"The
Queen's
Pond"

Scarlett Point

God's
Pocket

British
Columbia

Queen Charlotte Strait

Fort Rupert

Pultney Point

Vancouver
Island

Alert Bay

Tom and Susie's
float home

Voyage of the *Karen A*

....

Big Ship Route

– – – – –

1 inch = 8 mi. or 13 km.

N

Johnstone Strait

Minstrel Island

CHAPTER 6

By the Queen's Pond

 They were just tying up when the man came over and eyed them for a moment before speaking, obviously surprised.

"Just you two. All alone?" His voice had a quiet, melodious, almost singsong quality, his hair was dark and shiny, pulled back into a ponytail, and Annie knew from his face that he was an Indian. "You were close to the rocks. What if I did not come along? I'm Tom Skedans, by the way."

"Lars was too sick to get up," David said, all in a rush, "and the engine stopped and I changed the filters like he said, but it still wouldn't start."

"Who is Lars?" Tom asked, still a bit confused. "Is there anything we can do for him?"

"Oh, he's the owner, the captain," Annie explained. "He had a stroke last week. He seemed better when we left this morning, but then he couldn't get up. A doctor checked him a couple of days ago and he said Lars would get tired really easy. He just needs lots of sleep."

"All right, I will have a look at the engine soon as I sell my fish and get some groceries."

David told Tom that he was about to drop the anchor when he appeared.

"Too deep," Tom said. "Bad place." He shook his head once and walked back to his own boat, coiling the towline deftly as he walked.

"Hey, thanks!" the twins called out, but Tom made no indication that he'd heard.

"Well," Annie said when they'd ducked back aboard and out of the sleet. "I heard a generator up at the store, and if there's a generator, there might even be hot water. I'm going to check on Lars and see about a shower."

It was a rough-looking place. A sign over the ramshackle building said "Minstrel Island Resort." Cardboard boxes full of empty beer bottles were stacked unevenly around the porch.

She shivered again and pushed the door open. It was more of a bar than a store. Several groups of men were loudly playing cards at tables littered with bottles and glasses. She stood for a moment, uncomfortable and uncertain. A big man in a checked shirt turned to her.

"Yes, little lady?" He had gaps in his brown teeth, and one eye was unfocused and wandering.

"Um, you wouldn't have a shower, would you?" The man made her uneasy but the thought of hot water against her body was too much to deny.

"Two bucks," he said, handing her a key. "In the laundry building, around the side."

Annie dug in her pocket for the money, picked up the

key, thanked the man, and walked for the door, glad to get away.

The linoleum of the laundry room floor was worn through to bare wood in places. Tacked to a big sheet of plywood leaning against the wall was the skin of a wolf. She approached the skin gingerly, wondering who would want such a thing, but then was surprised at the careful skinning and flensing and the softness of the long, shiny coat.

The water was hot and she scrubbed and shampooed, feeling her worries about Lars, her anxieties about the trip, slipping away. "For two bucks," she thought, "I'll use all the water I want."

When she finally stopped, the windows were all steamed up. She rubbed a hole in the condensation and peered out. It was still half sleet, half snow, and Tom was walking along the float to his boat with a bag of groceries in his arms.

Suddenly a key rattled in the door.

"Hey," Annie said loudly, clutching a towel to her chest. "Someone's in here."

The door opened. Through the steam she could see the big man from the store.

"Hey," she said again, suddenly becoming frightened, "I'm *in* here."

He closed the door and carefully locked it, and turned around to face her, his one good eye gleaming. In two quick steps he crossed the room, ripped the towel from her hands, and stood back a moment, looking.

"Hey, get outta here!" she said, her voice rising quickly to a shout as she tried to cover herself with hands. "Hey! *Help!*"

And then a rough hand, smelling of tobacco juice and whiskey, was on her mouth. She bit into it instinctively, and the man pulled it back, swearing at her. She looked around quickly for something to defend herself with, but there was nothing, and the man came at her again.

The door opened with a crash, and a dark-clad figure came out of the steam clouds, driving into her assailant with a blow that slammed him into the dryer. It was Tom, she realized, the man who had towed them in.

"Get dressed," he spoke over his shoulder. "We should leave. They are all drinking. Better to leave."

Annie quickly pulled on her clothes, her heart still pounding.

The big man from the bar was sitting in the corner, sucking his hand, and there was a cut over his eye.

Tom drew out a long, shining knife, dropped swiftly to his knees and pulled the other man's head back by the hair. He put the knife to the soft place under the chin, pushing until the tip just pricked through the skin.

"I should skin you like that wolf," Tom said tonelessly. "Maybe I start down here." The knife flashed downward, severed the man's belt in a single stroke, and was back at his Adam's apple almost too fast to see. "Then we see if you bother girls again."

"Go to the boat," Tom spoke to her over his shoulder again. "Tell your brother we have to go." As Annie hurried out, she saw Tom putting the knife away and starting to work on the big man with his fists.

"David, David," she banged on the side of their boat, half stumbling in the snow and yelling at the same time. Her wet hair was already stiffening in the deep cold. "C'mon, we gotta leave. They're all drinking there. We gotta leave."

David looked out at her, not understanding. "Annie, you're not talking sense. The motor's not even running yet. We just got here. How are we going to leave?"

She wasn't listening to him, already starting to untie the lines. Tom came down the ramp, passed them wordlessly, leaned gracefully over the rail of his smaller boat and began walking backwards, paying out the towline behind him as he walked, all in one fluid motion.

"Time to go," he said, throwing the last loops of the line deftly over the anchor winch of the *Karen A.* It was then that David saw Annie's eyes starting to fill with tears. He instinctively realized something was very wrong and went up to the bow to tie off the towline. The other boat started up, the towline came tight, and the two boats moved away from the dock.

The big man came out of the laundry house then. He was limping, he had blood on his face, and he was holding his pants up with one hand. He yelled something at them, but it was lost in the snow and the sleet.

Annie collapsed against David, sobbing, and he pulled her into the pilothouse, sat her down, and tried to get her to tell him what happened. But she could only sob and shake and there was nothing he could do but hold her.

The sleet turned to snow, until the steep hillsides around them were hidden in it, and after a long hour, they slowed. He put Annie gently into the seat and got up and looked. Ahead, close to the steep shore, was what looked like a low, lumpy, white island, with three small buildings on one corner.

The two boats had slowed almost to a stop by the buildings, and David wondered how they could be getting so close to the shore, when he realized the lumps were logs. The island was a log raft. They tied up and a woman appeared out of the snow.

"Where's the girl?" she called up to David.

"Uh, inside."

The woman jumped quickly up and inside. When David finished tying up and turned around to go back inside, Annie was coming out with the woman.

"Are you okay?" David asked, glad to see his sister up at least, but surprised that she was apparently going off with a strange woman to some strange place.

Annie didn't answer and then Tom came aboard. "That's Susie, my wife. She can help your sister. Now, what happened to your engine?"

David explained about the filter and what had happened.

"Did you bleed it?" Tom asked.

"Huh?" David wasn't sure he had heard properly.

"Bleed air out of the fuel lines after changing the filter."

"Uh, no. How do you do that?"

For an answer, Tom went below, finding the filter on the side of the engine almost at once.

"See this bolt? It's the vent." He pointed to a small bolt on the top of the filter, found a wrench in the toolbox and loosened it, passed the wrench to David, and moved around him to the stairs. "Watch. I'll crank the engine. When fuel comes out, shout." Tom disappeared up the stairs, and a moment later the starter began turning the diesel over. After six or seven long seconds, fuel began spouting from around the bolt, and David called for Tom to stop.

"Okay, tighten it back up." Tom put the wrench into David's hand and watched as David tightened the bolt.

The engine started up smoothly this time, and after they'd run it a few minutes, and looked carefully with a flashlight all around the filter for leaks, David shut it off.

"Tom," David said, "thanks for showing me all this stuff. Now can you answer a question for me? What happened to Annie back there? I couldn't even get her to talk to me. I mean, did that man *do* something to her?"

"She's okay. Those fellows get drinking sometimes and get crazy. She was just scared. Susie took her to the cabin to warm up. You and your skipper are welcome there. Bad weather tomorrow." He waved out toward Johnstone Strait. "You stay here." Tom walked away over the snowy logs toward the cabin.

When Tom had gone, David went below. Lars was sitting up on the edge of his bunk in his gray long underwear. "You fixed filter, David. Good job." His voice was steady but his face was still very pale.

"No, Lars, I changed it, but I didn't know about bleeding it. We almost drifted onto the rocks, then this boat came along to help. But we're okay now. We're tied to this guy's log raft in some cove. We're okay in here. It's supposed to blow tomorrow." David decided it was better to give Lars the short version.

"Boy, listen." Lars drew David down to sit beside him. "Sometimes I have spells. Sometimes I don't see very good. But we must keep going! I worry about getting too sick to help and we never get to Alaska."

"We'll get there, Lars, don't worry," David reassured him. "You just rest. Annie and I can take care of things. The weather's supposed to be bad tomorrow, so we'll stay here. If you feel up to it, we're welcome to go up to the cabin."

"*Tusentakk*. Thank you, no," Lars answered. "I just rest here. You go up."

Lars's breath was sour, and his skin was becoming shiny and drawn. It reminded David of his grandfather in the nursing home, and he thought again of the long and winding line on the chart—all the distance they had yet to travel. All the fear and uneasiness about what was ahead filled him again.

At last light, David made sure Lars had what supper he wanted, tended the stove, then walked carefully over the logs toward the buildings. When he got closer he saw that the cabin and two smaller buildings were built on the flat plank platform of their own separate raft, which was tied to the side of a big log raft. Lars had explained that in some of the inlets, the land was so steep that settlers built rafts out of logs to put their cabins on.

The cabin was two rooms and a loft, and Annie was playing with Ruth, a toddler, on the floor. She put her down when David came in.

"I'm fine now," she said. "I was freaked out before, but I'm okay now. That man didn't do anything to me. I guess maybe he wanted to. But Tom came in." She held up a thin necklace of small, colored beads. "Look, I've been beading, Susie's showing me how." She turned away and went over to Ruth again, sitting with her on the rug in front of the woodstove.

"How is old man?" Tom asked.

"Uh, he's up and I made him some supper. He just seems real tired. I tried to get him to come, but I think he was afraid of walking across the logs. He was so great in Seattle and since we left . . . anyway, it's a good thing you were out there to tow us. I didn't know how to change the filter, and we couldn't get him to wake up. I mean, what will happen if it's real stormy or something? And we really need him, and he has one of those spells again?" David really hadn't meant to say so much, but once he started, the words just kept tumbling out.

Tom waved David over to the oilcloth-covered table. From behind a simply constructed bookcase, he pulled out a folded chart and laid it before David.

"Weather," he said in his soft voice. "In wintertime, you must always watch weather. High pressure comes from the north. Low pressure comes from the south. Sometimes they fight, bad weather for weeks. But sometimes there is a pause. It is then you must cross the Queen's Pond.

"Here," a calloused finger tapped the chart. "One day's travel to here. Boats always wait here. It is called God's Pocket—just a tiny cove, but very sheltered. You must wait there for good weather. Sometimes two, three days, or more. When the wind stops you must leave very early, before four in the morning. Get across before wind blows again. And here," the finger tapped on another place. "Safety Cove, on other side. You can get away from the wind here. But in between," his hand paused at a wide place on the chart marked "Queen Charlotte Sound," and he looked directly into David's eyes. "We call it 'The Queen's Pond.' There is no place to hide."

Later that evening, as the twins made their way back to the *Karen A*, the wash of the flashlight over the snowy logs created an eerie path, a labyrinth of odd, lumpy shapes among black and still pools of water. When they'd made the security of their own boat, Annie put her hand on David's arm and stopped him before he slid back the pilothouse door.

"Listen," she said, tilting her head out at the night. And there it was again, that hollow, roaring tide sound. Further away than at the Yucultas, but still the tide again, echoing against the snowy hills on either side of Johnstone Strait, fifteen miles away. Finally they slid the door back, relieved for the warmth and cozy smells of their little home in the wilderness.

When David woke, he heard a soft crying. He looked over and Annie's bunk was empty. He found her up in the pilothouse, sitting in the captain's chair with her eyes red and her cheeks shining with tears.

"Why did he have to do that, David? Why couldn't he just leave me alone? Up to now, I'd never thought too much about, you know, worrying about things. Worrying about if I have to be careful and be watching out all the time. It's like none of that stuff ever really occurred to me before now."

But David knew there was little he could say that would help. He draped his arm over his sister's shoulders and they sat together in the dark, comforted by each other's presence, wondering what the days ahead held for them.

Susie had made a big breakfast of hotcakes and homemade blackberry syrup. When it was almost ready, Tom came out across the logs, and they moved the boat so that it was beside the flat house-raft and not the slippery logs. They helped Lars out of the boat and into the cabin, and they all sat around the table together with Ruth in her homemade high chair.

While they ate, the wind and the snow came on strong, and they were glad for the hospitality and the cozy, protected cove. Occasionally a very strong gust would eddy down from the heights above and make the whole raft move, and David would get up, uneasy, to stand by a window and look out at the swirling white.

Afterward, Lars nodded off in a big chair by the woodstove, and Ruth came over to play around his legs. The others helped clear the table, then Susie and Annie sat down again across from each other with a cedar box of beading supplies between them.

"Come, David, I want to show you something." Tom held out David's coat to him, and together they stepped outside into the wind and the snow. David followed Tom, who strode confidently over a plank walkway hidden by snow, but marked by a thick rope strung between uprights. In a few yards the cabin behind them disappeared behind a blanket of white. David worried that if he strayed off the walkway onto the raft of snow-covered logs, he might not find it again unless the wind or the snow stopped. Then a darkening in the snow ahead resolved itself as a long shed with blue plastic tarp for walls, and a snow-blasted shingled building at one end.

They stepped through a door into the long structure. There was a sound of a generator starting up, and then overhead fluorescent lights came on, revealing a long shop, tidy and well lit with snow-covered skylights in the roof. A long machine dominated the thick plank floor.

"Sawmill," Tom said, pushing something that looked like a Volkswagen engine attached to a big band saw down a set of steel tracks to the end nearest them. "In big sawmills, the logs move through the saws. In little ones like this, it's easier for the saw to move. Here," he waved at the other end of the building, where a large log lay on an inclined set of steel rails, "You guide the log." With that, the two of them winched and manhandled the log up the rails and onto the bed of the saw, then locked it into place. Tom gave David a pair of gloves, safety goggles, and ear plugs, and explained how they would remove the sawed-off piece after each pass of the saw.

David couldn't wait to see the saw in action and felt the thrill of learning something new and exciting.

Tom positioned the gasoline-powered band saw at one end of the log, and started the engine. A moment later, the fast-moving steel band bit into the log, pulled by gravity through the log as it cut. In a couple of minutes it had cut through to the end of the log and the engine automatically slowed. Tom waved, and the two of them lifted the slice of wood with bark on one side and set it on a pile of others. Working together they rolled the heavy log ninety degrees, secured it, and the saw again bit into the wood. Twice more and the ten-foot length had been transformed from a round to a square, almost three feet on a side, and the saw started again.

"Piano spruce," Tom said when David took a closer look at the first plank off the log. "See how perfect the grain is?" The band saw was cutting so smoothly that David could easily see the grain of the wood. It was beautiful—all exactly parallel, without any tiny knots or any other flaws. "Most of what I cut goes for house lumber and stuff like that. But a couple of times each winter, I'll run across a perfect tree. So I saw it up, and ship it off in the spring to a man who sells to furniture and piano and guitar makers. This one board is worth almost a hundred bucks Canadian."

With three big logs to cut up, the day passed quickly, and when Tom finally turned the saw off, David saw that it was getting dark and could feel his stomach growling. Then he noticed the old photographs tacked on the wall over the workbench.

There was one of a lanky Indian, his hair pulled back and ribboned like Tom's, in a long, dorylike boat, with what looked like a tent and crates of supplies in the stern. The man sat there stern-faced with the ends of the oars in his lap, holding a great shiny double-bitted axe.

"Dad rowed," Tom said. "Gas boats were expensive in those days. Many people rowed. They lived in the woods, cut big trees with just axes, or two men with a big saw with two handles." Another picture, Tom's dad again with another man, standing on planks stuck into slots cut into the butt of a giant fir tree. But the background! Behind them were only the distant shimmering channels, with wisps of clouds in the trees. David looked closer and saw the blade and handles of a long whipsaw extending from either side of the tree.

"Those big trees swell at bottom for the roots. Too thick

to cut. You have to use springboards to get up where the tree is thinner. Easier to cut." Then Tom laughed gently. "Them fellows were *men*! They didn't have chain saws. Just cut everything by hand."

"What's this one?" David asked. Another picture showed Tom's dad standing on a raft of logs next to an old black tugboat with a tall smokestack. There were neat piles of cut firewood stacked all around the stern and along the sides of the tug.

"Sometimes they'd work all winter to get a raft together. They'd worry about a storm coming up and losing the raft. But then when the tug came for the raft, Dad would get paid. That was always a good day!" Tom smiled, remembering.

David asked about the firewood on the tug. "Yeah, that's for the boiler. Those old tugs burned firewood. Sometimes the crew would have to stop and chop wood for a day before they could keep going."

Tom stood, pulled a cord on the wall, and the lights dimmed as the generator slowed. He opened the door and the two stepped out into the early dusk.

"Look," Tom said, "the storm has passed. Tomorrow you can travel."

The sun was down, and in the short twilight the fresh snow on the hills around the cove was pink; the cabin lights shone cheerily out into the vast wilderness. New snow had drifted knee deep over the walkway, but it was light and fluffy, and the two of them took a shovel and a broom and quickly cleared it, and then made a wide path from the cabin to the boat.

When they stepped inside the cabin, the table was set and

piled with steaming venison, homemade bread, and a black-berry pie. They held hands: Lars, the twins, Ruth, Susie, and Tom, in a circle around the table, and Annie said a long grace, heads bowed. When the words stopped, David was struck by the peacefulness of the little lantern-lit cabin on that log raft in the cove, surrounded by the giant and empty land. Just for a moment all were silent, as if each one shared David's thoughts, and then it was gone, replaced by the clink of cutlery on plates and Ruth's renewed babbling.

After dinner, Tom and David worked side by side at the sink, where the wall was covered with thumb-tacked snap-shots from lifetimes spent in the North—of little boats and big fish and bigger trees; of smoking canneries in dark, forested inlets; of building the cabin on the little house-raft. And in all the pictures, the woods: looming, vast, silent, cloud-wisped, magnificent.

When they were done, Tom reached to the top of the bookcase. He brought down a wood canoe, all of a foot and a half long, carved and painted, with the high ends and wide sides of the Indian craft he had seen in pictures, and eight exquisitely made paddlers sat aboard, with a pile of carved wooden bundles between them. David held it gently, amazed at the detail of the carving, and looked for some mark on the bottom, to show that it was mass-produced. He found none.

"You made this?" he finally asked.

"Yes," Tom answered simply. "Sometimes in winter, storms stay for days here. Good weather to carve. For years, before white man and gas boats, my people traveled up and down coast in these canoes. Now, look how much better your boat is. Just watch the weather, and you will be fine."

"Come, boy." It was Lars, only limping a little, and the color back in his face. He looked so good it made David's heart sing. "Go look outside. The stars are out. Tomorrow will be good travel weather."

Outside, David's breath was white and thick in the air before him. But then his eyes quickly grew used to the dark, and he looked up, surprised at the brightness and number of the stars. He looked for a long moment, until he shivered from the cold. Inside Lars was waiting. "See, boy, good weather. We will get there for Christmas. We will do it!" David and Annie exchanged smiles, their spirits lifted.

Finally Tom got a big flashlight and they helped Lars outside and over the raft to the boat where they said their good-byes. The twins fell into their bunks for a night of dreamless sleep.

In the morning, David and Lars got the boat under way before dawn. The water was glassy and still, the stars were bright above them, and the spotlight played out across wisps of sea smoke as they kept a lookout for driftwood.

After a bit, Annie came up to the pilothouse to look out the back door. There was the tiniest dot of light in the vastness behind them, and she thought she could see the plume of chimney smoke rising straight and perfect into the still morning air. Then a fold in the hills came between them and it was no more.

Johnstone Strait, that wide and somber canyon where the

wind and tide fought sometimes even on the fairest summer days, was still. The sun rose to shine on white hills and dark water as their wake arrowed across the vast stillness of the morning. They all crowded into the pilothouse, the twins staring out, amazed at the land and seascapes unfolding before them with the coming of the new day.

Far behind them the hills came together at the place called Discovery Passage, where Vancouver's men had found and mapped the way north. And ahead the canyon narrowed, and there were more islands, ridgeline after ridgeline outlined in the morning's long, shadowed light.

In all that land and all that water, but for the snow-covered clearcuts high on the steep side of Vancouver Island, they could see no road, no town, no cabin, nor even another boat, and the twins felt humbled and very small.

When the sun had begun to arc over to the west in the afternoon of that short winter day, they angled in toward the shore and the row of houses that was the Indian village of Alert Bay, the first settlement they'd seen all day.

Alert Bay was a main fuel stop for boats on the Inside Passage. But on the fuel dock, the oil man came forward in his striped and faded blue coveralls and said there was no diesel fuel. The oil barge was late; it would be three days before it arrived.

Lars's face clouded. He said they had enough fuel to get to the next stop, but they sensed he was uneasy. So they went on, the sun hidden behind high, fast-moving clouds, and the wind coming on a little more. They passed a lighthouse and into wider waters where the wind raised occasional whitecaps. When the first spray began to hit the windows, they could see the ice crystals slide down the glass and the thin white rime begin to coat the railings, and they were afraid.

Susie had given Annie some herb tea, and she made some for Lars, then watched him carefully as he drank it, uneasy, worried that he could become disabled again.

"Is that the Queen's Pond?" she asked, pointing at where the land fell away to starboard.

"Way off, yes," he said, and they gazed ahead. In the cold winter air, the islands and trees created a strange mirage on the horizon, taking on a thin, elongated, distorted look.

The clouds grew thicker, and the light became flat, shadowless, painting all that lay before them in shades of gray. Even the twins, with their limited experience of northern waters, sensed in the sky and the air what more experienced mariners call a "weather breeder." It was an ominous time, the kind of afternoon when the sailor yearns for the most secure of harbors, a place where islands and arms of land enfold the entering vessel, and where the wind may blow all around with great force, yet the water remains almost unrippled.

They traveled just then a mile or two off the shore, near Fort Rupert, whose shores had once seen the first trading post of white men, the Hudson's Bay Company store. It was where the Indians had come in their high-bowed canoes and rested their paddles after journeys of many days. They would bring furs to trade for repeating Winchester rifles, bright cloth, and whiskey.

"Will we be there before dark?" David asked, anxiety plain in his voice.

"Look at chart, David," Lars answered, taking his eyes off the waters ahead only after a long while. "Remember what I told you." And so David took the shiny brass dividers and measured the distance from the tick on the chart that was their last position to the place where the pencil line entered a cove, their destination for the night, the place called God's Pocket.

As night approached, the wind blew harder and the spray flew higher. The twins' hearts were in their throats. The boat rose and fell in the seaway, struggling, and their old enemy, ice, began once again to accumulate. The very last light of day revealed only a bleak and cheerless scene of desolate snow-driven shores, with those awful wind-twisted trees.

"Turn, girl, turn," Lars said at last. "Turn to starboard now. It's God's Pocket; we are there." His knuckles rapped sharply on the glass and enough of the rime ice fell away for him to peer ahead. "And just in time, isn't that so?"

The boat swung, eagerly it seemed, and the sea and the wind died, and with the very last of the day's light, they tied to a half-sunk float by the snowy forest shore.

When the engine was silent, David could hear the wind. It had come up even stronger in just the last minutes since they'd made the turn and entered the cove. It roared through the trees above them, but only eddied gently down to where they lay, and the boat would come up tight against the slight slack in the tie-up lines and jerk softly.

"Wow," David finally said. "This is it?"

"Yah," Lars said. "We are in God's Pocket. We are safe now."

In the fo'c'sle, Annie had cooked a venison roast, and in

the middle of the small table set a nest of soft, plaited fir bough tips, in whose center she had placed three of the glass Christmas balls Susie had given her. Afterward, there were hot sweet rolls made with the jar of salmonberries from Susie's pantry. But there was about the meal something else: the deep and abiding satisfaction that only mariners savor and only, like the *Karen A* and her crew, upon finding shelter in the face of a coming storm.

The meal was not yet finished when a great wind came, moaning and howling and roaring in the trees on the ridges around the harbor. Something cracked sharply nearby, and then again—a muffled, crackling thump.

"Trees," Lars said when the noise came again. "Wind is knocking trees down."

But their boat barely moved, so complete was the cove's protection.

"There's barely a breath down here," Annie said in a soft, amazed voice, putting her bared arm out the door and feeling only the occasional softest eddies on her skin.

"You're better, aren't you, Lars? I watched you today," Annie said. "Was it the herb tea? Susie gave me plenty. You should drink a lot."

The old man stirred the light amber tea for a long moment before answering.

"I wish it so," he said softly. "Doctor said when you are old like me, spells come and go." He waved his good hand before him. "No reason, just comes sometimes. Yah, tea is good. Does it make me better? Will it keep spells away? Ah, child, is a thing I cannot say."

The roaring came again and something immense fell in

the forest. They all listened, and there was a foghorn, now loud, now snatched, carried totally away by the wind. The twins sat, awed.

"You see," Lars said when the worst of the gust had passed and there was only the low, distant roaring of the surf. "Now you know why we call it God's Pocket."

"We'll be there by Christmas, won't we, Lars?" Annie said. "It's the thirteenth now. I mean, once we get past the Queen's Pond, it won't be too bad. That's what Tom said."

"We'll get there, Annie girl," Lars said. "Maybe we wait a few days to cross the Queen's Pond, but is good going after that—narrow canyons where wind cannot reach til we get to Alaska border. Still, you always need luck when you travel in winter. Yah, we'll be there for Christmas."

Something woke David deep in the night and he sat up in his bunk, listening. The wind had come on even stronger, roaring in great gusts through the trees, and the surf was steady—a deep, heavy, low roar. But this was different, and it was a moment before he realized what it was: the throb of a big diesel and not very far away. He pulled on his heavy sweater and pants and went up to stand in the wheelhouse.

Before him was a very large tug, he saw at once, coming into God's Pocket with all her deck lights on. David slid the door back a little and looked with the binoculars, amazed at having a visitor. And then it struck him: the whole forward part of the boat looked oddly bloated and strange. He knew it was ice, and a chill ran through him. Two men in brown suits appeared with a sledgehammer, and what looked like a baseball bat. They made their way carefully up the sloping deck to the bow and began knocking the ice off the anchor winch.

He shivered and closed the door except for a crack, and kept looking, fascinated. Annie appeared behind him, her hair pulled down inside an oversized sweater.

"It's a tug," David murmured, "under all that ice."

They heard the rattle of a heavy anchor chain coming through the snow. As they watched, the shape of a huge barge appeared from the gloom behind the tug. The deck at the top of its massive, sloping bow must have been twenty feet off the water; above that it was piled almost out of sight with the steel container vans. Even the vans were iced up, shiny, glistening white, reflecting the spotlight's beam in the snowy black.

"David, look at the back of the barge." Annie's fingers dug into his arm. "Do you suppose it was like that or did they get knocked off?"

Then David saw it: the front of the barge was stacked four high with container vans and lashed with heavy chains. But part of the back quarter was empty except for a few scattered containers askew on the deck; loose chains hung over the sides into the water.

Another gust of wind came just then, and the tug and barge disappeared into the swirling white. A crack echoed down from the forest, so sharp and loud and close that the twins jumped. Yet still, barely a breath of air carried in to where they lay.

In the morning, the barge was drawn up alongside the tug, and in the thin light the twins could see men working on board, lashing the fallen containers to the deck and struggling to pull the long chains from the water.

When Lars was up and the oatmeal and hot chocolate

were on the table, a new sound carried in to them. David sprang up and watched as a green outboard skiff with two men aboard approached them from the tug. He pulled on his boots and heavy coat and went out on deck.

"Morning." The man in the bow seemed surprised to see such a young person. "Breezy one, eh?"

"Yeah," David answered. "Did you hear all those trees falling last night? That was some wind!"

"I'm Carl Larson," the lanky, ruddy-faced man in the bow said. "This is Rudy Peters." The other man wore green coveralls and a cap with "Foss Maritime—Always Ready" embroidered above the bill. "Do you mind if we use your radio? Ours aren't working." Foss was a major tugboat operator based out of Seattle.

"Oh, sure," David said, "no problem. What happened to you guys out there? Did you really lose some of the load on the barge?"

"Lucky it was just a few empty vans," Carl muttered as he climbed aboard. "It came on so quick. We could have lost the whole ball of wax."

Rudy followed him up and into the pilothouse. He quickly turned the radio controls, listened a moment, and then contacted someone called the "Bull Harbor marine operator" to make a call to Seattle.

"Hello, Foss Operations, Sam speaking."

"Hello, this is the Bull Harbor marine operator in British Columbia, I have traffic for you from the vessel *Wedell Foss*."

"Ah, go ahead, *Wedell Foss*." Sam's voice seemed instantly anxious.

"Rudy here, Sam. We're okay. We lost two stacks of containers and a couple of windows just as we were talking to you last night. But we're laying here in God's Pocket now, getting things squared away. We should have some more radios hooked up in a bit. We'll try you on the sideband then. Over."

"Anybody hurt? And where are you talking from?"

"Ah, *Wedell* back, no, nothing serious. There's a little troller in here, Americans, the *Karen A,* she's called. We're just borrowing their radio."

"Foss Seattle back. Which containers did you lose?"

"*Wedell* here. Ah, mostly empties. We're going through the numbers now. We'll have a full update by the time we get our radios back on line. Over."

"Seattle back. Okay, the *Henry* just transited Seymour Narrows northbound with two empty chip barges. If you need assistance, I can have her anchor the barges and meet you tonight."

"Ah, *Wedell* back. We'll call back in a couple of hours on that. That's all for now, *Wedell Foss,* WZF33134, clear."

"Seattle back, yeah, OK, Rudy, thanks for the call, and glad you guys are okay. We'll be standing by for your call on the big set. And we'll alert the Canadian Coast Guard about the vans."

Annie appeared on the stairs and asked the two men if they wanted coffee. They didn't need to be asked twice, and they all crowded down into the fo'c'sle. Lars invited them to the table and introduced them all.

"Twins are my helpers." Lars said to their inquiring looks. "My arm is bad, but with twins to help, we go north."

The big tug had been out by a place called Storm Islands when the wind came, Rudy told them. The barge was at the end of a long towline, so it was hard for them to see exactly where the vans broke loose.

"But after that wind came up and that cold, we had our hands full. Storm Islands are what we call the point of no return. Once you're that far across, you pretty much got to keep going; it's just as far back to Safety Cove as it is ahead to God's Pocket. Little boats like this," Rudy waved around him at the *Karen A*, "can sneak in behind Storm Islands. But for us, towing the big barge, we need a better harbor."

Then they'd gotten into a big tide rip, he said, and a real steep sea had smacked into the pilothouse and broken out two windows.

"Those tugs are tough," Rudy said. "I've been towing up and down the coast with her, summer and winter, and this was the first time we've had any windows broken out." He could see that his tale was upsetting the twins, so he changed the subject. "I bet you wouldn't mind doing a load of laundry or two," he said.

"You've got a washing machine on there?" Annie answered, surprised.

"Washer and dryer," Rudy said, smiling. "Movies, too. Get your washing together if you want, and all of you can ride over with us. We'll bring you back whenever you want."

"Could we?" Annie stood up. The men seemed friendly, people she could trust, and she knew David would go, too, or she'd never have asked.

"Twins go," Lars waved them off. "Old man just sit by stove."

The *Wedell Foss* was more like a small ship, and the twins were struck by how small the *Karen A* seemed as they drew away from her in the skiff. But for all the tug's size, a big piece of plywood covered two of her front windows, a sobering reminder of the power of the weather beyond the point.

There was something about the tug and her crew that made the twins glad she was there in the cove with them. A bull of a man in brown coveralls introduced himself as Isaac, the cook. He reached down and, one at a time, picked them up under the arms and effortlessly lifted them from the skiff onto the wide back deck. He led the visitors through a heavy metal door to the galley with its warm food smell and many bookshelves jammed with paperbacks.

"Wow," David said. "You guys must do a lot of reading!"

"Read?" Isaac laughed gently. "Oh, fifteen days up, fifteen days back on these Bering Sea runs. Oh, yes, sir, we get plenty of time to read."

Isaac set generous slices of pie and mugs of milk before them, then disappeared around the corner with their laundry. A few minutes later, he rejoined the twins, resting his thick, tattooed forearms on the table like a gentle giant.

"Why y'all headed to Alaska this time of year?"

And it all tumbled out, first from David and then from Annie: the moves from place to place, the foster homes, their mom taking off, then how they found Lars, and how hard it had been, traveling north so late in the season.

Isaac sat for a long while after that with his meaty hands templed under his chin.

"You say your dad's got a boat?" he asked finally. "Maybe

we could get ahold of him and he could charter a plane, get on down here and help y'all for the rest of the trip."

"They don't have phones in the cove," Annie answered. "And sometimes he's away hunting for days and days this time of year."

There was a crackle of static from a wall speaker, and then Rudy's voice: "KKI2641 Seattle, KKI2641 Seattle, come in, this is the *Wedell Foss*." A long silence followed before another voice answered, and the sounds of cheering and celebration erupted above them.

"Let's listen," Isaac said, cocking his head at the speaker. "They got the radios goin' again. That's a good sign!"

"Yeah, Seattle, *Wedell*, we're getting things patched up now. We're still inventorying containers, so you'll have to wait a bit on a list."

"Yeah, okay, *Wedell*, I was sure glad to get your call this morning. After I lost you last night, I called B.C. weather. They said the low that passed over the Queen Charlottes last night had the lowest pressure they'd ever measured on the coast since they started keeping records. After I heard that, I got real worried. Oh, hey, one more thing. That troller you were on this morning, if she was the *Karen A*, that's the boat that was on the news a week or so ago. Something about some runaway kids on board. They figure she's headed north, and the Coast Guard's been alerted to keep an eye out for her."

The twins looked at each other suddenly.

"*Wedell* back, nah. It was the *Katherine A* that's laying in here. No kids."

"Seattle back. Yeah, okay, Rudy, just thought I'd check. Okay, glad to hear your voice and we'll talk to you on the next regular schedule. Seattle clear."

"Okay, yeah. *Wedell* clear."

Rudy came through the door a moment later, got himself a coffee and sat across from the twins.

"Listen," he said in a kind voice. "I don't know what sort of trouble you're coming from down south, but I figure you've got enough problems without having the Coast Guard on your tail."

"Thanks," Annie said, relief pouring through her. She stood up and walked over to put her plate and mug in the sink for a moment before speaking. A porthole was mounted in the wall above the sink, and she could see past the tow winch to where the sea beat on the shore across the channel.

"It's not like we did anything bad," she said, turning to Rudy. "We just didn't want to go to a foster home again. We just wanted to get up North and find our Dad."

"Um," Rudy shrugged and pulled at his cap. "Like I said, what you did back south is no concern of ours. I'd just like to see you guys get safely where you're going. Too bad we're not going the same direction, or we'd keep you company out across the worst of it."

"Do you think it'll be okay after the storm passes?" David asked. "I mean, we might have to wait a day or two, but we'll be able to get across, won't we?"

Rudy got up suddenly, as if remembering something. "C'mon upstairs, kids. There's something I can show you."

They thanked Isaac for the snack and followed Rudy around the corner and up a set of narrow stairs to the pilot-house. It was enormous, running the full width of the tall deckhouse, with a wide chart table along the back wall, above which was a whole wall of radios and other electronic equipment. But on the starboard side, two of the windows were covered with plywood, and the wind whistled around the edges. The compass lay askew in its gimballed holder, the glass top smashed, the fluid gone. Two men in coveralls had removed the access panels beneath it, and they worked among a maze of plumbing and wiring. One of them had a bandaged face.

David reached gingerly over the men to feel the window frames, twisted and bent inward by the force of the water. If he hadn't seen it for himself, he wouldn't have believed that such damage could have been wrought to such an able-looking ship by the force of a wave.

"It was bad, kid," one man said quietly. "You're from that troller, aren't you?"

David nodded.

"Well, listen," the man was suddenly aware of Rudy frowning severely at him. "This wouldn't ever happen to you. When you're in a little boat, you got to be picking your traveling weather this time of year. But for big rigs like us, we pretty much travel right through, weather or not."

"David, Annie, look at this," Rudy called them over to the chart table. A wide piece of paper was scrolling out of the weather fax machine on the wall. When it stopped, he ripped it neatly off and set it, smelling faintly of copier fluid, before them.

It was a weather map that comes over the radio, Rudy explained. It covered the whole North Pacific from Japan to Alaska, and had Hs and Ls for high- and low-pressure areas.

"But what it means is this: you'll get a blast of wind

tomorrow when this next low tracks through, and maybe the day after that, but then, my guess is that this high will push in, maybe just for a day, maybe even less, but just enough that you might be able to slip through between storms."

Rudy set the weather fax aside, drew out a damp chart and set it before them.

"When you think it might be a chance," he said, "you gotta go out and look at it. If there's any kind of traveling weather at all, usually it'll be early in the morning, so you gotta plan the night before to be out here just at first light." His finger fell on a dot called "Pine Island." One of the other men had begun to caulk around the edges of the plywood, but the wind still moaned through the places he hadn't filled yet, and Rudy could tell the twins were not excited at going anywhere before there was light to see by.

"Here's the good part, though," Rudy ran his hand over a maze of narrow channels leading north above Queen Charlotte Sound. "Once you're across you'll have easy traveling in protected channels almost the rest of the way to Alaska."

Isaac called them all down to a table loaded with food. Afterward the twins took showers, folded their laundry, and stuffed it into the duffel. Annie picked a video from the big shelf and the two of them nested in big, overstuffed chairs and forgot, for a short while, where they were and where they yet had to go.

When the movie was over, daylight was failing. Isaac gave them a box with hot food for Lars, and Rudy took them back across the cove to the *Karen A*.

David looked back at the size of the big tug and then at

their own little boat, snuggled in against the shore. He felt the cold breeze on his face and looked up to the ridgeline above the harbor. The wind was still working up there, and tall stands of trees waved back and forth like so many leaves. He was afraid, and the fear was like a cold stone in his chest.

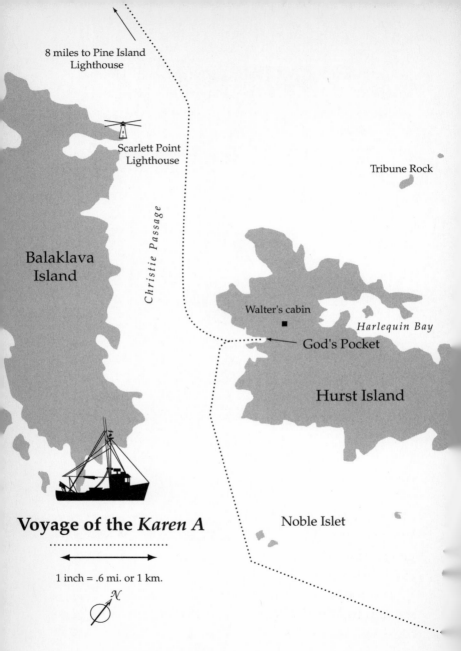

8 miles to Pine Island
Lighthouse

Scarlett Point
Lighthouse

Tribune Rock

Christie Passage

Balaklava
Island

Walter's cabin

Harlequin Bay

God's Pocket

Hurst Island

Voyage of the *Karen A*

Noble Islet

1 inch = .6 mi. or 1 km.

N

CHAPTER 7

In God's Pocket

 Sometime after midnight, the clanking of metal against metal woke David, and he went up into the wheelhouse rubbing his eyes, and slipping into his sweater. It was the tug, half hidden by swirling snow. The *Wedell Foss* was leaving, and David's heart sank.

As the tug moved into the channel and the snow grew thicker, a whiteness washed over their lights. At first he thought it was snow, but then he could see the bow slowly rising and falling in the seas, and he knew it was spray, which would freeze quickly on the exposed metal in the bitter night. A snow squall came and swallowed up the lights as if they had never been. In the blackness, David shivered involuntarily and admired the men for going out on such a night, and he felt very alone again.

Annie woke when the light came and, without looking, she already knew that there wasn't a chance of leaving. She could distinctly hear the low roar of the surf, the foghorn, and another big wind working on the hillsides and ridge tops. Finally she got up to look around, to see if perhaps the night had brought company, like it had before.

But there were only the bent and twisted trees on the hills, the wind-darkened water, and low, snow-thick clouds. She snapped on the little AM/FM radio, turned it way down so as not to wake the others, and tried to find a station. At first she thought there was something wrong with the radio, but only after she'd scanned both AM and FM, getting only one faint and faraway station, did she grasp the truth: there weren't any stations within range. She snapped it off and slumped back in the seat; even when they'd lived in the cove with Mom and Dad, there'd been stations on the radio.

They were subdued at breakfast. While Annie made pancakes, first David and then Lars went up into the pilot-house to have a look, only to return and sit wordlessly.

Once there was the sound of another tree falling in the forest—a sharp crack followed by a rustling thump, and they all flinched.

"Geez," David said, "after a while you'd think there wouldn't be anything left to blow down up there."

Just then the boat settled slightly to starboard. There was a sharp rap at the door and a hoarse voice cried out, "Lars Hansen, you old criminal, are you in there?"

David got up slowly, totally stunned. When he stepped up into the pilothouse, he could see the outline of a person peering in through the glass, and he slid the door partway open.

"What's this, by gum, a kid?" A strange-looking man stood in the doorway, clad in dirty, snow-blasted rain gear.

Runny eyes peered out from a bearded and winter-reddened face. David just stood there a moment, speechless, for he could see past the strange figure to the cove beyond, and there were no other boats but theirs.

"Ain't this Lars Hansen's boat?" David recoiled from the man's bad breath. Before he could answer, the man turned aside to direct a thick stream of tobacco juice onto the deck outside.

"Um, ah, where'd ya *come* from?" David finally managed to stammer at the stranger.

"Come from?" The man stuck a thick finger into his mouth to adjust his wad of tobacco. When he withdrew it, glistening with the dark tobacco juice, David noticed that the last joint and fingernail were gone. "I *live* here, boy, that's where I *come* from. Now is this old Lars's boat or ain't it? And if it is, where is he?"

Lars came up the stairs just then, and the stranger pushed in past David to wrap Lars in an oilskin, tobacco juice, and snow bear hug.

"Well now, Walter Gorst, might you be?" said Lars, stepping back finally to get a better look. "And here I am thinking you was dead and buried."

"Not dead," Walter said, "Close." He shucked off his rain jacket and pulled down the neck of a thick homespun sweater to reveal an ugly mass of scars. They started up under his beard, covered half his neck, and disappeared under the edge of a disgustingly dirty set of long woolen underwear. "Close, by God, a hunnert and sixty-three stitches close, but not dead."

Walter came below to sit at the table with Lars, and the

twins retreated to the pilothouse steps to sit and listen. Walter helped himself to the coffee while Lars introduced the twins and explained, in a few short sentences, how it was that he was northbound so late in the year.

Walter glanced around, taking in the twins and the old man's bad arm.

"So, old Lars with a set of twins for company. Ain't that something? Well, now, Lars, this ain't the season to be running along up North with a bum arm. It's hard enough to get through this time of year when all your parts are working."

"More than just company, Walter," Lars tapped his head. "I had stroke. Twins run the boat, see? Now we must have your story, Walter. What happened? I heard your boat blew up, all lost. And now, here you are. What is true story?"

"We had a powder boat," Walter said softly, addressing the twins as well as his old friend. "When the truck showed up in Seattle with a load for us, I could tell the dynamite was too old to be safe. Hell, there was nitro oozing on the outside of some of those sticks, but freight was scarce, especially for us powder boats, and if I'd have turned it *all* down, which I should have, there was two or three other hungry fellows standing right behind me."

"What's a powder boat, mister?" David asked. At first he'd been afraid of the man, but as Walter had talked, David had sensed that a kind heart lurked beneath the gruff exterior, that living alone in such a place might make a person a little rough around the edges.

"Coast Guard rules, son. To carry dynamite—we still call it powder—boats have to be built special, the holds have to be lined with wood, that kind of thing. There were just two or three of us powder boats on the coast. It was a good little business, running dynamite and such to all the little mines and lumber camps. When you get up-and-down country like this, you got to use a lot of dynamite to build even a logging road."

"Well, what was that part about the old dynamite? I don't get that part."

Walter drew a small tin can from a pocket, held it close to his mouth, spat carefully, and set the tin down on the table before him. Then he turned to David again, "You ever been around dynamite, son?"

David shook his head.

"Funny stuff, dynamite," Walter said thoughtfully. "When it's not out of date, you can hammer it, burn it, even shoot it, and she won't go off except with special primers which we keep in a whole different part of the boat. Mr. Nobel did a big service when he came up with that stuff. But the bad part is when it gets old, the nitroglycerine, like, sweats sometimes on the outside of the cartridges. And when she gets like that, watch out. It's liable to be real unstable. So anyway, I checked it all over, the whole load, and the worst of it I wouldn't touch, no way, but I took the rest, and there must have been more bad stuff that I couldn't see."

Walter stopped for a moment to load up his cheek with pungent-smelling tobacco from a flat tin in his pocket.

"Lord," he said, shaking his head slowly, "we always tried to be so careful with them rigs, shut off the oil stove even when we went in to unload. Must have been one of them loggers. The unloading crane at this logging camp way back up one of those inlets was busted, so we rigged our own, but we were shorthanded, so three of them logging fellows come aboard to help us unload. Maybe they was sneaking a smoke up in the paint locker or something, or maybe it was just oily rags catching; we'll never really know. She started smoking bad up out of the locker in the bow, and then flames broke out real quick. I was ashore, talking to the foreman, telling him about the condition of the dynamite. Then I heard the commotion and looked outside. As soon as I saw the flames, I started running down the dock, telling them boys to get the hell out. We would have stayed and fought the fire if the dynamite wasn't so old, but you get that nitro on the outside, and it's bad news! Won't take nothing to set it off." Walter stopped for a moment, and the twins could see he was having a hard time telling this part of the story.

"I didn't get but halfway down the dock, and I remember seeing my engineer, old Charlie Knissen, just coming up the deck with the hose going full bore and starting to play onto them flames when she blew. Took the end of the *dock* with her, by god. A piece of it broke my neck and laid me open. Missed the artery, but if the camp first aid guy hadn't been right there, I'd a bled to death anyway."

"How about the guys on the boat?" David almost whispered his question, and Walter shook his head for a long time before answering.

"Just bits of smoking wood in the water. Nothing else was left. Three of them loggers, the three fellows that was with me, all gone." He snapped his fingers. "Just like that."

Afterward, he explained bitterly, the logging company sued him. He lost the insurance money, his home in Vancouver, and all he'd worked for.

"You work all your life, building something up, and then she's all gone. Nothing left, and sometimes it ain't even your fault!"

No one said anything, and after a while, Walter stood up. "Well, come lads, you're not going anywhere today, so I'll show you around here."

The twins were intensely curious, for they hadn't even noticed any sign of life around the shores of the cove before. David and Annie put on their gear and helped Lars over the slippery part of the float and ramp to shore.

They followed Walter to his cabin along a path that was tramped in the snow. The cabin was set in a clearing so small that the branches of the trees met above the roof. One end of the house looked as if it had burned, and the burned part had been replaced with driftwood planks and boards that had been carefully cut and fitted together. But the windows were lit cheerily from within, and a cozy plume of wood smoke issued from the chimney.

Inside was one big room, with a smaller room off the end. It was tidy, with two big full bookcases on the wall and a table that looked like it was made of driftwood, but what most surprised the twins were all of the blazing lights. They didn't hear a generator.

"Wind power," Walter boomed, waving out at the trees outside. "That's free electricity going by out there most of the year. I cut the top off one of them big ones last year, got me a windmill and put the batteries under the bed."

David settled in at a window over by a driftwood desk. Walter, or perhaps the previous occupant, had cut a slot through the trees, a corridor just wide enough to see out to the Queen's Pond.

It was a wild and frightening sight. The seas seemed to be leaping straight up, fifteen or twenty feet in the air, and he knew that their little boat could never survive out there. He lost track of time, just staring out at the wild maelstrom of windswept ocean, and feeling the fear grow a big knot in the pit of his stomach.

"Tide rip, boy, big tide fighting against wind." Lars's big hand rested on his shoulder, and he turned away from the window. "Don't worry. We wait and wait, and *boom*, a chance will come and we will slide across. Don't worry."

David felt better, but he turned back for one last look and knew that for all Lars's reassuring words, it was a very big place out there and their boat was very small.

The inside of the cabin was all driftwood planks. Most were straight, without the shape that might indicate they were from a boat. Barges might have such planks, David thought, or floats or docks.

In the corner, to the left of the sink, were two curved shelves. Massively built, much larger than they needed to be, they were adorned with lettering on their curved fronts, and it was a moment before David realized what they actually were: transoms, the upper bulwark planks of the sterns of two vessels near the size of their own *Karen A*. "*Bernice*—West Van. B.C." The other one was *Western* something, but the twins couldn't read the rest.

"Walter," said Annie when there was a pause in the adult conversation. She waved at the two transom shelves. "How many boats actually have trouble out there?"

Walter stroked his beard and peered out the window a

bit before answering softly. "Hardly any, really." His thick hand rested for a moment on the lower shelf. "The old *Western Ace* was abandoned on the beach; little more than firewood when I got here. This other, I believe she had engine trouble, blew ashore out there below the lighthouse. But all the fellows got off." He looked out the window again. "When we get a good blow, especially spring and fall, traveling time for the boys, we get a few boats come in, maybe busted a window out or tore up their rigging a bit, but most everybody gets across or elsewise ducks back in here to lick their wounds, so to speak."

Annie nodded, but somehow the answer hadn't been as reassuring as she had hoped.

The twins knew that even once they'd gotten across the Queen's Pond, it still might be days before they had the daylight and the place to take a walk. So they left the men yarning and took the trail up to the windmill tree.

For a little way, the trail was in the lee of the ridge; easy going, the wind screeching through the treetops but carrying little down to where they walked. But then they got to the top of the ridge and stopped, amazed.

The place looked as if a bomb had hit it. The windmill tree stood alone, guyed off with five or six wires in a vast jumble of fallen timber. At first David thought that someone had to have cut the fallen trees, for the trunks of the bigger firs were three and four feet thick. But he looked and saw all the big root bases pulled out of the ground and he knew it must have been the wind. They made their way gingerly through, walking along the tops of the biggest trunks until they got to the ridge itself and found a place where the wind moaned by, just over their heads, but which still gave a good view out and around.

From the vantage of the ridge top, there was a sort of terrible beauty to the vast sea and landscape spread out below them. To the right and the left, the sea frothed and hammered on the shores of several bleak and inhospitable islands. Below was the channel and the lighthouse, its regular flash welcome and reassuring. The wind drove long lines of white spume down the faces of the seas, and in the higher gusts, the spinning blades of the windmill over their heads gave off an unusual and deep throbbing hum.

"We're going across it, eh?" Annie had to put her mouth close to David's ear to be heard.

He kept looking out before answering, trying to correlate what he was seeing with his study of the chart.

"I got it now," he shouted back. "There's another lighthouse way out there, see, on that island? That must be Pine Island."

Annie looked and finally saw the sweep of another light from a dot of the island on the horizon.

"We go out the channel to Pine Island, then we turn about almost thirty degrees to the right and keep going until we're up inside the shelter of the land again."

They both gazed for a long moment, out across the windy, whitecapped plain to the horizon, hoping for the faint loom of the land on the other side, but there was nothing. Finally the wind and the cold were too much, and they retraced their steps back toward the cabin.

"Hey, a tree!" Annie stopped in front of a perfectly formed fir about three feet high.

"Okay, a tree." David almost bumped into her.

"No, I mean a *Christmas* tree! There's just room on the engine box for one, and we can decorate it with some of Lars's trolling gear, remember, like we used to do with Dad. Remember? And I got a couple of glass balls from Susie. Let's see if Walter has a hand saw in his shop."

They cut it, then rummaged in Walter's scrap wood pile until they found a piece that could serve as a temporary base, and took them both down to the boat. Like the coconspirators they were, the twins quickly decorated the tree and anticipated the surprise for Lars.

When it was done, David stood back a moment. "Annie, it's really nice. We needed it. All of us."

Walter had hot tea waiting for them, and as the twins sipped, he placed a photo album on the table.

"Here, now everyone thinks this is the worst spot." He waved out at the sea beyond the window. "They forget what Seymour Narrows was like before we got the contract to blow it in '58."

The men turned back to their talk, and Annie, not really understanding what Walter had meant, opened the album. The first few photos were of rapids in a narrow river canyon, but after a few minutes of studying them, she grasped that in some photos the water was running in one direction, and in others, another.

"Walter," she asked. "This isn't salt water, is it?"

"Yes, child," the gruff man said gently. "That was what Seymour Narrows looked like before we blew her open. You probably came through Yuculta Rapids, like most small boats. But big boats always had to go through Seymour."

Walter tapped a photo that showed a maelstrom of white water. "Now imagine that you had to go through that each time you went up or down the coast."

"But, these are when it's running," Annie said, remembering what Lars had taught them about the slack water every six hours. "If you go through at slack, it's okay, right?"

"Ah, right you are," Walter said, his eyes glistening. "But slack, *true slack* only lasts fifteen minutes. In the Yucultas, if you were a little bit late or early it was still okay. But at Seymour it was different. Look sharp now, see this?" Walter pointed at the place where the water always seemed the whitest. "There was a rock right in the narrowest part. And the tide pushed you right against it. The current runs a lot faster than in the Yucultas. Two, three boats a year would sink there, either hitting the rock or just getting overwhelmed by the whirlpools."

Annie turned the pages, remembering the roar of the Yucultas in the night and the size of the huge whirlpools. There were other pictures, of a camp in the woods, of a group of hard-faced men standing next to what looked like the shaft of a mine, and of flash-lit miners in hard hats posing with their equipment in an underground tunnel. Then came two whole pages of an explosion that looked like an underwater volcanic eruption. The twins studied the explosion pictures a long while, for the immensity of it was daunting: the tall trees along the shore dwarfed by the giant geyser of dark water and bits of rock.

"What happened?" Annie asked, awed.

"Why, we *blew* her, blew 'er the daylights out of there."

"You were there?" David asked.

"There? Why, hell," said Walter, scratching his cheek reflectively with the slightly dumbbell-shaped end of his finger. "Probably if you looked hard enough, you'd see the end of this here finger going up in that blast. I was lead powder man on the Seymour job. That was a high-honored job. When we blew her, it was the biggest shot anyone ever done. Every powder monkey on the B.C. coast was itching for a crack at it. Almost three million pounds of Nitramex. The newspapers said it was the largest nonnuclear blast in the history of the world."

As Walter spoke of the drilling and blasting of the tunnels—570 feet down, then 2,400 feet over, then 300 feet up—gingerly working inside the rock, underneath the churning waters of the rapids, the lights in the room sometimes grew very bright, and the twins knew it was a wind gust hitting the windmill up on the ridge.

"Look at my hair now, gone totally white. When our shift went in that morning, it was jet black. We were working up inside the rock, underwater, under the narrows. The engineers had given us the go-ahead to drill. So Johnny Davis started in with the two-inch main drill.

"I don't know how them engineers could have missed such a big fault, but his drill broke through into the water outside. We were almost a hundred and fifty feet under the water, and the force of it pushed his drill out and knocked him off his feet. Man, I want to tell you, didn't that water come a shootin' outta that hole! Fifteen years I'd been working powder in the mines and I never seen nothing like the force of that water."

The lights briefly brightened to the intensity of tiny

suns, and momentarily they all turned their attention to the moaning of the wind that carried in to them. Then Walter continued.

"We tried to hammer in the wooden plugs we always keep handy, but they were nothing against that water. After a few minutes, it was up to our knees, and we knew it was time to give up and retreat back past the floodgates into the main tunnel.

"But that fellow at the floodgate must have gotten in a panic with all that water running down at him, and he shut the floodgate, without ever checking if we was still alive! We was trapped. Well, we rapped on that door a while with the water filling in around our knees, and then we figured if we didn't get back and stop that leak somehow, we were all done."

Walter shifted his weight in his chair, savoring the deliberate pause and the twins' eager eyes that urged him to continue.

"So then what?" David finally said.

"Well, see, the worst part was that the slope of that side tunnel was slightly downhill to miss another fault they'd found, so by the time we got back to the face, we were damn near swimming. She was still gushing, but I managed to whittle down the shoulders of one of them wood plugs so we could jam her in there a little tighter. Where we lucked out was when Johnny got to fishing around underneath that water and found a drill rod we could jam in under that plug when we drove her in. And on the last crack at it we got her. I drove the plug in and John wedged the drill rod in between the floor and the plug, and she held!

"But see, those doors are designed so that the force of the

water keeps them closed. There wasn't any way they could open them until they pumped out the water. But the pumps kept jamming, and it was damn near two days before they got the water down enough to open the door. 'Course, we was just about spent from the cold and the bad air. I had to keep holding Johnny up at the end or he'd have fallen and drowned in two feet of water.

"When they got the door open, I passed Johnny through, but when I came through the men seemed like they were afraid of me, and that's when I found out my hair had all gone white, just like that." He smiled a tobacco-stained smile and ran his fingers through his snow-white hair.

"I stayed for the blast; we were almost done then anyway, except for placing and wiring the charges. We'd come too close for me not to get in on the fun part of the job. But after that, I wouldn't go down the mines no more. I just figured I'd used up all my chances. I bought the boat and started running powder. I knew all them fellows anyhow, so they put the work my way."

Walter stopped talking and the twins leafed through the photo album again, picking out the handsome man with the shiny, jet-black hair in the pictures. The lights got very bright and the wind moaned, and old Lars rose stiffly. From the looks of the sky, the day had already started to go, and he didn't want to try the trail after dark.

"Why don't you join us for dinner on the *Karen A*?" Annie asked Walter.

"You bet, but only if you let me bring the main course," he said. Walter quickly wrapped up a king salmon filet that he had been thawing.

As the foursome made their way down the path, they stopped for a moment when they came around the corner. The *Karen A* and the cove lay before them. Out in the middle, the water was alternately dark in patches where the wind gusts would strike it. There was no light on their boat, and the blast of a lighthouse foghorn came to them on the wind. Something was indescribably bleak and lonely about the scene. Then Walter broke the silence, as if he knew what the twins were thinking.

"Remember this, you guys: I've seen boats that were less than the *Karen A* make it across in some terrible weather. And just think back to them Natives in their big canoes—I talked to some of those old chiefs, and they'd lay in here or over across at Safety Cove for two, three weeks sometimes, waiting for their chance. One old chief told me one time his paddlers couldn't sleep for three nights thinking about it. But finally they got across." No one spoke, and after a bit they made their way down the ramp, onto the float, and Walter helped Lars aboard.

Annie went down the stairs first into the foc's'le and turned on the light over the tree. Walter helped Lars down the steps and they both stopped as the twins yelled, "Surprise!" The small and perfectly formed tree stood on the engine box, the ornaments shining in the light.

"It was the perfect size," Annie said. "It made us think of Christmases we had up North with Dad. We never really had much ornament money, and we'd use Dad's trolling gear and make stuff. It doesn't really take up much space. Can we keep it up?"

Lars' eyes shone and it was all he could do just to nod at

her. He took in the tree, bright with the copper, brass, and chrome lures and spoons that he'd dragged for decades through miles of endless, dark waters. Once more, he wondered at his good fortune to have these children in his life now, when he so needed someone.

Lars filled short glasses with rum for himself and his friend, and the hum of their conversation mixed in the air with the rich smell of baking king salmon. They toasted each other, the *Karen A*, and even Queen Charlotte before dinner was ready. And as the four of them ate, pressed knee to knee around the small table, the weather report came on the radio. As one, they set down their forks to listen.

"A strong ridge of high pressure from interior Alaska may bring a brief respite to the North Coast tomorrow after the present Pacific disturbance passes through. However, another low in the Gulf of Alaska is gathering strength, and mariners are advised that a gale or storm warning may be issued later in the day, if either of these systems gets any stronger. Mariners are urged to listen at all regular times, and be advised that an emergency storm or gale warning may be issued at any time."

"We may still have chance. We will wait and watch," Lars said to two fallen faces. "Is best to play it safe." And they went back to their meal.

When at last they had said their goodnights, Walter stepped outside into the cold and black. The twins and Lars went to bed early, in case the morning's weather was better— at least a "chance," as Lars called it.

David rose at 4:30 and slipped quietly into the pilothouse to slide the door back and listen to the night. But to his surprise,

Lars was already there, sitting in the captain's chair.

"What do you think?" David asked, relieved that Lars would be able to make the decision for him.

"Not yet," Lars said, and he slid down a window for David to listen. "We check again at daylight."

The wind still rushed through the trees, but with less force than before.

"What about leaving early?" David asked. "I thought you were always supposed to leave early to get across here."

"Is good *idea* to leave early, yah," Lars said. "But sometimes, only chance comes later, sometimes even in the afternoon. Still, it might be only chance in two weeks."

"But shouldn't we wait until everything's just right? So we can get across in daylight?" David knew he would have to steer if it got rough again, and the thought of being out there after dark and having to steer terrified him.

"David, boy," Lars said gently, "do you want get north for Christmas, or stay here? Sometimes on the North Coast at this time of year, many weeks pass before perfect chance comes."

At daylight it was no better. David volunteered to make breakfast, so Annie coached him through poached eggs on toast. As they ate there was little talk. They could hear the roar of the surf from the partially opened pilothouse door. And when the breakfast things were put away and the galley was cleaned up, they all went back to bed, for their spirits were very low.

Voyage of the *Karen A*

·············· Big Ship Route ·············

← 1 inch = 11 mi. or 18 km. →

N

Lama Passage

Pointer
Island

Burke Channel

Fitzhugh Sound

British
Columbia

Safety Cove

Rivers Inlet

Cape Calvert

Windows
broke here

Queen Charlotte Sound
or
"The Queen's Pond"

Egg Island

Smith Sound

Cape Caution

Pine Island

God's Pocket

Vancouver
Island

CHAPTER 8

The Jeffrey Foss

Annie noticed it first: the roaring of the wind was gone. She looked at her watch: 10:30 A.M. In a moment they had started up, and lowered the tall trolling poles and locked them down in the fishing position so they could use the big metal triangular stabilizers to reduce the boat's roll if it got bad.

Out beyond the point, the swells were huge. But there was no wind to build up the crests and make them roll and break. They passed the lighthouse at Scarlett Point. The dot on the horizon that was Pine Island got closer and closer, and there was little talk. On the tops of the biggest seas the twins kept craning their necks, looking out beyond Pine Island and trying to see Cape Caution and the land on the other side, or the shoulder of the mountain that hid Safety Cove, but there was nothing except the heaving, watery plain.

There was a lot of driftwood in the water. All the bigger pieces had seabirds on them, mostly dainty Wilson's phalaropes and the larger, graceful arctic terns. As their boat approached, the birds would stand, move restlessly about, then sit again after they passed. Once they passed a deadhead, a log floating vertically, the very tip of it rising only occasionally above the surface. Its size struck Annie most of all, and the slow, ponderous way that it moved frightened her. To strike a timber or a small branch of a tree was one thing, but the deadhead was a good four feet in diameter and anyone's guess how long. It was, she noted, almost impossible to see, appearing above the surface of the water only irregularly and momentarily. She looked several times after they had passed it, but caught no glimpse of it again, and she shuddered, sensing how frail the *Karen A* was.

The Canadian flag hung, oddly limp, from the pole at the Pine Island lighthouse, and they took turns looking with the binoculars. The twins could see curtains in the lighthouse windows, and once a person passed in the room inside. But the island itself was high and steep-sided, with no cove for a boat to get out of the waves.

At Pine Island, they turned more to the east and there was only the uneasy, slowly heaving water of the Queen's Pond ahead of them. It was an anxious time and no one spoke. Only the knowledge that this was the last big piece of really open water on the way to Alaska cheered the twins.

Finally, land began to swim up over the horizon and into visibility. First the high country behind the shore: inhospitable-looking, snow-covered peaks and buttes, and then a little later, the shore itself. They still had twenty-five miles to go to reach Safety Cove. Yet all the same, it was land, and a welcome sight. For the first time since they'd left

God's Pocket, the twins began to relax.

The tide turned then, and their steady forward progress slowed. To the east and north, all the water from Rivers Inlet and Smith and Fitzhugh Sounds began pouring out, chasing the moon, running almost directly against their course.

The darkness seemed to come up out of nowhere. One moment it was light enough to see the hills and trees along the shore, and the next there was only the flash of the lights at Cape Caution and Egg Island. The first tentative conversations that had begun when they'd neared the shore sputtered out with the going of the day, and in the unexpected black, the noise of the engine was especially loud.

David steered with the spotlight shining out ahead into the night, to help him look for wood in the water. They climbed up the faces of the big swells and slid into the watery valleys beyond, over and over in an endless, almost hypnotizing procession.

Lars slid the door back and stepped outside for a few moments.

"Wind coming soon," he said when he returned.

David cocked his head, listening for any new sound, but could hear nothing.

"How can you tell?"

"Is much colder," Lars said. "Cold brings the wind."

David stepped outside. Lars was right: it was noticeably colder. They went over the top of an especially big swell just then, and there was a light breeze on top that hadn't been there before.

Annie had heard Lars, and she came up from below to stand by them. They passed the lighthouse at Egg Island and then the shape on the radar screen that was the emergency anchorage at Millbrook Cove fell astern. They all peered ahead, waiting for the wind.

It came first in little eddies, humming occasionally through the rigging when they went up and over the tops of the big swells, but there was no real force behind it, and sometimes there would be no wind at all.

Finally the light at Clark Point came abeam. Safety Cove was only four miles away, and the twins had started to relax when the real wind came. The first gust rattled spray like hail onto the windows, freezing instantly.

"Okay, David, now, stabilizers out." Lars elbowed David out of the way, pulled the throttle back to half, then turned on the deck lights.

When David pulled the door back, he was amazed at the difference just a few minutes had brought. The wind howled shrilly through the rigging, and in the circle of light the water was all white and confused. Less than five minutes had passed since the wind had come and already the crests were breaking loose and tumbling down the slopes of the swells.

But they were as ready as they could be, and David unlashed and awkwardly manhandled the heavy, flat, metal stabilizers over the side and into the water. With the stabilizers in, traveling at half speed, the ride was steadier, but their progress toward Safety Cove became even slower. David made his way inside, glad to slide the door closed against the cold, windy blackness, and took up his position behind the wheel again.

He felt the bow rise steeply into an incoming sea, and instinctively pulled the throttle back to a third. Even so, the crest smacked heavily into them, and he could see the iced-over windows sag in briefly from the force of the water outside.

"What about Millbrook Cove?" he called anxiously to Lars over the drumming of the wind through the rigging. "It's so cold we're going to ice up bad. What about running downwind to Millbrook Cove? Didn't you say there was shelter there?"

"Too far downwind. Then we have to run sideways to get in." Lars made a motion with his hand of a boat trying to run sideways to those big seas. "Seas would be worse down there. We must make Safety Cove before the ice gets too bad."

Another breaking sea slammed into them, and a moment later they dropped sickeningly into the trough on the other side. The seas were too much for the autopilot, and David had to quickly kick it out of gear and take the wheel.

The roaring of the big crest, coming suddenly and louder than all the others, caught David's attention and made him involuntarily turn away from the window, an action that saved his eyes. It was impossible to rise quickly enough into the steeply breaking sea, and the top of the window over the compass exploded inward, blowing water, ice, and broken glass over David and the inside of the cabin.

"Ahhh!" Annie cried out, more frightened than hurt, just as Lars pulled the throttle back to a third.

David turned around, stunned, and put a hand to his face, expecting to feel it covered with blood. But he was lucky: only a single shard had penetrated into the fleshiest part of his cheek.

"Towel, get a towel, girl, quick!" Lars called over to

Annie, worry evident in his voice. Just then the bow rose into another sea, and with surprising quickness Lars whipped an oilskin jacket off the pegs and used it to cover the automatic pilot motor just as another gallon or two erupted through the broken top of the glass, soaking David's already-wet front.

"We've got to turn around, Lars," David said loudly, shivering and stunned at how quickly things were happening. Annie appeared with the towel, pale-faced and shaken. The bow rose again, and more water shot through the glass, but David stepped aside that time and it cascaded onto the floor.

"Here," Lars waved up at the window and then over to Annie. "Cover hole with towel. I will get plywood."

"Lars," David said, more anxiously this time. "Did you hear me? We've *got* to turn around. We'll lose another window if we keep up."

"No, boy," Lars said, brusquely pushing past David and disappearing into the fo'c'sle. "Is worse out there," he spoke over his head as he rummaged for something in one of the lockers under the bunks. "Tide rip, you cannot see, the seas will be worse. We must head for the land. Steer now."

"David, get a grip and *steer*!" Annie called out to him. "I can't cover the hole and steer, too." She was trying to spin the wheel, head them around back upwind again, and hold the towel over the hole all at once.

They felt the boat lifting again, and another big one slammed into them. More glass and water broke through and onto the floor. David edged around his sister to take the wheel, but the wind was driving the spray into the cabin like small pellets. Blinded, he had to turn away, and felt them rising suddenly into another sea.

"Look, there's a boat out there!" Annie pointed, amazed, out the windy hole that was the front window, then deftly stepped aside as another couple of gallons of frigid water poured through.

What looked like a big tug was bursting through the top of a wave less than one hundred yards away. Suddenly the tug's spotlight went on and shafted dramatically across the water to them.

Just as quickly they forgot about the tug as they nosed up into another big sea. The roaring was louder this time; in the spotlight beam they glimpsed another big, breaking sea tumbling down toward them.

"Plywood, boy, plywood!" Lars roughly thrust something into David's side. "Quick now, cover window."

The roaring was even louder, but David grasped the plywood and quickly fitted it into the window cavity, holding it with all his force when the sea hit. It was a loose fit and the pressure of the water pushed David back enough for water to squirt in around the plywood. He saw the side window sag in heavily, and he knew that it was just a matter of time before that failed, too.

"Watch out, David. I nail. You steer." Lars' voice had a sort of strangled sound to it, and David saw he had a half-dozen nails between his teeth. Working with amazing dexterity, considering he only had one good hand, Lars pushed each nail's point enough into the plywood to stick, then quickly hammered until it was secured, covering the window. Satisfied, he disappeared back down into the fo'c'sle.

The boat dropped heavily over the crest of a wave, angled downhill steeply and started to accelerate. David pulled the throttle back, not wanting to bury their bow in the trough of the sea, traveling blind with no vision forward, trying to feel his way through the big seas.

The bow rose as the bottom of the sea passed, and he speeded up so as not to lose way and slip slideways as another big one came down on them. Then he heard it again: that great, gathering, tumbling roar from the darkness outside.

"*Look out!*" He gathered Annie instinctively to him and ducked down behind the steering wheel just as the wall of water struck the boat a staggering blow, and the starboard front window exploded inward with a tremendous rush of water.

The boat tipped downward as the crest passed, and David fumbled for the throttle in a panic, terrified that another big crest would hit them.

"Annie, quick, get Lars. We need another piece of plywood, *quick!*

Annie got up reluctantly, soaked and terrified, and staggered halfway down the steps, aghast at what she saw. Half a foot of water was washing back and forth on the galley floor, along with boxes of food that had burst out of a cupboard with the impact of the sea. Lars was on his knees in the water, with one of the floorboards up, his good hand fooling with something unseen beneath the floor.

"Lars, Lars, is there any more plywood? Another window broke!"

He nodded toward the bunk, his voice tense, "Look

under bunk. Use plywood hatch. Is big, but might work. I have to fix pump."

The boat started uphill, and Annie winced as another big one slammed into them and more water cascaded into the broken window above her and down the steps around her.

"More plywood!" she heard David calling out. "We gotta get that window covered!" She could hear the panic in his voice, and she stumbled across the flooded floor, pushed the sleeping bags as far forward as she could to try to keep them dry, and found the plywood hatch cover, the nails, and hammer.

Annie made it back up to the pilothouse just as the bow was lifting. She could hear the roaring from outside the windy hole that had been the window. Reaching up awkwardly, she tried to jam the hatch into the window opening, but it was too big to fit into the recess, and then the crest was on them. The sea was smaller than the others, but still, enough water hit the plywood to throw her back painfully against the door as more icy water cascaded in through the hole.

When she had recovered her breath, she stole a quick glance into the fo'c'sle. The water was noticeably higher. Lars still hadn't gotten the pump going, and she could feel that the boat was more sluggish in the water with the increased weight. A terrifying thought suddenly struck her: they were going to sink. And the raft was probably too iced up to use.

The boat pitched down and started to gain speed on the face of the wave. Annie slowly got to her feet, trying to lift the plywood up into the window again, but knowing that it was fruitless without help.

Just then the cold that had been gusting through the window stopped and the bow pitched up. David throttled up for the next sea, and the roaring from outside seemed further away. Annie put the plywood down and approached the broken-out window cautiously, afraid that another big one might roar through it at any moment.

They came over the top of the sea just then, but there was no breaking crest. As they pitched down onto the next one, their spotlight played on what looked like a sheer cliff beyond the next wave, and Annie recoiled in fright before she realized what it was: a big barge, full of stacked containers, traveling along at about their speed. The tug had pulled in ahead of them to break the seas with the barge.

"Fishing boat off Safety Cove, *Jeffrey Foss* calling, got it on, Cap?" The radio startled Annie. The call was repeated, and then she realized it could be that tugboat, calling them.

Dazed and shivering, Annie reached for the microphone, thinking how lucky they were that the radios were mounted on the overhead where the water hadn't reached them.

"Uh, yes, over." She tried to remember how Lars had talked to the other boats, but drew a blank.

The tug called again and she answered again, but they didn't seem to hear her.

"The button, Annie, the *button*. Are you pushing the button when you talk?" David half turned to her when he spoke, and she realized he had his hands full keeping the waterlogged boat on course.

She called again, pushing the button when she spoke, and then releasing it when she was done. The tug answered her immediately.

"Yeah, this is the *Jeffrey Foss*; we saw you guys out there. It looked like you were having some trouble, so we pulled in ahead to give you a little protection. How is it back there now? Any better?"

"Oh, *Jeffrey Foss*," Annie's words came all in a rush, "this is the *Karen A.* Just keep doing what you're doing. The waves broke two windows and Lars is working on the pump. It was *terrible!*"

"Okay, well, listen." The voice on the radio was very calming. "Just stay in behind the barge and you should be able to make it all right. Are we getting too far ahead of you?"

Annie peered out into the windy black, picked out the barge in the spotlight, and noticed that it did seem to be a little farther away.

"Uh, yeah." She pushed the button again, trying to control her violent shivering, immensely relieved that there was someone else out there with them. "Could you slow down some more? It looks like you're farther away." She released the mike button and hung it up on the hook, hugging herself with her arms to try to get warmer.

"*Jeffrey Foss* back. Okay, we'll slow down a little. We want you to try and stay as close to the back of the barge as you can. It's pretty wild out here, but there should be a little lee behind the barge. Is everyone okay aboard there?"

Annie picked up the microphone with an effort. "Yeah, yeah, we're okay, just real cold, and there's a lot of water in the boat."

Lars came up just then. In the dim light the spotlight was reflecting back from the barge, she could see his face was streaked with grease and there was a short cut with freshly clotted blood on one cheek.

"Pump is going now," he said, leaning back heavily against the exhaust pipe box. "We will be all right." Then he started forward as he glimpsed the barge outside the broken-out window. "What is that?" he asked suddenly.

"It's a barge," Annie answered. "The *Jeffrey Foss* is out there, breaking the waves for us."

The old man took it all in before taking the microphone gently from Annie.

"Ah, *Jeffrey Foss*," he said in his accented voice. "*Jeffrey Foss, Karen A* here. How you copy?"

"*Jeffrey* back, yeah, read you fine now, Cap. You got everything in control back there now?"

"Ah, *Karen A* back. Is better now with pump working. It was bad there for a little while. But listen. Are you going into Safety Cove? We need piece of plywood for our window." Lars spoke in a flat voice with long pauses between words, and Annie realized he was having a hard time catching his breath.

"*Jeffrey* back. Yeah, that's fine, Cap. You just stay in behind the barge and give us a shout if we start getting too far ahead. It's getting pretty wild out here, and we need to check some of the reefer units on the barge, so we'll lay into Safety Cove for a couple of hours."

"Ah, *Karen A* back. Yeah, that's fine, Cap. We will follow you into Safety Cove."

Lars handed Annie the mike to hang back up, and she tried to look at him closely in the dim light but it was too dark to see well.

"Lars, that plywood saved us. Now how are you?" Annie

put her arm on his shoulder.

He struggled with a long, phlegmy cough before answering. "Just tired, girl. Just tired."

Suddenly Annie felt very cold and realized she was soaked. She started down the steps, then stopped; three or four inches of water still sloshed back and forth on the floor, and the stove had blown out. She fumbled behind her for her boots, splashed across the floor to the bunk area, and was immensely relieved to find the sleeping bags and clothing hammocks dry.

"Well, at least the bunks aren't wet," she yelled up into the pilothouse.

She rummaged around until she found dry clothing for all of them, and started up to the pilothouse before she realized there was no room for anyone to change with all of them up there. She decided to wait for a few more minutes until the pump cleared the water off the floor.

Lars came down the stairs. In the sharp-edged light from the single bulb, he looked pale and drawn. Not looking at Annie, he sat down heavily on his bunk and started to lay back.

"Lars!" She jumped up, realizing he was as soaked as she and David were. "Wait! You should change. If you lie down like that, you'll soak the bunk. Hey, David?" she called as she climbed the stairs. "Let's trade places. Lars needs a hand getting out of his wet clothes."

David pulled him upright, and half-lifted, half-guided him to the galley bench.

"Here," David said as he began unbuttoning the old man's shirt and the wet woolen long underwear beneath.

"Annie says we're lucky—the clothes and the bags didn't get wet. Isn't that great? We'll be able to get warm if we can keep the bedding dry." He rubbed Lars's chest with a dry towel, and pulled a dry T-shirt up his arms and awkwardly over his head, for he seemed only semiconscious and was barely able to lift his arms. Putting on the button-up flannel shirt was easier.

Then came the awkward part, changing his pants without letting the dry ones sag down into the water sloshing back and forth on the floor. Somehow he managed, struck at how frail and weak Lars seemed. The old man was immediately asleep. Then David changed quickly, relit the diesel oil stove with a flaming piece of paper towel, and went up to the pilothouse.

"Your turn to get into dry clothes," he said. "The pump took care of almost all of the water."

Annie was steering with one hand, while trying to wrap the rest of her body around the warmth of the engine exhaust box. She was shivering violently and her teeth were chattering. She'd found a piece of plastic and did her best to staple it to the bottom three-quarters of the window frame. A bitter cold breeze still blew in through the viewing slot.

"Okay, Annie, I got it. Go on now." He thought to himself that he sounded more together than he felt.

She just nodded, too cold to talk, and disappeared below.

David took the wheel, positioning himself so he could see out the two- or three-inch slot between the plastic and the top of the window. He could only really see for a few moments on the downhill slope of each sea, but it was enough to glimpse the shape of the huge barge ahead and the big tug struggling with the seas.

Finally the tug's probing spotlight played on a wide opening in the hillside, and they all began a slow turn into the shelter of the land. Annie returned and took the helm again after persuading her shivering brother to go warm up in his sleeping bag. As they turned onto the new course, the wind and seas came on their starboard beam, and the *Karen A* took some violent rolls, but the tug's skipper had crabbed over as close to the shore as he dared before making the turn, and they made it out of the storm and into the sheltered cove without any more damage.

"Ah, *Karen A, Jeffrey Foss*. Okay, Cap, you still back there?"

Annie jumped at the sound of the radio and picked up the mike. "Yeah, we're okay. It's a *lot* better in here. This must be Safety Cove, right?"

"*Jeffrey* back. That's right. Now you know how it got its name. We'll go up as far as we can and anchor, and then you guys can come alongside and warm up."

"Thanks. We've got on dry clothes now, but we all got real cold out there." Annie was getting all the meager heat she could from the exhaust stack, but she was still shivering.

The tug began to slow, and Annie pulled the throttle back, stood on the tips of her toes and peered out into the black. The tug's big floodlights were on and the reflected light played on the dim shapes of snow-covered forests rising steeply from the water's edge.

She let the boat drift and went below to get David. He was curled in his bunk in a fetal position, still shivering violently, and only after a long time was she able to get him to come up and help her. The tug's anchor was down by then. Annie pulled on her boots and coat and went to open the door, to get the lines out to tie up, but it was frozen shut and she couldn't budge it. David put his back to it, too, without result. Finally, they called the tug to explain their situation.

Three of the *Jeffrey Foss* crew stood on the back deck, waiting for them.

"Good lord, look at that!" The mate gaped at the craft that was emerging into the pool of light behind them. For the wind had been very cold, and the flying spray had frozen, covering all of the *Karen A* except the very lowest part of her hull planking and the hot exhaust pipe. The rigging out to her trolling poles was thickened with ice, and the radar and raft were just round lumps atop the pilothouse. Even the anchor, in its chock on the very bow, was a smooth, frozen, tear-shaped blob.

As they watched, a hand emerged from one of the broken-out windows, waved briefly to them, and withdrew.

David brought them carefully alongside the tug, and two men in brown coveralls jumped aboard. But the ice on the back deck and around the door was much thicker than the men had anticipated, and they had to call for heavy screwdrivers to get it all off and the door open.

The twins slowly emerged from the cabin and stopped on the back deck, blinking in the unexpected brightness of the deck lights shining on the ice, the sudden stillness broken only by the soft purr of the tug's generator.

The tug's crew was stunned by the youth of the twins. Bundled up in coats and watch caps, it was obvious from the twins' faces that they were but young teens. To encounter such an inexperienced crew on such a small, ice-encased and storm-battered craft, in such remote northern waters in December, was totally beyond the men's experience.

"I'm Annie. This is my brother, David."

The men nodded their heads, and finally the mate found his voice. "The other man. He talked on the radio. Is he okay?"

"That's Lars," Annie answered, inclining her head back toward the pilothouse doorway. "He's sick. He's sleeping down below." Her voice stuttered as another wave of shivering and teeth-chattering came over her, and the tug crew realized how cold the two of them must be.

"C'mon," the mate waved them over to the tug. "C'mon aboard. You can get in our showers. We got plenty of hot water. We'll check on Lars. C'mon now, both of you, you're chilled."

The two men helped the twins over the rail and onto the tug. Just before they went inside, the twins stopped and turned to stare at the little craft that had taken them so far.

Seen in the glare of the tug's decklights with the dim shapes of the desolate snow-covered hills beyond them, the *Karen A* seemed more like a ghostly apparition than a boat. Wrapped in ice, dully shining in the light, with her two trolling poles rigged out to either side, she was unrecognizable as the craft they had boarded in Seattle.

As the twins stared, a wind gust, a williwaw, whirled down from the hills around the cove. Snow-laden and bitter cold, it swirled briefly around the boats and just as quickly blew away off to the west. A shivering fit overtook Annie. The warm interior and waiting shower beckoned, but she lingered, looking one more time at the *Karen A*. Suddenly, unexpectedly, a feeling of warmth and gratitude washed over her for the little boat that had taken them through such a difficult time.

"Was it a close one?" she asked, through chattering teeth.

"C'mon, young lady," the tug's mate said in a kindly voice, "you'd best get inside and get warmed up." He nudged her toward the door.

But Annie resisted, asking again, "No, tell me. It was a close one, wasn't it?"

The mate studied the iced-up boat again before answering. "Almost too close," he finally said in a faraway voice.

When she'd followed her brother inside, the mate climbed back aboard the *Karen A* and stopped below to look in on Lars. The old man seemed to be sleeping well enough, and the mate decided it was best to let him be. He adjusted the stove to warm up the damp room, then something in the corner of the small fo'c'sle caught his eye. It was the little fir Christmas tree. The balls were all put away, but a few bits of shredded aluminum foil still clung to the upper branches. He wondered what would take such kids, children almost, away from their homes at Christmastime, to take such risks, in such a small craft with a sick old man.

He stopped in the pilothouse on the way out to take some measurements of the windows. When he was done, he looked around one last time at the smallness of it all, the bits of broken glass still on the floor, and remembered his wonder at seeing them out there, caught in the beam of his spotlight, iced up, windows broken, far from land. And then the twins, stepping out onto the back deck when they'd finally gotten the door open. He tried to remember what the news report had said about them that night in Seattle. *Runaways*, he thought, that's it. They'd run away from their home. One quickly gets a sense of people, he thought, especially with children, and this pair had seemed very fine, and he wondered what sort of home they would run away from.

The tug's captain came out on deck just as the mate jumped back aboard.

"She shipshape enough to make it the rest of the way on her own?" he asked.

"Oh, she's pretty stout really. Her skipper's asleep below, and I took some measurements where the windows were busted out. We've got some plexiglass to go over them. That's the worst of it." He nodded out toward the windy harbor mouth. "Did you talk to those kids?"

"Just for a minute; they were both pretty cold." The captain took his hat off and scratched his forehead. "But what the hell's a nice pair of kids like that doing trying to get north this time of year? You saw those guys out there, if the *Wedell Foss* hadn't told us to be on the lookout for them, and if we hadn't come along just when we did, do you think they would have made it across? Hell's bells, the worst part of that tide rip was after we pulled in front of them with the barge."

They both looked at the *Karen A* for a moment, and then the captain continued.

"Well, anyway, that was Seattle on the radio. They're chafing for this freight up north. I told them we'd be underway as soon as we checked out the reefer units." He nodded out toward the barge, just dimly seen astern at the edge of the circle of light. "Start winching the barge in, and Roger can check it out. You do what you can for the kids and their boat. They sure need whatever we can do for them." The captain turned to go, but the mate pulled at his sleeve. "You didn't say anything to Seattle about the kids, did you?"

"No. I wish we could take them with us, or help them more, but no, I didn't say anything to Seattle. I figure they have problems enough."

Annie stayed in the shower as long as she dared, still dazed and amazed at their rescue just when it had seemed there was no way out. She wrapped her hair in a towel and came out to sit in the galley with David, who'd finished his shower, too. The cook set heaping plates of spaghetti in front of them, and they ate ravenously.

The captain came into the galley with a chart in his hand and explained that the bad weather was over for awhile, they might face snow ahead, but no serious wind.

"That was the worse part, out there." He waved his hand toward a porthole and the wild and windy night beyond the cove. "You've got pretty much sheltered channels all the way from here to Alaska. I think tomorrow should be good. It'll be a little breezy right in front where the tides mix, but the farther north you go, the better it'll get. I marked a chart to show a back way around Milbanke Sound; that can get a little breezy too, and I wrote down channel 77. That's the channel all our company tugs stand by on."

A husky man in insulated coveralls came through the galley door and the captain turned to him.

"Barge is all squared away," the man said. "Ready for

the anchor?"

"Anchor up," the captain nodded and turned back to the twins.

They both flinched as one.

"You're leaving?" Annie half rose from her chair. She hadn't fully grasped that the warm, cozy, friendly tug was leaving.

"Couldn't we follow you?" Her voice was shaky. The thought of being left all alone in that cove at night, after all they had come through getting across, was suddenly terrifying to her.

"Well, I guess you'd be welcome to try," the captain said doubtfully. "We'd be clipping along pretty good to make up lost time though. I don't think you'd be able to keep up, and then you'd be all alone out there, and what with these big tides and the logs in the water . . . " His voice drifted off.

David stood then. "Uh, can you wait a few minutes? I'll have to break the ice off our anchor winch."

The mate gently put a hand on David's shoulder, "Don't worry, son. We already took care of that. You just go ahead and finish."

When it was finally time, the twins zipped up their winter coats and went out onto the back deck, where the wind and snow eddied around them.

David started to shiver as soon as he stepped through the door, and his face paled when he saw how small and frail their boat seemed next to the tug. He saw that the tug's crew had knocked off much of the ice on the pilothouse, around the anchor winch, and back deck.

A heavy clunk sounded from the tug's bow as the big

anchor came home against the hull, and the captain came down from the pilothouse to talk to the twins one last time.

"You want us to wait until you get your skipper up?" Another cold williwaw eddied down from the hills around them, and Annie started to shiver.

"No, he needs his sleep. We'll be okay," she said in a voice that sounded stronger than she felt. "We've anchored before. Just let us get the engine started."

The cook came out then with a big bag of hot food. Annie thanked him and turned to the captain.

"Thank you for helping us like you did out there," she said. It was all she could do to keep from crying. She inclined her head off toward the barge and the windy dark beyond.

The captain was struck by how warm and soft her hand felt. The engine on the *Karen A* started up then with a puff of smoke from the stack, then David came out of the cabin and climbed onto the tug to offer his hand to the captain also.

"We'll lay here for a moment with our lights on," the captain said. "Just go on up to where it shallows up to five fathoms and drop your anchor there. It could blow a hurricane and you'd be fine."

Then it was time to go. The men threw the tie-up lines back aboard, and David gingerly backed away until he could make his turn and be sure to miss the tug's house with their trolling poles. The Fathometer slowly came up and they did their routine with the anchor—David operating the winch, and Annie reversing slowly until they could feel the boat gently lurch as the steel anchor bit into the bottom.

The twins shut the engine down and stood shoulder to shoulder in the open doorway, looking out at the tug and the night. The throb of the big engine grew deeper, and the tug's bright deck lights shone on the high, snowy hills around the cove. And then the big lights winked out, and there were only the white masthead lights and a red running light on the barge. The tug throttled up a little more, a williwaw from the hills stirred up snow around the cove, and the tug and barge lights were no more. Once again, they were alone.

David went down into the galley to stand by the oil stove and check on Lars. After he had finally begun to get warm, he heard static on the radio from the pilothouse, as if Annie was looking for stations. She found a faint one, tuned in better and turned up the volume a little. It was a Christmas carol, a choir singing *Away in a Manger*. Hearing it so unexpectedly suddenly brought Christmas to mind, and he went up to get closer to the music.

He found Annie crying, dry soundless sobs shaking her whole body. He put his arms around her and held her until the song was over.

"Why did Mom have to leave us?" She shook her head and stared out into the darkness beyond the windows. "I know it wasn't the greatest, but still it was home. I was going to get the tree this year and decorate it, and I was going to make presents for you and her. Now look at this: everything's damp, we're in the middle of nowhere, and we'll never make it to the cove for Christmas. Not at this rate."

"Hey, Annie," David said gently, "at least we're alive. If that tug hadn't come along, we might not even be here at all." As strong and tough as he wanted to be for Annie's sake, David tried not to give in to the tears that were stinging his eyes.

Then another Christmas song came on, Bing Crosby this time, singing "White Christmas." The twins stared out the side windows at the ominous snow swirling all around them, then looked at each other and spontaneously began to giggle. The theme of the song struck both of them as hysterically funny. "A white Christmas," David choked out. And every time their eyes met, the strangled laughter would begin again. The station was down in the States somewhere, far away, and the song faded in and out, sometimes coming in clear and strong, and a moment or two later, fading away to almost nothing. And so did the laughing spell, ending with loud sniffles, red eyes that needed wiping, and full sighs that seemed to cleanse them of their sadness.

In the morning light, Safety Cove was revealed as a large, almost circular basin, with snow-covered trees rising right from the water's edge. Annie turned up the stove and made oatmeal, and put toast in the oven. Lars stirred while they were eating, and David helped him up and over to squeeze in around the back of the table.

"How do you feel today, Lars?" David put milk, butter, and brown sugar into a bowl of oatmeal, and set it before the old man. His face looked pale and drawn.

"Bones ache," he said. "Chest hurt." He swung his head slowly around so he could look out the wooden periscope built into the roof of the fo'c'sle. "Ah, Safety Cove. It is good going from here. The wind doesn't reach down to water so much." But Lars seemed distant, as if reciting a litany he had said many times.

"It doesn't seem too bad out there, outside in Fitzhugh Sound. I think we should try it." Annie said.

"We must have look, can always come back if it is too rough," Lars said. He finished eating his oatmeal and sat back heavily before speaking again. Then he waved at the engine and up to the pilothouse. "Check juices, lay out your courses on the chart. Anchor up at dark. Is easy going: deep all the way to beach. If you find is rough in middle, sneak up along shore." He slumped back heavily, as if the effort of speaking had exhausted him.

The twins got the engine going and anchor up, and David carefully steered out of the cove. He wished that Lars had come up to be with them instead of lying back down. The tide rip was right where they wanted to go. It wouldn't be so bad if they could head out more toward the middle of the wide sound; he was used to that, but steering down the side in the narrowing band of water between the tide rip and the shore made him uneasy. About a mile out of the harbor, the tide rip began moving in toward the beach, at first slowly, and then in a rush.

"Annie, Annie, I'm running out of room. Quick, get Lars!"

She could hear the panic in his voice, put down her book, and tried to shake Lars gently awake, but with no response. She went up to see what was going on.

Then the tide rip was upon them, with short, white-capped seas and a few slowly revolving whirls pushing them directly in toward the beach. The wide lane of calm water between the rip and the beach had disappeared.

"Steer out, David. Can you get out into the rip? It's not that bad."

David had no choice. He throttled back to half and turned offshore. The bow dipped sharply into the tide rip, and he felt his heart in his throat.

But the seas were lower than he had expected. The spray seemed to jump up vertically and there was little wind to drive it. The boat lurched to one side then another, violently at times, but barely enough ice formed on the windows to obscure their vision, and in a few minutes they were through and into the calmer water on the other side.

"Whew!" David looked back in surprise when they were through. "We're through. That wasn't too bad!" He carefully turned on the automatic pilot, waited as the machine oriented itself and settled down, and then engaged the clutch. The steering wheel began to rotate as it did when the pilot was working properly, and David stood, carefully watching the compass as if surprised to see that it still worked after all they had been through.

Annie came over and put her chin gently on his shoulder. "I wish there were some other boats or something," she said, looking out ahead. "It just looks so unfriendly out there."

"I know," David said, looking out ahead. They were proceeding about a mile off the western shore of a wide channel. A gray, low sky lay on top of the snowy hills, and in the distance ahead, they could see the tops of more snow-covered hills poking above the horizon. The whitecaps were all in the tide rip behind them, but a breeze had begun to darken the water. The twins yearned for the sight of a settlement along the shore, the welcome plume of wood smoke rising into the winter air, the hull and rigging of another boat growing bigger on the horizon, or a lighthouse.

But none of those things appeared, and it was an uneasy time. David had the chart laid out on the table, the courses all penciled in from the night before. They steered a course very close to the line, and the shapes on the radar screen resembled the patterns of land and water on the chart. Each half hour, David would carefully study the radar, take the dividers and pencil and draw the smallest line across their course. Then he'd faintly write down the time. If they were actually where he drew the line and the number, he couldn't be sure, but there was something reassuring in it, and it was what Lars had showed them to do.

The twins agreed on two-hour watches so that each would have a chance to go below to sleep or snack while the other was steering. But neither left the pilothouse when their watch was over, except to check on Lars or make a sandwich or cocoa. Each came back up to sit or stand with the other, taking turns with the binoculars, scanning the shore and the water, seeking signs of life. But there were none, just the endless march of snowy hills and occasionally a channel leading back into some remote and little-visited bay.

They changed watches again, and the sky seemed to press a little lower to the water, the light begin to fail, and still there were no boats or settlements.

"A light, oh, a lighthouse. Oh, look, David!" Annie had seen it first: the sweep of a light, and then the familiar white pillar, and comforting lightkeeper's house emerging from behind a point of land perhaps two miles ahead and to port.

The daylight was fast going from the sky, and they shared the binoculars back and forth, savoring the sight of the great, slowly sweeping beam and the brightly lit windows of a tidy cottage set back from the high bluff of a small island.

"It's the turn, see? We're right here, that's Pointer Island light!" David tapped his finger on the chart excitedly.

"Let's anchor there, David. Let's anchor right by the lighthouse so that we can look out and see it tonight."

David studied the chart for a long moment before answering. It was growing rapidly darker, and he yearned to drop the anchor in some wonderfully protected cove, especially if there could be a lighthouse nearby. But the lighthouse was on a high and steep-sided island, with no place to lie where a wind would not reach.

"We've got to go just a little farther," he finally said. "It looks like there might be a good place around this next point." But there was anxiety in his voice. "Would you go look in on Lars, if he's awake? Maybe he could come up and help us go into this anchorage."

Annie returned a moment later. "I shook him, but he's still out."

David throttled back even more and watched the Fathometer carefully. Annie came to stand beside him as they entered the narrow channel at the point, and the land unfolded around them, revealing fifteen or twenty acres of dark and still water. Snow blanketed the trees, and the shore was a razor-drawn line of white and black where the tide had melted the snow and then withdrawn.

David studied the chart and Fathometer for one last time, and took the engine out of gear before pulling on his boots and winter coat and stepping outside into the last of the day's light. The anchor rattled over the roller, the boat's way was checked with the little tug of the anchor biting into the bottom, and David gave Annie the motion for "Shut 'er down," a finger across his throat. Suddenly all was still.

He stood a long moment in the quiet. The wind had gone with the daylight, and they lay absolutely still, the chain vertical in the water. His ears rang slightly in the silence, and the boat, lying there with the trolling poles still rigged out, seemed to him like some graceful bird. Annie had started to make supper, and the light was on in the galley, shining up through the skylight in the cabin roof. That cheery light, shining out into the wild, lonely land all around them, and the boat lying so safe and secure in still and sheltered waters after those long, hard-fought passages filled David with an immense and powerful satisfaction.

He made his way carefully around the side of the pilothouse to the back deck, and stopped one last time before going inside. "We made it!" he howled out into the dark and silent night. "We made it!"

Annie appeared suddenly at the door, startled. "Are you all right?"

"We made it!" he cried out again, and then turned to his sister. "Can you believe it, Annie? We did it! A whole day by ourselves. Lars didn't get up all day, and we made it anyway! I'm sure we're going to make it now, all the way up to Dad's for Christmas. Everything's going to be okay." And he pulled her out onto the frozen and dark back deck, hugged her tight, and whirled her around.

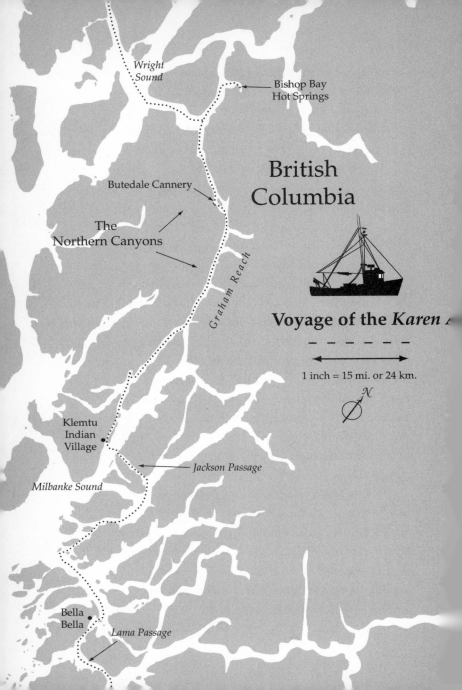

Wright Sound

→ Bishop Bay Hot Springs

Butedale Cannery

The Northern Canyons

British Columbia

Graham Reach

Voyage of the *Karen*

1 inch = 15 mi. or 24 km.

N

Klemtu Indian Village

Jackson Passage

Milbanke Sound

Bella Bella

Lama Passage

CHAPTER 9

The Northern Canyons

 The morning came with the muffled silence that means snow in the North. Annie was up first to stand in the pilothouse in her night clothes and to look out upon a world in shades of white and gray: the boat, the deck, the water, and very faintly, the shore. Quietly, she slid the door partially open and stuck first a hand and then her face out into the falling white.

David came up, startling her. He'd been looking for the wind, and there was none.

"Let's go," he said. "It's supposed to be all sheltered waters for most of the day. See, I laid all the courses out on the chart last night before I went to bed."

David showed her the chart, checked the juices, started the engine, and had the radar and radios on and tuned up before she even had time to change her clothes.

Lars woke when she was done changing, and she helped him over to the table. He craned his neck and looked out the periscope skylight for a long while, changing his position so as to see all that the two mirrors would reveal.

"Lama Passage," he wheezed out. "Good; the wide waters are behind now for a while."

Amazed that he could tell where they were by what little the periscope might reveal, Annie looked up. The veil of snow had lifted slightly and the shape of the cove was revealed, but still, there were no particularly distinctive land-marks that she could tell.

"How can you tell?" she asked. "It just looks like any other cove to me."

"Ah," he said, a smile cracking his pale face, "see, old man not so dumb. Now tell David the channel will seem very narrow—especially with radar. Targets fill screen. But just stay in middle. No wind, good traveling."

At first David was anxious when the land disappeared into the snow, constantly alternating between the compass, the chart, and the radar. But that first part of the channel was the widest, and after a bit, he grew more confident, mov-ing the chart over to the table, engaging the autopilot, and sitting back longer between chart scans.

When it was her turn to steer and watch, Annie was less practiced and a long while passed before she began to get comfortable with just the radar and the chart to guide her through the snowy world outside.

As the day drew on, and still there was no clearing, no lightening of the sky, no easing of the steady snow, the twins grew more subdued and spoke less. Twice the channels grew very narrow, closing in around them on the radar screen, and they had to go very slowly, almost idling, until the channel was wider.

The wind came in the middle part of the day, when they neared Milbanke Sound. The seas heaped up, and through a thin place in the snow, they glimpsed breakers, big and white on the ledges, and fear crept in again.

"It's getting cold again," Lars said when he came up, and his words chilled Annie. "It will be rough in Milbanke Sound. Better we go Jackson Passage."

More snow came with the wind, cloaking everything around them even more thickly, and she sensed that even Lars was anxious.

The radar targets closed in around them, and she knew they'd left the main channel. She edged over to the chart table and saw that the new line the tugboat captain had drawn passed through a place little wider than the pencil's mark.

Lars's curled hand pulled back the throttle to just a third, and in a soft, flat voice, he began giving steering commands to David: "Port ten," he would say without taking his eyes off the screen. Or, "Starboard a hair, steady now." David would watch the compass intently, trying to steer exactly as he was told, coming up on the new course without oversteering.

An alarm buzzer went off on the Fathometer and Annie jumped. Without even taking a break in his ceaseless scan of the radar, Lars found the machine and silenced it.

Lars put the engine in neutral and they coasted slowly ahead, watching the Fathometer closely. Annie looked out and glimpsed trees through the snow to starboard, so close they looked as if their trolling poles would snag them. This was the way north, through such a constricted and shallow channel? She hadn't known what to expect when their course took them almost off the edge of the chart, but to traverse such a place when they could barely see seemed foolhardy.

They felt a stirring against the bottom of the boat, as if they were passing over something. Annie looked and there was kelp and seaweed lying on the surface of the water all around them.

"Thin spot," Lars said, and put the engine in gear once more, advancing the throttle up a third. They were through then, and back onto the main chart. Lars had a coughing spell and went below, and the twins were alone in the snow again.

Whenever the shore appeared through the snow, Annie would scan it with the binoculars, searching for boats or houses or people. Surely, she thought, now that they were in more protected waters there would be more settlements. There had been a Native village marked on the chart earlier, just an hour after they had started, and she had glimpsed a line of buildings and the smudge of wood smoke against a hillside. But then the snow closed in again, and there was nothing.

The snow came harder, obscuring their running lights, and when they tried the spotlight to watch for wood and logs in the water, the snow only reflected back a dazzling, blinding whiteness, and they had to turn it off.

The channel grew narrower, a canyon piercing the coastal mountains. The walls seemed to press in upon them from both sides on the radar, and the miles slowly passed. Neither spoke.

The night came, quick and snowy. Inside the pilothouse there was the dim radar display, the faint red chart light, and a nickel-sized circle of light on the front of the compass card. But outside there was nothing. And still they went on, into the blackness with the snow swirling endlessly outside the windows.

Two hours through the black they traveled, relying totally on the machine's display of greenish shapes of land and water, and few words passed between them. The anchorage Lars had penciled their course line into was a small dead-end bay, and David throttled all the way back, as if reluctant and uncertain about leaving the main channel.

"I guess we'll lay in here tonight," he said uneasily, dressing to go outside. Somehow he had expected a town, a settlement, other boats. But the chart only showed the steep-sided shore and a small shelf of bottom shallow enough to anchor.

When the anchor and chain had rattled down into the darkness and the engine was stopped, he stood a moment, hood up, gloves on, listening and feeling the soft fall of the flakes around him. His ears rang in the sudden engineless silence, but there was no sound at all.

He went in then, put his outside clothes on the hook, went below, and stopped. Annie had put a tablecloth and lit candles on the table, and there were small glasses of something that looked like champagne. She'd resurrected the tree after the soaking in the Queen's Pond, and decorated it with a dozen star-shaped flat candleholders clipped to the branches. There were small, lit candles on every one. The effect was magical: the ornaments shone in the candlelight, and she had crushed some of the tree's smaller branches so that their pungent fragrance filled the small space.

"To Christmas up North," she said, handing him a glass. "It's just sparkling cider. I wanted to get Lars up for this," she waved at the table and the tree, "but he was coughing so much, I thought I'd just let him be."

"To Christmas up North," David said and lifted his glass to her.

"It's the seventeenth today," Annie said. "We'll make it to Dad's for Christmas, don't you think, David?"

"I just wish it wouldn't snow so much," David answered, "and I wish Lars were better."

"I looked at the chart today," she said brightly, "and I tried to figure out how much we'd traveled before, on our good days. Even if you figure on a couple of days when it's too stormy to go, then I'm pretty sure a week should be plenty to get us there."

"I just wish it wouldn't snow so much," David said again, hoping his words wouldn't betray his deep uneasiness.

But in the morning, it was white and thick again outside. There were no swells or even waves that day. They yearned for a glimpse of the shore, always seeking, always turning their necks to port and to starboard, but only seeing the wall of falling white. In other places where there had been snow, the channels had been much wider, or Lars had been right there beside them, and they'd felt easier. But these channels were like canyons, the land filling up most of the radar screen, the water only a narrow strip down the middle. The person steering always had the unsettling feeling that if their attention strayed for half a minute from compass and radar, they'd be ashore.

They kept hoping Lars would get up and make his way up the stairs to sit by them comfortingly. But he only slept, ate a little, and went back to bed. Each time, Annie would sit with him at the table and help him with what he wanted, but he was distant, disoriented, and difficult to reach. She worried.

At the edge of dark they slowed and let the boat drift in neutral while they went outside to raise the tall trolling poles. They didn't want the poles in the way when they went into the fuel dock at the cannery that was their destination that night. The lines were iced over, and it took longer than they expected before the big poles were up and lashed.

"I wanted to get in before it got dark," David said, when they'd started up again with only the very thinnest light of the day left. "It's too spooky running in the black when it's snowing." And then it was night, though it was not yet four o'clock. A long while passed and no one spoke.

Annie studied the radar as they went along, and finally turned to her brother, "David, didn't we go past that cove a little while earlier before we took the poles up?" She pointed at the shape of a narrow indentation on the shore, to their port.

David studied the radar for a long moment. When he turned back to the compass, his face was visibly flushed in the dim light. He pulled the throttle slowly back to half, knocked the autopilot clutch out, and swung the wheel around. "I can't believe it! We must have gotten totally turned around when we were out there getting the poles up," he said quietly. "Good thing you noticed it. We could have steamed for hours back south if you hadn't noticed that cove."

At six o'clock, a narrow cove wrapped its arms around them on the radar. David slowed and ducked below for a moment to talk to Lars.

"Butedale Cannery," he said stiffly, as if he were in pain. "There's a big dock at the head of the cove. Float at north end. The water's plenty deep. But watch for a current off the dock."

Most small-boat radars are unable to display targets closer than around twenty or thirty yards away, so as David steered gingerly in toward the shape that was the dock, the target disappeared into the center of the display before he could see the dock through the snow. He tried the spotlight, but it only reflected back from the snow, blinding him, and he had to turn it off, hoping there was a light at the cannery or on the dock that he could see.

"David, David, stop!" Annie called from the back deck. "There's something out there."

He jumped at his sister's warning, throwing the boat into reverse until he could feel their forward motion stop, and went out on deck.

Annie had shrunk back against the door, as if she was afraid of something. Then he heard it and flinched: a muted, roaring sound. First thinking it was the engine and bow wave of a steamer, he darted back into the cabin and flipped the range switch on the radar until he could see the whole cove, assuring himself that there was no one in it but them.

He went outside and a wet sort of mist settled over the back deck, replaced a moment later by the snow again. The mist touched something in his memory and he realized what it was.

"Annie, it's okay, it's a waterfall! That's what the roaring sound is. There's a waterfall right next to the cannery. I remembered reading it in the *Coast Pilot* book last night."

The radar was useless at such close range, and David nudged the boat in and out of gear, approaching where he thought the dock was. The Fathometer still showed over a hundred feet of water, but it gave him little comfort, for he'd studied the chart and knew that here, like a lot of other steep-sided coves, it might be a hundred feet deep, only fifty feet off the beach.

The roaring got very loud, even inside the pilothouse, but outside was only black.

"There's a light," Annie said excitedly through the window, "just off to port, can you see it now? It's definitely a light."

He saw it then, the dimmest halo of white in the night. He turned the wheel slightly to port, leaning forward, trying to get some sense of perspective, of what the light might be.

A white shape grew out of the night below the light, and he was almost upon it before he grasped that it was an empty float, a place to tie up, lit by a single light on top of one of the pilings that held it in place.

Annie dug down into the snow, tied a line to the cleat, and moved back amidships where the deck was lower to the water, the rest of the line in hand, ready to get off and tie up.

Finally David reversed, the boat scrunching gently against the float with the very last of her momentum, and Annie climbed over the side, testing the solidity of the float with one foot before committing all her weight to it. The snow was deep, and the roar of the falls very close. She kicked around until she found something to tie up to, and even then had a difficult time making a knot. When she got back on board, David had shut the diesel down and the roar was even louder.

"Why don't you go up and see if someone can pump us some fuel?" Annie spoke over her shoulder as hung up her coat.

David looked out at the single light bulb and the untracked snow on the float. "Not without you; it's too weird."

Annie responded with a sigh, immensely glad just to be tied up to a dock again. "Okay, but I'm bringing our grocery list in case the store's open."

"Store. Here? Annie, this place seems like a ghost town. You mean there's a store?"

"Yeah, this is our big grocery and fuel stop, don't you remember?" But Annie's voice was uncertain; the place seemed so strange and lifeless.

"They'd better have fuel," David said. "I don't know where the next stop is, but we're about dry. I didn't want to tell you, but I was worried about getting in here tonight."

On the snowy float, the place seemed even stranger. They had left the boat's back deck light on, and as they stood on the float, the snow swirled in the cone of the light, and the boat loomed above them, spectral and ghostly.

The tide was down, so the ramp up to the shore or dock was steep. They ascended it with difficulty, clutching onto the side rails, and stopped at the top. There was no light and the snow was so thick the flashlight beam was useless.

Annie started out uneasily through the snow, then David clutched at her shoulder and spoke hoarsely in her ear, "Annie, what if there's a hole in the dock or something, or if we come to the edge, but don't see it? Let's just wait until morning." She didn't need to be persuaded, and they retreated carefully back down the steep ramp to the boat.

In the night, after Annie had gone to bed, David got up again to stand in the cool pilothouse, his breath white in the air before him, looking out the door one last time. The snow was lighter, but the dock light was still haloed by swirling white. The waterfall was loud and close. He slid the door shut, snapping the lock for the first time since he'd been aboard, for the feeling the place gave him was unsettling.

Morning brought more snow, and it was almost nine before enough light penetrated to call it day. The twins stopped at the top of the ramp, orienting themselves with the waterfall to their right before proceeding slowly ahead, feeling their way through the curtain of thick flakes, wary of hidden obstructions or holes in the dock.

A snow-blasted building emerged from the white ahead, startling the twins. There were lights on inside, and a big faded sign over the door: "Canadian Fishing Co.—Butedale, B.C."

The snow was untracked and knee-deep right up to the door. They approached and peered inside: a store with well-stocked shelves of canned goods, every light on, but no one in sight. The door was unlocked and they opened it cautiously, struck suddenly by the dry heat that filled the room.

"Ring for service," Annie read as she pressed the bell push on the well-worn wooden counter. Somewhere behind one of the doors in the back of the store there was a muted buzzing. A dog barked in answer and a door that was set into a wall of canned goods flung open. A red-haired young woman of perhaps seventeen walked in with a big black-and-white husky. The dog bounded over to the twins.

"*Customers!*" the young woman said in a lilting voice. "Wolf, they're customers, don't eat them!" Although he must have weighed all of eighty pounds, the dog was obviously a puppy, and the twins relaxed and put their hands out for the eager dog to lick.

"And *kids*," she added, looking the twins over. "We never get kids up here this time of year. It's been two weeks since anyone's been through. Can you stay for a while? I'm Jeanie Peters."

Her friendly manner put the twins at ease immediately.

"Wait a minute," Jeanie stood with her hands on her hips, her head tilted slightly to one side, as if she was trying to remember something. "Now I know. You're the runaways from Washington that they talked about on the radio. And you got all the way up here. Way to go!"

The twins' faces fell and involuntarily they turned for the door.

"Wait a second, wait a second," Jeanie said. "Hey, I won't tell. I think it's great you're running away to Alaska. And around here, who's to know? There's just Mom and Dad, me and Wolf. There's no one else within fifty miles of here."

"What about diesel fuel?" David asked finally. "We're almost out. We were lucky to make it in here. And does anyone know medical stuff? We're worried about our captain."

"My mom was a nurse years ago," she answered. "And we've got plenty of diesel. All you want. Could you show me your boat, too? I get so lonely for company this time of year." Jeanie disappeared through the doorway for a few minutes and returned wearing a heavy coat and knee-high rubber boots.

"I spoke to my mom," Jeanie said. "She'll be down to the boat in a bit. She says welcome to Butedale, by the way."

Outside, on the float, Jeanie turned a valve and kicked around in the snow until she found the right hose. She gave it to David, and while he filled the tanks Jeanie stood with Annie in the relative warmth of the pilothouse.

"Mom is the runaway, not us," Annie said plaintively. "We came home from school one day and the furniture was gone. The landlord showed up the next day and called the police. We had to leave, either that or get sent to a foster home again. We're just trying to get up North and find our Dad."

"Oh," Jeanie replied, "you know how the news is. They don't tell you any of that part." Then her voice dropped. "How bad off is the captain? The radio said you were traveling with a sick old man."

"Lars has spells. The doctor said they were small strokes," Annie said. "There were times when I was worried he wouldn't be able to help us when we really needed him, but he always pulled through." She pointed down into the fo'c'sle and lowered her voice. "He's been sleeping a lot these past couple of days. I think going across the Queen's Pond took a lot out of him." Annie pointed up at where the plastic had been screwed over the outer window frames. "We lost two windows coming across. Big waves broke them out. If a tug hadn't seen us having trouble and come over to help us in to Safety Cove, I'm not sure we would have made it."

"Wow," Jeanie answered, going over to feel the plastic, her eyes big. "That must have been really bad."

David appeared at the door just then. "All done," he said to Annie, "but Lars said he wanted me to change the oil, too, so I guess that'll take a while."

"C'mon, Annie," Jeanie said. "Bring your laundry and your shower stuff—we've got plenty of hot water. Then I'll show you around. Mom should be down soon."

Butedale was a water-powered cannery, Jeanie explained once they were back in the store and out of the snow. A big lake in the hills fed the waterfall. The builders had put a small dam near the falls and constructed a big wooden penstock, or big pipe, that carried the water down the mountain to the powerhouse, where it turned a generator that provided electricity, enough to light and heat the whole cannery complex, plus power all the machinery.

They traveled from one building to the next in wooden passageways. Outside, through the snow, Annie glimpsed other buildings, all brightly lit, but empty.

"What are all these buildings for?" asked Annie, as they entered yet another well-lit and heated, and apparently empty building.

"Oh," said Jeanie, "In these remote areas, canneries are basically like whole little towns for all the workers and their families. There's bunkhouses, shops, a mess hall, plus houses for married workers."

"So . . . where is everybody?" Annie asked.

"The cannery's just used for storage now. In the wintertime, it's just us," Jeanie said.

Annie finally grasped what Jeanie was telling her. "You mean you and your mom and dad are the only people in all these buildings? What do you *do* all the time? And how come the lights and the heat are all on? Isn't it a waste?"

"It's not good to run the generators without a load, so we

just keep everything on. Dad works on stuff that needs fix-ing, Mom does schooling with me, and Mom and I run the store . . . when anyone comes."

"How often do boats come by?"

"Well, we hadn't seen anyone for two weeks before you showed up. But spring and summer get real busy. A lot of fish-ing boats go through." Jeanie stopped in front of a small building and pushed open the door. "This is the powerhouse."

"This is it?" Annie had expected a huge, noisy room filled with complicated machinery. Instead the room was small and the machinery—two dryer-sized units set into the concrete floor—only hummed. Outside the window the penstock caught her eye. It was at least four feet in diameter, coming from beneath the powerhouse, sloping steeply upward and disappearing into the white.

"That's the pipe from the lake," Jeanie said. "It's really neat: wood with big metal rods around it to hold it tight. Sometimes it gets a leak and the water blasts way up in the air. I wish there wasn't so much snow; there's a long set of steps next to it that goes all the way up to the lake. We could go up."

They went out and down the snowy walk, finally stop-ping at a room with eight pairs of washers and dryers, and a big bath off it with rows of toilets and shower stalls. Jeanie left her, and Annie put in a load of laundry, then took a long and luxurious shower, feeling somewhat guilty that her brother was toiling away down at the *Karen A.*

After she moved the laundry into the dryer, a refreshed Annie followed Jeanie's instructions on how to find the old cannery superintendent's house. Jeanie's parents still were off somewhere, working in the immense complex of buildings, and while the snow swirled silently outside, the girls sat on the soft rug by the woodstove in the big living room. They played cards at first and then Scrabble, and then they just talked.

"You know," Annie said quietly, "it's been a real long time since I've just, played, you know, just had fun with a friend? For that last year or so with Mom, she wasn't around that much, and even when she was, she didn't do much. I was doing all the cooking and cleaning and shopping and stuff. It just seemed like there was never time just to be a kid."

"What'll happen if they catch you?" Jeanie asked quietly. The burning wood made a friendly popping sound in the woodstove.

"It's not like we're criminals. All we want to do is find our Dad!" Annie shook her head. "I don't know. I try not to think about that part. I wouldn't ever want to go to another foster home again."

David came in just then and looked around at the big room, the woodstove, and the girls sprawled on the rug. "Nice place," he said. "Hey, Jeanie, your folks came down to the boat. They're really fun. Lars was awake and your mom checked him out. She says he's just really worn out, and we should let him sleep as much as possible. But we need to keep him warm and make sure he has plenty of hot drinks." Then he noticed that Annie's hair was still slightly damp. "Hey, can I get a shower, too?"

And finally when all the chores were done—clothes washed, oil changed, boat refueled, twins showered, and boxes of groceries packed down the snowy ramp to the boat,

Annie and David lingered.

"Couldn't you stay?" Jeanie asked, in the pilothouse with them, sharing a last cocoa with Annie.

"We're trying to get home for Christmas," Annie answered simply. "We lost so much time waiting for weather, and Lars was sick for a while. We sort of have to go when we can."

"But in this?" Jeanie waved out at the swirling white beyond the windows.

"We can see pretty well with the radar," Annie answered. "At least the wind's not blowing. It's the wind that makes it bad."

"Why don't you go to the hot springs tonight? It's not far. You'll love soaking in it. We go a lot."

Both twins perked up.

"Here." Jeannie turned to the chart that was already laid out, took the pencil, and circled a little cove, close to the pencil line that Lars had already drawn. "You just go straight in. There's even a float to tie up to. Just walk up the ramp to shore, and the springs are in a little building on the left. There's no one ever there this time of year. You gotta go."

David looked at the chart carefully, then at his watch.

"We can make it," he said. "We can go now and make it before dark."

He started the engine, tuned the radar, and all was ready. Annie and Jeanie hugged each other, close friends in just those few hours. And then the lines were off, and the snow was closing in around Jeanie waving good-bye.

"I could have stayed," Annie said, "you know that? I could have stayed." But David didn't say anything and she went below to put away the groceries.

In a place called Wright Sound, Lars came up into the pilothouse for the first time in a day and a half, studied the radar and the chart, and finally settled into the chair next to David. He seemed very weak, but David was immensely glad that he had come up.

"When I was young man, I work on steamer," Lars said heavily, waving at the land and channels out beyond the snow. "Up, down, up, down, with a few days at either end to unload. We unload everything by hand. Erling Erikssen, another boy worked with me. No radar then, just chart and handbook." He thumped the green *Hansen Handbook* with all the courses and marks, and drawings of the different points along the way.

"Erling and me, we play little game: each time one of us come up for steering watch, we had to guess where we were without looking at logbook or chart. Just guess by looking out window at land and water."

"Guess?" David said, surprised. "How could you guess without looking at the chart? Even then you'd have to know where you were. It just all looks the same to me—even before it started snowing."

"Ah," said Lars. "First few times it looked that way. But imagine going up or down every week, then you would know route pretty well." He thumped his heavy hand down on the chart. "But look at this here, all channels and bays come in here, all look the same, almost look the same on radar. Wright Sound would always stump us. Is hard to pick out right channel. See, you must watch very careful now." He turned the radar up a range so the whole sound was displayed with all its arms and channels leading off in different directions. "Now, which way to go?" Lars asked, motioning at the radar.

David studied it for a moment, then tapped his finger down on a channel. "This one, right?"

"Ah, see," Lars said. "Even with radar it is hard. No, boy, is *this* one." He pointed to the next channel over. "See, is important to follow compass course in book, always watch chart."

Lars went below after a bit, ate a little, and went back to sleep. Another hour passed before David steered them carefully into the channel Jeanie had told them about. The slowing of the engine woke Annie with a start; she hadn't meant to fall asleep. When she went up the stairs, she found David bent over the chart table.

"I found a better chart," he said. "Lars has been in here before; the course line is marked. And see? The snow's letting up a bit."

Annie gazed out in awe. The snow had almost stopped. They were just coming into a cove at the head of a long bay. The water was still; the tide was high and the snowy tree limbs drooped down into the water. Ahead, two big tree trunks formed a simple ramp down to a snow-covered float. On shore, steam was coming out of a small building.

"Get the lines, Annie. We'll tie up and surprise Lars."

When they woke him, his head turned quickly to the periscope window and a wide smile crossed his tired face.

"Good job, Annie; good job, David!" He slapped the twins heavily on the back, and motioned to the kerosene lamp fastened on the side of the cabin. "Bring light, matches. I will show you."

The twins put on swimsuits under their clothes, gathered the lamp, matches, and towels, and helped Lars along the walkway to the shore and the small building, now wreathed in steam. The anteroom had hooks on the rough plank walls for clothes, and the water vapor was warm around them, smelling faintly of sulfur. Lars surprised them both, taking off his clothes down to his shorts with a rapidity they hadn't seen before. They hung their clothes on the pegs and lit the lantern, for the day was dying fast in a red cloud over the cove. Lars took the lantern with his good arm and they followed him into the stone pool that took up most of the floor space in the little structure. He put the lantern on a shelf, and sank with a gleeful cry into the hot steamy water.

"*Eeeeee*, Annie, David!" He waved them into the water and both twins cried out in pleasure as they slid down into the delightfully hot water. Only their heads and necks stuck out.

For a long time, they spoke little, just savoring the deep heat penetrating their bodies. Wall openings revealed misty views of the snowy cove. It was almost dark by then, but Annie had left a light on in the fo'c'sle so they could find the boat after dark, and it shone cheerily out into the peaceful evening.

Lars pointed at something on the walls. David turned the wick of the kerosene lamp higher, and saw words that were carved into the rough wood planks.

"*Polaris* April 26, 1951—107,000 pounds," Lars called out, reading the inscription without his glasses, for he knew it by heart. "We loaded her in two days in the Bering Sea." And another: "*Attu* October 17, 1957—102,000 pounds.

Thor Olson was her skipper, tried to beat our record; hah!"

And then the twins understood: when Lars had been a halibut fishermen decades earlier, the long, white boats had sometimes stopped in at the hot springs, and the crews had carved the dates of especially big trips into the walls.

The old man smiled in the lamplight and steam, and the three of them felt the cares of the difficult journey fade away as the hot water soaked to their very bones.

Back on the *Karen A*, dinner that night was a homemade stew that Annie had had simmering on the stove for hours. She had laid out the good glasses and the sparkling cider, and when they had all sat down, she said a simple grace and looked up, lifting her glass.

"To Alaska," Annie said, her eyes shining.

"To Alaska!" responded David and Lars.

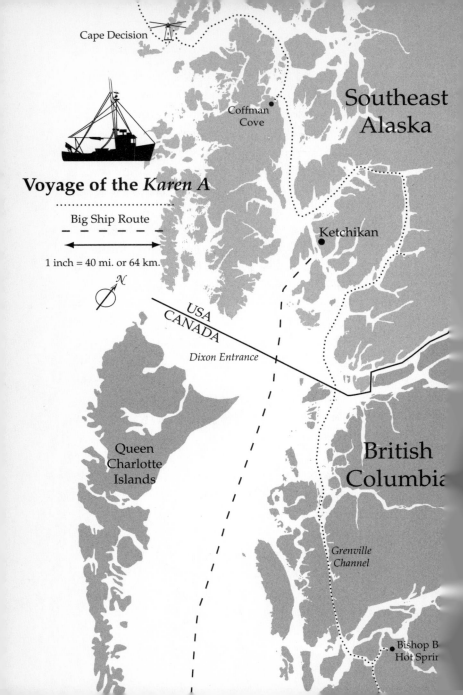

Cape Decision

Voyage of the *Karen A*

· · · · · · · · · · ·

Big Ship Route
- - - - - - - -

← - - - - - →

1 inch = 40 mi. or 64 km.

$\mathcal{N}$

Coffman
Cove

Southeast
Alaska

Ketchikan

USA
CANADA

Dixon Entrance

Queen
Charlotte
Islands

British
Columbia

*Grenville
Channel*

Bishop B
Hot Spri

CHAPTER 10

Race to the Cape

 The light, pale and shimmering on the glass of the cabin skylight, woke Annie, and she lay there a long while, looking up. At first she thought it was the moon, seen through racing clouds, but the color changed, from a thin, cold white to a delicate pink, and she knew it had to be something else. She moved to wake her brother, but then thought better of it, not wanting to be chided for her fears if it turned out to be nothing.

She got up quietly and went up into the pilothouse. It was even colder there than down below; her breath hung still and steamlike in the air before her. The windows were partially frosted on the inside, and it was a moment before she could see out.

Then she knew: northern lights, the aurora borealis, but more vivid and dramatic than she ever remembered. She snatched her coat off the hook, drew it tightly around her, and eased the door back.

The sky was alive with color and motion. Sometimes the

lights would take the form of shafts, or great, thin, almost vertical beams hanging over the cove. Pale, pastel colors faded and changed one into another. Yellows, greens, and reds, but all muted, like glowing curtains working in slow motion above snow-laden trees.

Sometimes it would fade away almost entirely to reveal a great splay of stars on a vast dome hung above them. Once, when the aurora had died away again, and she thought the show was over for the night, it suddenly flared up without sound or warning, a vast and multicolored curtain, shooting out unexpectedly until it appeared to hang over the very tops of the rigging. Unconsciously, Annie waited for the boom, so dramatic and lightninglike was the display.

She woke David, and when he went outside, he started to speak, but stopped in mid-sentence, so compelling was the drama in the sky.

Once it was like a spotlight shafting red and orange up into the sky from the entrance to the bay. Then it came over the ridge, focused and bright, like the beam of a great locomotive's spotlight, sweeping over the hills and valleys on steel rails that shone in the night. Silent and shimmering, changing into a curtain again, ethereal, mysterious.

Only after a long while, when it had gone momentarily dim, did David find his voice.

"Do you remember it like this, from the cove?"

"Yes. I mean, no," Annie answered, searching the sky for the beginnings of another great wash of color and shape. "I remember it, sure, don't you? It was almost a regular thing on nights when it was cold and clear like this. But I don't remember it quite like this, you know, moving and changing so much and being quite so bright. How about you?"

"Same here. I remember it okay, but not like this." Another great colored curtain grew, in a moment, from a few quivering rays to a wide, rippling display that covered two-thirds of the sky.

Only when they were both shivering did they turn and go below and stand by the fo'c'sle stove. David turned the stove up and made two cocoas.

"Hey," Annie said in a hoarse whisper when he handed her the cup. "Hey, David, we could go!"

"What do you mean? It's only 5:00 A.M." He answered in a soft voice so as not to wake Lars.

"I mean it's stopped snowing. I don't think the wind's blowing. We can actually see! We could leave."

"Well," David's voice was hesitant. "Don't you think you should ask Lars?"

"We did it before and that was in snow. He's so tired now, he needs rest," Annie answered. "The worst part is logs. There's no snow now. We could use the spotlight easy to look for logs, like we did before. Before the Queen's Pond, remember? And besides, in three or four hours, it'll be daylight, anyway.

"It might be our only chance," she said after a long while. "You know, to get to the cove by Christmas."

When she went out to untie from the dock, the engine exhaust purring in the night air, she realized suddenly why the cove had been so striking under the aurora: it had frozen in the night.

She grabbed the boathook, jabbed it over the side, and penetrated the ice, but not easily; it was perhaps an inch thick or more.

"David, come see!" she called in a stage whisper. "The cove's all frozen. It's iced-up!"

She jabbed again when he came out, but the boat hook failed to penetrate.

"Oh, great," he said warily, "and it's thick. What if we can't get out?"

The thought struck her unexpectedly, and she slumped back into the door frame with the immensity of it. The weather forecaster had spoken of colder weather from the arctic air mass. What if they couldn't get out? The ice would just grow thicker and thicker. They might not be able to get out for months.

"I don't think it's *that* thick," she said uneasily. "Who'd have thought that salt water would freeze up that quick? I don't remember our cove ever freezing over."

They untied the lines, but when David put the engine in gear, they didn't move.

"What if we're stuck?" he said over the sound of the engine. David advanced the throttle until the tachometer showed 1200 RPMs, what would be suitable for a good, slow cruise. The stern settled noticeably into the water, but without any forward motion, and David felt his hands tense on the wheel.

Suddenly with a lurch that rocked both of them back, the *Karen A* moved ahead, crunching through the ice in an arc away from the shore and toward the deeper water. David felt his sister's arms around him as he straightened the wheel and reduced the throttle until they were smoothly moving through the ice at a pace that was slightly faster than a walk.

They had swung around then to face where the ridgeline around the cove was the lowest, and the sky was revealed with its light dancing and changing, reflecting in the black sheet ice below the snowy mountains. It was a stunning sight, and David reduced the throttle even more until they were moving just enough to steadily break through the ice without lurching to a stop.

"David, you have to come out here! I'll steer for a while," Annie called from outside the back door, waving out at the shining ice. They swapped places and he could see what she was so excited about. For as they broke their way through the glassy ice sheet that covered the cove, the hundreds of little pieces broken by their passage skittered slowly away from them over the ice, like so many tiny crystal hockey pucks. The engine was idled back enough that he could hear the sound of the breaking ice, a sort of brittle, hard-edged hissing.

"Just steer straight, okay?" he called in to her. "I'm going up onto the bow and have a look. It's incredible!"

The spotlight was still on, and David knelt carefully so he could see over the bow to the exact place where it pierced the ice. The amazing thing was that the ice itself seemed to be flexible, rising in a gentle and unbroken curve as the boat approached, then shattering, the pieces falling to effortlessly slide away from them on the ice. A little water followed the pieces, only to be arrested, turned to slush, and then frozen hard within a few feet. It was fascinating to watch. The ice in the outer bay became thinner until finally the rumbling through the hull stopped, and they knew they had passed into open water.

There was no wind and they entered the canyon that was

Grenville Channel: vast and still, with the walls stretching ahead, shining, immense, and silent. David squeezed in until he was right beside his sister, the autopilot did its slow dance with the steering wheel, the miles passed, and they just stared out at the snowy mountains and the play of light in the sky. Twice, while the aurora danced and shone above them, they passed inlets where a channel was briefly revealed, winding back through the hills to bays where they thought they could see the glint of new ice.

After an hour or so, the aurora disappeared as suddenly as it had come, replaced by a great tapestry of stars. They had come to a wider part of the channel and Annie moved to the back door and stood a long time, looking behind them. In the dim light from the stars, Grenville Channel was a faintly shining canyon that disappeared back into the land.

As the canyon walls fell away and the sky grew bigger and more brilliant, David said, "Look, that must be the Milky Way, right?" The sky they saw that early morning was a sight few city folk ever see, so black was the sky and so bright the stars. There was in the atmosphere neither the airborne dust, smog, and microscopic smoke particles that slightly occlude vision, nor the light pollution—the glow from towns or even small settlements that hides the faintest stars. And so the Milky Way was displayed that night with unusual clarity and intensity, the flattened plane of a spiral universe, seen on edge.

It was nine o'clock before the first light of the new day came. First the black paled to blue, then the blue to yellow, spreading north and illuminating the sky above the low saddle where the Skeena River had worn down the mountains in its push to the sea. Annie was making eggs when David's excited voice carried down to her.

"Annie, come up quick, you can't miss this! I think I can see Alaska ahead. The sun's just about to come up. It's killer—you got to see it!"

She joined him and stood, awed by the vista ahead. The sun had just risen and was shining on a high and snowy mountain wall that rose from the sea at the far end of the channel that lay before them.

"That's Alaska," he said again, excitedly. "I'm sure of it; look at the chart."

For a long moment she stayed at the window, for the sun hit the mountains in such a fashion that all the rest was in shadow, and Alaska seemed to tower, shimmering and bright, above all the lower land before them.

When Annie finally went below again, Lars was there, sitting at an odd angle at the table, his face pale and tense.

"Lars, what is it? Are you feeling all right?"

"I cannot move my arm now. Leg feels slow, maybe asleep, hard to move. Oh, Annie, I don't want go like this, one piece at a time." He shook his head and there were tears in his eyes.

She helped him into a more comfortable position and went up to talk to David.

"It might be another stroke," she told him quietly. "I don't know enough about it to tell."

"Is he resting okay? Is he in pain?" David asked.

"He's sitting up, but something has definitely happened."

David studied the chart, looking up and comparing it

with the land to the east until he could make out a faint plume of smoke from behind a low island against the shore.

"Over there," he said, "see that smoke behind the long island? That's the sawmill at Prince Rupert. It's like the center for this whole part of the coast. They'll have to have a doctor." He stepped in front of Annie, kicked off the autopilot clutch, swung the wheel until they had steadied on the new course, east, toward the smoke, and engaged the pilot deftly with his foot.

"What is this?" Lars was suddenly at the stairs, struggling a little with his left leg. His unexpected appearance startled the twins, and he made it to the top of the steps before David went over to help him.

"Is okay!" Lars brusquely brushed away David's offer of help. "Why do we go to Rupert?" He demanded, waving out the window and clearly upset.

"We wanted to get you to a doctor, Lars. You might have had another stroke or something. We should get help."

Lars kicked off the autopilot and swung the wheel around with his good arm to put them once more on course toward Alaska.

"How long have we waited for weather like this?" He stared at the twins. "Dixon Entrance can be bad. We must go now. You want to be home for Christmas? We must not delay!

"And what happens if we go to Rupert, and Customs finds out we don't have right papers? Or doctors say I must stay in hospital? Or Coast Guard remembers *Karen A* as boat with runaway twins? How do you get to cove then?"

"Listen, Lars," David started gently, not wanting to

upset him again. "I know it's really important to get across, and Annie and I really just want to get to the cove, but if something happened to you that a doctor could have prevented, well, that would be terrible. I guess what I mean is that we want to be able to help you as much as you've helped us."

They went along in silence while Lars studied the chart. Then he put his good arm on David's shoulder. "I know is hard to know what to do. Old man, winter, long trip. You and Annie do not know too much about all this." He nodded around him at the pilothouse and the water beyond. "Doctor will just say 'Must have plenty of rest,' and how can I rest when I worry about twins going to foster home and not finding their father?" Lars's frustration over his ailing body seemed to gather, and he slammed his hand down next to the compass. "Listen! I know my boat. I know the way to the cove. You can steer, even take care of engine, but is best for me to just be here." Just as quickly, his outburst ended and the emotion seemed to sap his energy. "Now. We have chance to make cove before Christmas, but only if we push hard. Leave early, go late each day. And hope weather is good."

"Okay, Lars, okay," David said. "You're the boss. But what do you think about traveling at night? We got a good early start, I measured it all out, but we'll never get across before it gets dark."

Lars thought for a moment before answering. "I listened to weather. It is a good chance. We can keep going."

Finally David helped Lars go below, and Annie took a long watch at the wheel. Once when she was sure there were no logs ahead, she took a moment to stand at the door and look out astern. The low sun beat on her face through the glass, and their wake trailed back, straight and true. Of the long and winding channel they had taken only a few hours earlier, there was no sign. The shining landmass that covered the horizon seemed a mountain wall, and she looked and looked, but saw no sign of Prince Rupert's smoky mills, nor any other sign of human existence.

As Annie watched the sun slipping toward the horizon, she felt as if her southern life, her stateside life, her city life, was slipping away as well. She knew they'd been gone only three weeks or so, but already all that she had been through in Seattle seemed remote, veiled by time and distance, as if it had all happened many years before.

Lars returned to the pilothouse just then. Coming up the two steps had tired him out, and it was a moment before he could catch his breath enough to speak.

"Alaska," he said, pointing out ahead. "Two, three hours to Alaska." He paused, and Annie looked and noticed his eyes were wet.

"Lars," she said as she turned to face him better, "what's the matter? Does your chest hurt again?"

"No, no." He pushed her away weakly. "Nothing hurts. Is just . . . I never thought I would see her again, my Alaska. Now here we are. You think I help you, but is the other way around: you help old man." He dried his eyes awkwardly with his sleeve, and when he was done, Annie put her arms around him, and they rode up there together while the sun found the mountains in the western islands, and the snowy mountain wall to the east shone dramatically in the sun's last light.

The night came, and it was full dark by 3:30, for it was

near the shortest day of the year. David turned on the spot-light and it shafted out ahead, showing the cold, white vapor rising from the water. It was the first time the twins had steamed for very long into the night, and they weren't comfortable with it. They should have been able to see the Tree Point Lighthouse, just over the Alaska border, but it was hidden by the sea smoke, and without any stars or light in the sky, it was easy to become disoriented. The spotlight showed a strange, moving tunnel of vapor and half-seen water, through which David strained to see logs.

Twice little squalls came up and the spray flew obliquely across their bow to quickly freeze on the windows where it hit. After a few minutes the plastic was almost opaque, and David had to struggle to find a place clear enough to see through. The wind stopped after the squalls, and the fan was able to melt the ice again, but David felt the muscles in his back and shoulders knot with tension.

Once when Annie was steering, they thumped into a piece of driftwood, and everyone jumped. Lars's hand was instantly at the engine controls, throttling back and putting the engine into neutral, so as to avoid propeller damage. A moment passed without any further noise or vibration, and they resumed speed again.

After Lars had finished spending a particularly long time at the chart table and the radar, shifting ranges and using the variable range marker to fix their position, he looked up and said, "Alaska. We are there now." A smile lit his craggy face.

"We've waited so long for this, I want to go out and see if I can see anything," David said as he grabbed his coat and stepped out into the black. His eyes struggled to find some fixed point of reference, some light on the horizon beyond the occasional glow of the spotlight reflecting from the sea smoke, some—any—sign that the land they had been trying to get to for so long was out there. He waited until his eyes grew accustomed to the dark, and then peered around until he began to shiver violently in the bitter night air. Finally he went inside.

"Nothing," he said though chattering teeth, and went below to stand by the stove until he was warm enough to take the wheel again.

"How about anchoring in Foggy Bay tonight, Lars?" Annie pointed to a place on the radar, just a few miles ahead. "I read about it in the pilot book earlier, it seems like a good anchorage, don't you think?"

"Wind hole," Lars said simply. "We must go two more hours."

Finally they entered a channel again, Behm Canal, and the welcome arms of the land closed around them. And after another long hour, a smaller bay, lightless and still.

The anchor chain sang its little song and the engine was silenced. David stayed on the bow a moment before going into the cabin. But there was no sound and nothing to see, only the strange way that their lights shafted out into the sea smoke, hiding the land and the stars.

Annie made a small supper of soup and toasted sandwiches. Afterwards she brought out the last of the sparkling cider and the little glasses, and held hers high. "To Alaska!" she toasted.

"To Alaska!" They clinked the glasses together for a

difficult passage made. But there was little chatter; it had been a tedious day, and the tension of the long, last leg in the dark had drained them all.

The gray morning light of 9:30 woke Annie, for they had all slept in. She got quietly up, turned up the stove, refilled the kettle, and stepped up into the pilothouse, for she wanted to be the first to see Alaska. But when she looked outside, her breath caught in her throat.

The sea water had frozen again in the night, and a light snow had come after the freeze. They lay at the head of a constricted bay whose outlet was hidden by a high headland to the west. There was no open, unfrozen water; it looked like they were in a frozen lake.

At first she was frightened that they would be unable to free themselves, then a gust of wind eddied down from the high land above the bay and pushed on the boat. As the boat moved, she could see the anchor wire easily saw through the ice and could tell it was thin.

"David, look!" she said excitedly when her brother came up. "It froze and snowed in the night. Isn't it magic?"

David looked at the ice and his face fell. "Here we go again . . . "

"It's not that thick," Annie said, sensing his concern. "You can tell where the anchor wire goes through."

"Did you turn the stove up?" he asked. "It's really cold up here." The outside thermometer read just above zero; so far, ten degrees was the coldest they'd seen.

"Guess there's no 'Welcome to Alaska' sign, huh?" David said finally, taking in the austere and clifflike sides of the cove.

"I think we're over the worst, David. Just three more days

and we'll be there, can you believe it? Yesterday wasn't too bad after all." As she spoke, she remembered how anxious she had been, worried about Dixon Entrance, that they'd be weather-bound for days, that Christmas would come and go before the wind let them pass.

"I didn't like steering in the black. How about you?" David said.

"No, I didn't like it either. I get disoriented too easily, and I really hated it when we hit that log last night. I couldn't see it at all. At least before we came across the Queen's Pond, we'd see a boat every now or then. I mean, we've haven't seen another boat in four days! It's like, did everyone leave?"

"I know," he said thoughtfully. "It is kind of weird. I keep looking for boats or houses or anything on the shore with the binoculars, and you sure don't see much. I was so glad just to see that smoke yesterday, just to know that there was a town there, even if we couldn't actually see it."

David looked out at the cliffs before continuing. "I remember looking from the airplane, that time we flew down with Mom, when we left the cove. I had the window seat. You could look down and see all the islands." He stopped, and when he started again, his tone was more somber. "It just didn't seem so far. The flight only took an hour or something."

"I know," she said. "I never thought it'd be this far."

"Whoa, what's that?" David cried excitedly, "Something's moving under the ice."

Annie looked in the direction he was staring. A boat-length in front of them, the ice suddenly pushed up, as if a small animal was trying to break through. Then a dark head did break through and look around: a seal. It was close enough for the twins to see his whiskers clearly, and then he was gone, leaving a circle of dark water, stark against the white snow-covered ice.

"He was so cute!" Annie said, wishing the seal to return.

A little wind devil whirled off the cliffs as they watched, picked up the snow on the ice and danced across the cove with it, a spinning white column forty or fifty feet high, leaving a darker, snowless trail on the ice behind it. Twice it lifted off, traveled a few hundred feet, and touched down again with a burst of snow.

"Maybe we should go," Annie said, after the whirling column had disappeared into the whiteness. "It's really cold. The ice is probably still getting thicker. Do you want something to eat before you start up? I got some instant oatmeal at Butedale."

"We have to wake up Lars," David said.

"Why? You didn't wake him yesterday or the two mornings before."

"That was different. We were just following the little green book he always uses. It's got all the courses and distances and stuff written in it. It was easy to go from the book to draw out the courses on the chart. The book goes past Ketchikan, not way over here." David showed Annie the chart.

"Well, we could figure it out, couldn't we?" she said, looking at the chart. "I mean, here's Ketchikan over here, where all the old course lines go to. We're over here behind this island. We could just go back and around and past town and keep on using the book, couldn't we? I looked at the book before and it keeps going past Ketchikan."

"There's a Coast Guard base in Ketchikan," David said. "It's right on the channel, Lars said. We'd have to go right past it. And you're supposed to stop and go through Customs, too. You heard what those tugboat guys said: they're looking for this boat."

Annie bent to study the chart again. "Well, we could just keep going up this way, couldn't we? Through those little islands, and then way down here, above Ketchikan, we'd be back in the little book and we wouldn't have to go past the Coast Guard, right?"

"Except we'd have to go through all those little islands. You're supposed to have a different chart. I looked last night and we don't have it. See, on the big chart it doesn't tell you how deep the water is or where the rocks are or anything. It's all just blank except for the outlines of the islands."

"What would Lars do without the chart?" Annie asked.

"He just knows it," David said. "He's like that. You remember those places on the trip up, he just knows them, with or without the chart."

It took a long while to get Lars up. They both had to help him over to the table. It was like before: he had difficulty speaking and breathing came hard. He was disoriented at first, saying, "We must keep going!" over and over after he was seated.

"Lars, it's okay," Annie said. "We're still anchored up. We got to Alaska, remember? It's okay. We're going to start up as soon as you help show us where to go."

David brought the chart and set it on the table and asked him about the islands and the passages between.

"East channel," he said in a hoarse whisper, finally

focusing on the chart. He flopped his good arm awkwardly out and pointed at the islands that had concerned David. "East channel, just stay in middle. Plenty of water."

When David went out on the bow to pull the anchor, his parka hood up and his breath white before him, he was struck again by the somber mood of that iced-over bay. A bald eagle circled low over the ice, as if in bewilderment at what had happened to the water.

The ice broke easily before them at one-third throttle, and they cut a wide, curving turn. When they looked behind, the boat had cut a path no wider than her narrow hull, revealing a strip of dark water that smoked in the bitter air, intensely black against the white of the ice.

They came around the point that formed the entrance to the bay, a place that gave David a view out to the wider channel beyond, and once more he felt the cold stone of fear within him. For the ice didn't end at the entrance as he had assumed, but rather stretched across, into the distance, flat, featureless and white. The boat slowed then, as if the ice had gotten thicker at the bay's entrance. How could so much ice have formed in a single night? He looked at the outside thermometer again, and shivered involuntarily: it had struggled up a couple of degrees to maybe five, but he could still feel the cold through the thin walls and single-pane windows of the pilothouse.

The ice grew thicker and their progress slowed a little more. He had to advance the throttle and he could feel the boat lurch and bounce, and he worried about the propeller.

Annie came up with some hot tea for him. "I'm really worried about Lars," she said. "I've never seen him quite like this. He's still real confused. I know he'd get really mad if we tried to find a doctor for him, but maybe we should think about it."

David didn't answer until they had shouldered their way through the thicker ice at the bay entrance, and gotten out beyond, where it was thinner again.

"It was real thick back there," he said. "I wasn't sure we could get through. It seems better here. Maybe the tide pushed the ice together as it was freezing or something. Wait a minute, I know what I was thinking before it got thick: there's a *nurse* at the cove. Millie Roberts, or Robertson, or something. Don't you remember, she's the one who gave us our shots?"

"You think she'd still be there?"

"Should be. She *lived* there. She was married to a fisherman. Their cabin was four down the beach from ours, remember? Annie, listen, we should be there the day after tomorrow. Tell Lars that, tell him about Millie. It's Roberts. Millie Roberts. He'll remember her."

The day was very still, and when they got out into the middle of the channel, there were places of a few acres each where the ice had not yet skinned across. When David saw one, and it wasn't too far off their course, he would steer for it, and the boat would surge ahead eagerly, free of the ice, and they'd pass through sea smoke as high as the pilothouse windows. Then they'd enter the ice again, and he would try to feel if it had gotten any thicker, for he could see the new ice growing on the edges of the open spots.

It was even thicker at the islands and in the channel Lars had told them about. A ridge of thicker ice had formed, probably from the action of the tide, and they searched carefully for a way through.

Out and beyond, they could see open water, still and unrippled, with the sea smoke lying in thick, foglike clouds. So near and yet so far, for the ridge of thicker ice arrested the boat's progress. David backed out of the slot the boat had made and went from one side of the narrow strait to the other, hoping for a thinner place in the ice. Even if it didn't lead to the channel Lars had chosen, the tide was coming in, so if they went slow and touched bottom, he reasoned, the tide would float them off.

But there was no place that looked any better, and finally David came back to where they had started. The slot he had made had already skinned over with new ice, and he pushed the throttle up to half and felt them gather momentum. He worried about making a hole in the boat, but did not know what else to do.

They hit with a lurch that threw them to one side of the pilothouse and knocked the pencil and dividers to the floor.

"David! Stop! We'll put a hole in the boat!" Annie said loudly. She rubbed her back where she had hit the chart table.

David didn't answer, but dropped quickly into the foc's'le, threw back the rug, and lifted up the floor hatch to check the bilge. It was dry. He returned to the pilothouse and looked around: they had made fifty or sixty feet before the ice stopped them.

"We're not leaking," he said with relief evident in his voice. "And I think we might be through the worst of it." He backed up and plowed forward again as he whispered, "Come on, baby, come on!" The first push had gotten them past the thickest part and he didn't need as much throttle to finish the job. "All right!" he exclaimed as they entered thinner ice that continued to get thinner and thinner until they passed into the open water beyond. He and Annie exchanged high-fives, and then the sea smoke rose up and enveloped them.

In some places, the vapor wasn't thick at all and they could see two or three hundred yards. Or they might run for ten minutes and hardly see beyond the anchor winch. Other places there were corridors or passages in the strange vapor. The twins were uneasy until they understood it was more like traveling at night, relying on the radar and marking a tick on the penciled course line every hour to know where they were.

Moisture-laden as the vapor was, it instantly condensed into frost on any part of the boat it touched, creating delicate-looking frost feathers on the rails and rigging. Even with the fo'c'sle stove turned up, the pilothouse was cold; the fan could only melt a plate-sized hole for them to see through in the front window.

More alarmingly, the picture on the radar slowly grew fainter as they traveled. At first David and Annie thought the machine itself was failing, and they began to slant over to the western shore of the wide strait, so as to have a course laid out into a cove for the night if the radar died completely. Then Annie recognized the problem as the same they had encountered when they iced over on that terrible night: frost from the sea smoke was forming on the radar antenna, thick enough to blind the machine.

David slowed and took the engine out of gear. He and

Annie dressed in their parkas, hats, and gloves as the boat slowly coasted to a stop. It was eerie outside, and he was glad she had come out with him. There was no wind, and the frost accumulation on the boat was light, nothing like it had been when they had really iced up.

Yet there was something about the stillness of the day that made them uneasy. David carefully climbed up the ladder and gently removed the thick hoarfrost from the antenna with the windshield scraper. When he was done, he sat back on the top of the pilothouse as Annie turned on the radar again and waited for the picture to come on.

There was no sun nor any break in the clouds to even show where it might be, but he could feel the short day already starting to fail, and knew he didn't want to be out there after dark.

"Okay, got a good picture now, good job!" Annie's words brought him out of his trance, and he gingerly made his way off the roof and down the ladder.

Annie took over next, and when they had begun to move again, she picked a wide cove and headed toward it. Another cove was nearer, but it was narrower, and she worried about the ice forming in such a place on such a bitter night. With sixteen hours of darkness ahead until they could travel again, it might build up fast enough to lock them in.

David studied the chart as the daylight began to fade.

"Look here, Annie. There's a village here, in Coffman Cove. There might be a nurse or something. Such a small place wouldn't have a Coast Guard station. Let's stop."

"Or maybe just a place to warm up," she said.

They came around the point, eager for people, to get

attention for Lars, and they could see the settlement in the failing light: two neat curving rows of buildings set on the southern shore of the cove, with a dock and a float.

But there was something odd about the place. At first Annie assumed it was the sea smoke that hid the lights, but as they drew closer she couldn't see any lights at all, nor vehicles, and the snow was untracked, unplowed. The village was abandoned for the winter.

"Uh, you want to tie up anyway?" Annie asked as she slowed and brought the boat around in a wide curve toward the float. For some reason she wasn't eager to spend the night tied to a dock at a village without people.

"Let's not," he said, echoing her feelings. "I'm not sure how well I'd sleep tied up there."

Annie took the boat out of gear and it slowed, thirty or forty feet off the float, and they went out onto the back deck to have a look. The light was failing fast and the late afternoon air was even colder than before. David began to shiver, even inside his coat. There was a sign on the float: "No Trespassing. Coffman Logging." They went inside then, motored over to the western shore, where David pulled on his hat and gloves once more and dropped the anchor. He stood up once it set, and stayed a moment up on the bow, easing a muscle ache in his lower back. Annie tapped at the glass and made the finger-across-the-throat engine shutoff sign, and he nodded at her.

In the engineless silence, he looked out one last time at the settlement, hoping at least to see the glimmer of light in a caretaker's cabin, but it was all black; there was nothing. The clouds above the cove pressed down on the land, and the light was almost gone. There was about the place a desperately bleak, lonely, and forlorn feeling, and he began to shiver again.

"What do you think happened to the people?" Annie asked quietly when he had come down into the fo'c'sle.

He was still very cold. The stove was turned all the way up, but the cabin hadn't been designed for such cold weather. The skylight was frosted up, and frost had formed on the bolts and hull fittings that penetrated to the outside.

"I don't know," David said, trying to stop his teeth from chattering. "Maybe it was too cold for logging or something."

"I fed Lars a little earlier. All he wanted was a little toast and some leftover stew," Annie said. "At least I got him to drink some hot tea."

"How did he seem?" David had finally stopped shivering, but he still wasn't warm. "I wish he'd been up with us today. I hated going through the ice and then being out in the sea smoke. I never thought it would be like that, I never thought we'd have to be breaking ice. Lars said we had ironbark, some kind of really hard wood, all along the waterline, to protect from the ice, but still, some of that ice was really hard. Could you tell how freaked out I was?"

"No, you did great. You got us out of there. I was the one who freaked out." Annie stirred the stew with a long wooden spoon and lowered her voice. "It's like Lars was before, you know: like he's hardly there. He doesn't seem to really hear me when I talk to him. It's awful. I had to help him out of bed, but he wouldn't say if he was in pain or anything. He just ate and went back to bed."

"You know," David said, "I wonder if the cold has something to do with it. He was in totally great shape when we were in the hot springs. Old people are supposed to be more susceptible to the cold. Maybe that's it. I know I'm cold. I've been cold all day. Can't we turn up the stove any higher?"

"It's already all the way up," Annie said. "It's been on high every day since God's Pocket. I'm cold, too." She paused, then added, "Just two more days."

"Yeah, tomorrow night we'll be at Cape Decision," David said. "We're back on the courses in the book now. And then the day after that, we'll be there."

But there was something in the way he said it that made Annie uncomfortable. "What's the matter?" she asked. "You sound like you're unhappy about something."

"Oh, I just wish Lars were up to help us a little bit more. It's like there are two ways to the cove after Cape Decision. One is way longer, like two more days. You gotta go up and around all of Baranof Island, and through a bunch of narrow channels and stuff, where the tide really runs hard. But it is inside, protected."

"How about going outside?" Annie asked quietly.

"That's the problem," David answered simply. "It's outside."

David unfolded the chart on the table. For the first time since they had left, their evening anchorage and their final destination were on the same large-scale chart. Annie marveled at it wordlessly. For so long, their old home, a cove on Baranof Island, had seemed impossibly far away, and there it was, way in the upper left-hand corner of the chart.

"I see what you mean," Annie finally said. For in contrast

to the sheltered island maze through which they had been traveling since Dixon Entrance, the short way home took them out into the North Pacific, exposed for some thirty-five miles. "Tomorrow's the twenty-second. We won't make it by Christmas if we go up and around, will we?"

"Uh-uh," David shook his head.

Annie didn't say anything, but she looked at her brother as they ate, and thought how far he had come since that first afternoon out of Seattle when he had been afraid to steer the boat into the harbor. How far they'd both come.

Before 8:30 they were both in bed. In the intense cold, their sleeping bags were the only truly warm place on the boat.

Annie woke David in the morning, and he sat up, his breath was white before him, even in the fo'c'sle. "It's still water," she whispered. "It didn't freeze. It's warmer, too, almost ten degrees."

He ached all over, and knew he'd be cold again as soon as he got out of his sleeping bag.

They traveled north in the morning, through a narrow channel called Snow Pass in the middle of the day, and west in Sumner Strait all afternoon. Even with the stove on high, the cabin was cold and they swapped off steering watches, retreating to their sleeping bags when their watch was over. Neither saw any other boats nor smoke on any shore. The emptiness and vastness of the country humbled them, and they said little to one another when they changed watches.

Lars got up in the middle of David's twelve-to-two watch. When David saw him, he went below to make him tea and toast while the autopilot steered them steadily through the still water.

The skin on the old man's face looked as if it had shrunk, clinging tight, shiny, and parchment-like to the bones. As David made the tea, now and again a shiver would come to the old man and his whole body would twitch for a moment and then be still.

David brought the big chart down, the one with most of Southeast Alaska on it, and spread it out beside the tea and toast.

"Lars," he said slowly and clearly, "I need your help. There are two ways to go from here." He tapped his finger hard on the chart. He had marked out both courses clearly. "Unless we take the outside route, we won't get to the cove by Christmas. The weather sounds as if the high pressure might last a little longer. What do you think? Should we take a chance and go outside? Or play it safe, and go around, and maybe miss Dad?"

But Lars didn't seem to hear him, turning away before David was halfway through asking, reaching out and touching the frost on the iron chainplate bolted to the wooden side of the fo'c'sle.

David asked again, and finally Lars turned toward him. His eyes were clouded, his look faraway, and his lips moved for two or three seconds before any words came out.

"Just keep going," was all he said, two or three times, with that hoarse, raspy voice and sour breath. But he wouldn't say where or how. And when he had eaten, he began to shiver again all over. David helped him back into the bunk and went up to steer again. At the end of his watch, he quickly went to bed himself, huddling in his sleeping bag, feeling even more lonely and uncertain than before.

Annie came to David when her watch was over and shook him on the shoulder again and again until he got up and stood by the stove. The day was almost gone; he could tell by the dim light through the heavily frosted-over skylight.

"We're almost to the cape," she said. "I'm going to get some supper ready."

For an answer, he just nodded, pulled on his heavy coat, and stepped up into the pilothouse where he got behind the wheel, peered out and tried to orient himself. Not even 3:30 and already almost dark. He started to shiver and pulled the zipper of the coat up as far as it would go.

Annie had crossed Sumner Strait during her watch, and they were approaching a long mountainous point that came from the north. At its very tip, on a high and forbidding headland, was the Cape Decision lighthouse. It had been automated several years before, and the windows and buildings that the twins had hoped would be filled with people and light were empty, boarded up, and dark.

David anchored in a wide and desolate cove. Dinner was fried canned ham and baked beans, and he ate in his coat, wanting only to finish and get back into his sleeping bag again. Annie looked pale and drawn and neither spoke of what the next day might bring.

They were both in bed before seven, but sleep came hard.

A wind came up after midnight, and David got up quickly to watch for a while, to make sure the anchor wasn't dragging. Idly he turned on the little AM radio to look for a station that might keep him awake, finally finding one, way at the end of the dial. The same big Midwest 50,000-watt boomer they had heard earlier in the trip was playing carols again. "Silent Night," "Little Drummer Boy," "White Christmas," and others, fading in and out.

The bow started to rise and fall and the rattle of spray came, flung up and against the windows. The fear came again, big and unreasoning, and all David could think about was having to go out into the wind and the black and the freezing spray, pick up the anchor, and get underway. The cheering music faded, and David began to tremble violently, knowing he could never, never, go out there on such a night.

But it was only a night breeze from the strait, not a storm coming through, and after a while it lay down and the anchor wire was silent in the chock. David turned off the radio and went below to huddle in his sleeping bag. It was a long time before he stopped shivering enough to sleep.

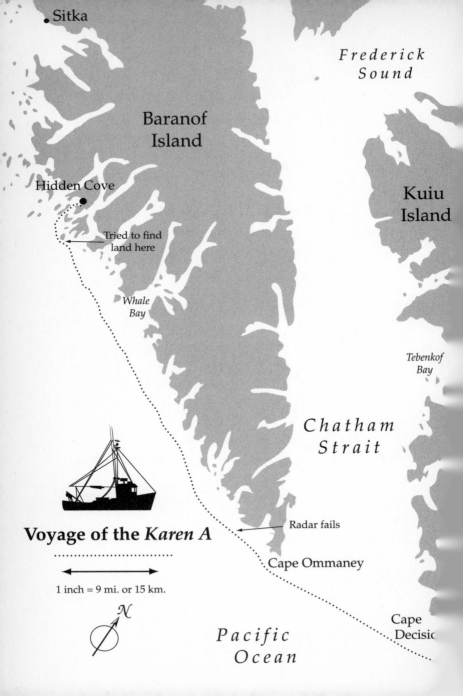

Sitka

Frederick Sound

Baranof
Island

Kuiu
Island

Hidden Cove

Tried to find
land here

*Whale
Bay*

*Tebenkof
Bay*

*Chatham
Strait*

Radar fails

Voyage of the *Karen A*

1 inch = 9 mi. or 15 km.

Cape Ommaney

Cape
Decisi

N

*Pacific
Ocean*

CHAPTER 11

The Homecoming

"David, David," came the voice from far away. "We'll be home tonight; we'll be *home*!" Someone was shaking him, and groggily he got up on one elbow. Eight o'clock; dawn was still almost two hours away. "C'mon, David," Annie said again. "It's not blowing—we can get around, we can make it home for Christmas!"

"Give me another hour," he said hoarsely. "I can't go out into the black again; I'm too cold." He retreated into the warmth of the bag. He remembered the wind after dark, the spray freezing over the windows, and the unreasoning terror that had filled him at the thought of leaving the shelter of the cabin to step into that bitter, lightless night.

The hour passed like nothing, and Annie was at his shoulder again, shaking him insistently. "Okay, David, you've had your hour. I've checked the distance on the chart. If we don't leave now, it'll be way after dark before we get to the cove. You get dressed and I'll get the anchor up."

She had a mug of cocoa all ready for him, and he pulled on three shirts and heavily sat down to drink it, feeling stiff, sore, and immensely tired. When they were finally underway and passing Cape Decision and its lighthouse, they could see that the water ahead, Chatham Strait, was a vast place, and it made them uneasy to be so far from the land when Lars was sick and unable to guide them.

"What do you think?" David asked in an uncertain voice. Something about the day seemed ominous.

Ahead, to the west, was the dark shoulder of the southern tip of Baranof Island, low on the horizon. Beyond it was the Gulf of Alaska, or the North Pacific. It was a vast and restless ocean, and a long swell began to make its presence felt.

"Let's look at the charts and see what those bays look like on the other side of the cape—in case we need shelter." Annie's voice was tight, and David could tell she was feeling the same kind of unease over the decision they had to make.

"I remember Dad talking about those bays," David said. "'Blowholes,' he called them."

"Yeah, I remember," Annie said. She brought out the charts and they looked at the bays—narrow and deep without any bends that would shelter a boat from the wind.

They went on in silence, headed for the cape, the outside route along the exposed coast of Baranof Island.

"I just wish we'd see somebody. I wish there'd be other boats," Annie said.

"I know," David answered.

A little wind came at the cape when they were a mile off the place where the land made its last stand, a bold, high headland, before dropping steeply into the water. It wasn't a big wind, only darkening the faces and backs of the swells at first, but it was a wind, and it was the ocean, and it was winter. They heard a sound from the fo'c'sle, and Annie hurried down the two steps.

When she came back up, her face was tense. "David, it's Lars. He's throwing up."

David looked out the window before pulling the throttle back to an idle and going below with her.

Lars's breath was foul; his face sweaty. Annie held the pan for him and afterward David wiped the old man's face, and helped him lie down again. They tried to get him to speak, to advise them where to go, but he was too exhausted, and David went back to steer.

It was decision time, and David's chest was tight with anxiety. They must commit themselves to one course or the other. If he turned northeast, in less than an hour's time the mountain flank of Baranof Island would shelter them from whatever wind was coming. It would be an easy run along a protected shore.

But their evening anchorage would be another uninhabited cove, and the same on the day after that: Christmas Eve. The stove would struggle against the cold and they would shiver in their sleeping bags. On Christmas Day, they'd have a tideswept narrows and many miles still to cover before they got home. Dad often took an extended hunting trip right after Christmas. If the weather delayed them, he might have already left. And Lars seemed to be failing now; it was clear he needed help as soon as they could find it.

"What do you think?" he said when Annie came up from seeing to Lars.

"We have to get help for Lars," she said. "That's more important than anything right now. I can barely get him to drink, and he's getting so weak."

David nudged the autopilot out of gear with his foot and altered course farther offshore to put more distance between them and the unforgiving land, in case the wind got stronger.

"Let's go for the cove," he answered. "Pray the nurse is there. And pray it doesn't blow."

"All right, we're doing it," Annie said, sounding more certain than she felt.

The snow came on lightly at first, softening the features of the land and the sea, but after an hour it grew heavier and the shore disappeared into the falling white.

David turned on the radar but there was no picture. The machine and the controls were illuminated, but there was no display on the screen. As Annie steered, he ducked outside to look at the antenna, thinking perhaps it was the ice. But the antenna wasn't rotating at all, and he went back inside to wiggle the plugs on the back of the machine. Nothing made any difference, and he felt the tightness in his chest again.

David went over to the chart table, instantly wishing that he had marked exactly where they were when he finished their jog offshore and changed course back parallel to the coast again. Wasn't there a point on the land they were just coming abeam of? He wracked his memory, but couldn't remember for sure. He had gotten sloppy, assumed that the radar would work when they needed it. He knew in his heart that Lars would have always taken a good fix at a course change, radar or no radar, and he felt as if he had betrayed the old man's confidence in him.

"See now, Davie, sea will always be waiting for you to let down your guard. You must always be vigilant." He remembered Lars telling him again and again to always double-check his navigation as they went along.

David checked the handwritten table that Lars had made and posted on the wall; it showed how fast they'd be going at different engine speeds. Making his best guess on their position, he marked it on the chart, adjusted the throttle back to 1500 RPMs—just eight knots on Lars's speed table, and settled in to look out ahead for driftwood or logs.

Though it was one o'clock, the light already seemed to be weaker, penetrating with difficulty through the thick clouds. The snow wasn't steady, but rather came and went. When it eased, sometimes he could see the faintest hint of the shore through the veil of white. And he wondered if he shouldn't alter course and head in toward the beach until the land appeared. He hoped to fix their position better.

Then the snow came on thicker, and the chance was gone.

Three times David laid out their course to the cove, each time with different speeds, to see whether they could make it before dark if he speeded up. But even the fastest had them approaching the narrow entrance a good hour after dark. He bitterly regretted the extra hour he had taken in his sleeping bag after Annie had called him that morning.

Annie came up and they looked again at all the bays on the chart between them and the cove. They were all the blowholes that they remembered their father speaking of: exposed to the ocean, too deep to anchor in securely, safe only in summer and good weather.

"I guess we better hope it stops snowing," he said anxiously. "Maybe I can find my way in after dark . . . if the snow stops."

"And if it doesn't?" Annie asked.

"All we can do is try and duck into one of those bays and get the anchor down. I don't know what else to do." David was having a hard time keeping his voice even, for he felt trapped with the darkness coming on and no secure place to go.

A big sea roared out of the gloom and they rolled heavily to starboard. "Stabilizers," a voice in his head spoke. "Lars would put the stabilizers in now."

David dashed outside, shaking in the cold even with the heavy coat on. It took him a few minutes to get the stabilizers into the water, and when he made it back inside, he was shivering badly again.

The sound of Lars's coughing drifted up the stairs just then, and Annie hurried to him. It was a little while before she returned, and her face was pale and drawn.

"Lars is throwing up again," she said. "This is not good. It looks like there's blood mixed in with it. David, we've *got* to get help for him tonight. He's struggling just to breathe. I think we should call the Coast Guard or somebody."

Annie went down again and David studied the chart shakily, thinking of where he would say he was. Maybe the Coast Guard would take them to Dad, instead of all the way back to Seattle.

"Call, David, call now! This is getting bad," Annie shouted up to him, and the fright was in her voice as well.

David was still shivering, from the cold, certainly, but

also from the knowledge that he didn't have a firm fix on their location, and he didn't know if he would be able to even find a bay to anchor in if the snow kept up. He reached for the radio, but the knob turned with difficulty, and the radio didn't light up as it had before. He wiggled the connections on the back and one of the wires came right off in his hand. He looked at the end of the wire dully, seeing the white powder of corrosion and electrolysis. Probably it had gotten soaked when they had lost the windows in the Queen's Pond, he thought, and no one had noticed it until then.

Another big sea roared out of the gloom, smacking the stern heavily and slewing them to starboard, but the stabilizers kept them from going completely sideways to the seas, or broaching. Outside it seemed a little darker than just a few minutes before, and David felt nameless terror clutching at him, and he began to shake again.

"I can barely turn the knob," he said loudly so Annie would hear, trying to control his voice, trying not to show the terror he felt. "It's all corroded in back. Water must have gotten inside."

"How about the other one, the CB radio?" Annie came up into the pilothouse. "Maybe that one still works."

David slowly reached up, stunned that their main radio was useless. The CB, a short-range radio, was next to the marine high-frequency radio, and it lit up instantly when he turned it on.

He heard the roaring of another big sea, felt the boat start its sickening rush forward again and suddenly realized the autopilot wasn't working. He grabbed the wheel just as it started to spin rapidly to port as the boat tried to broach before the big sea.

"Okay, okay, there are forty-eight channels. Does the Coast Guard stand by on sixteen, like on the other one?" David asked, trying to get used to steering with the big seas trying to slew the boat sideways. His heart was beginning to pound in his chest.

Annie picked a moment when the boat was more or less on an even keel, reached up, turned the knob to sixteen, and grabbed the microphone.

"Uh, Coast Guard, Coast Guard. Mayday, Mayday, this is the *Karen A*, do you read?" The red transmit light went on as she spoke, but when she let the talk button go, there was no response, only the whistle of static and what might have been voices, but far away and too faint to decipher. She repeated her message, but only got the same result.

David craned his head around to the window on the rear door, hoping to get a glimpse of what was behind them, but it was solid, opaque ice. He felt totally blind, with no visibility in any direction.

"David, David," Annie suddenly said, excitedly. "It's channel twenty-two, isn't it? The one everyone around the cove used to talk on. Remember? It was twenty-two." David struggled to remember, but trying to keep them pointed downwind in the right direction was about all he could handle just then.

She reached up and twisted the knob again over to twenty-two. Instantly the pilothouse was filled with the cheery voice of a woman talking about how to make turkey stuffing. She was so matter of fact, so totally oblivious to what might be happening just a few miles away, that it stunned the twins, and they stood there speechless.

"I got some of those mailboat apples last week, and they weren't too bad. I ordered Granny Smiths, nice and tart, but all they had in town was those bland Red Delicious. I told Ronnie Davis that I had ordered the Grannies, but he said those Reds were all they had."

"It's Millie, the nurse—she's there! In the cove! Remember her voice?" Annie keyed the transmit switch. "Hello, hello, Millie, it's Annie, Annie Ross, remember me? We're in Lars Hansen's boat, the *Karen A.* Lars is really sick, and our radar's broken and we're out in the ocean trying to find the cove. It's real snowy and rough and we can't see anything. Oh Millie, can you help us? Mayday! Mayday!" She let go of the button, and they both listened eagerly.

There was a long soft static whine, and then a tentative voice.

"Millie? Somebody walked all over you on that last one. I couldn't get it all, but it sounded like somebody in trouble, and they said something about old Lars and the *Karen A.* Um, this is Hidden Cove, back to the call, how do you read?"

"Oh, Hidden Cove, Hidden Cove, this is Annie on the *Karen A.* Lars is really sick, and our radar's broken. We're trying to find the cove, and it's snowing so thick we can't see anything. Please, we need help."

Another big sea slammed into their stern, and they could hear the water rushing around the iced-over pilothouse. There was a thump on top of the roof, something rattled for a moment and stopped. When Annie let go of the transmit button to listen, there was only silence. No static, or distant voices, just silence, even though the channel dial was still lit.

Several drops of water fell suddenly by the compass, and the twins both looked up, surprised. The water was coming from the CB's antenna wire, where it made a big loop between the place where it went through the ceiling and the radio itself.

David reached up and pulled gently on it, as if to seat the wire a little better into the silicone sealant he had put on it in Seattle. Instead, the wire pulled easily in his hand, and before he could stop, it came completely through the ceiling, and water dripped steadily through the hole.

"Busted off," he said in a dull, flat voice. "It must have iced over heavy and snapped off with the weight."

"They must have heard us," Annie answered. "How about hooking the CB up to the other radio's antenna? That might work." David could hear the sharp edge of fear in Annie's voice.

"I don't know. It's about all I can do just to steer." David was having a hard time thinking. His arms were aching from fighting the steering wheel in just the short time since the autopilot stopped working.

"Here, can you take over?" He throttled back and waved his sister in behind the wheel. "I want to make one last try at finding a harbor, but I've got to get some of that ice off the windows. Steer around ten degrees. You got to hold on tight because the big ones try to throw you around. Don't let it happen with me out there. I might get swept off."

"David?" She was terrified at the thought of him going out there, of what would happen to all of them if they broached and he went over the side. But then the spokes were in her hands, fighting her, and the effort of trying to keep them headed straight took all her attention.

He had to use the big screwdriver to lever the door open, and even with it, struggled to get it wide enough to get through.

They were iced-up even worse than he had thought, the pipe rails swollen and bloated. He could feel the boat's motion get slower and heavier, and he knew if he didn't find a harbor and chip the ice off, they would capsize before morning. He clipped the safety line around the railing and cautiously inched forward to scrape the windows.

"Okay," he said when he got back inside the cabin, taking over the wheel from Annie. "Let's edge over toward the shore again one last time while it's still light. When we get in a little closer, I'm going to have you steer, and I'll look from outside, okay?" He could see more through the windows than before, but once they got in close, he wanted to be outside, in case the seas started breaking behind them.

David worked the wheel over to starboard, edging them closer to the shore, alternately watching the Fathometer and peering ahead through the snow. Ahead were only dark seas and swirling white, and the depth flashed steadily at 120 fathoms—more than 700 feet. Then, in the same moment that the flasher began to display shallower and shallower water, he could feel the shape of the big seas changing and getting steeper.

He slowed the engine, gave the wheel to Annie, and stepped out into the swirling snow again to try to see. It was very cold, and the light was failing fast. He desperately wanted to find a harbor for the night, and knew this would be their last chance. In another half hour it would be full dark.

With the snow, approaching the land without radar would be impossible.

The whirling wall of white to starboard seemed to thicken for a moment. Was it land? He peered off to the side intently, unable to tell for sure.

"Slow down some more," he shouted, "I think I see something." Annie jumped at the sound of her brother's voice, pulled the throttle back and tried to see ahead.

The snow stung David's eyes, but the form in the swirling white took shape, and then he was sure what it was: the steep rock face of the shore itself, with the filigreed shapes of snow-covered trees above the frozen rock.

Annie and David yelled out "Land!" almost in the same moment, and she steered off to port to try to parallel the shore at the edge of visibility. David strained his eyes peering into the gloom. The land disappeared and there was only snow. There was a noise, too, that he didn't recognize. Then suddenly he saw land: to port, starboard, and in front, too, and it hit him with sickening clarity—the noise was the roaring of the surf in a blind cove, with land on three sides, shelterless, rocky, a death trap.

The shoulder of the sea ahead of them suddenly rose unexpectedly high, blocking his glimpse of the land. Then his sister's voice came, shrill and terrified, "David, it's getting shallow!"

The great hill of water before them seemed to shudder and then sink with great tendrils of spray blown back toward them. He knew it was breaking and he knew what to do. All at once he was in the pilothouse, shouldering Annie aside, turning the wheel violently to port and, as soon as they were two-thirds the way around, shoving the throttle all the way against the stop, to maximum speed.

And then they were over the top of the next big sea, the engine racing for a moment as the propeller came out of the water. They surged downhill, and David throttled back instinctively so as not to bury the bow in the trough. The sea behind that one was a little less steep, and he knew they had escaped.

His whole body shook, cold from being outside and terrified about closing in on the land again. He felt Annie's arms around him, so tight he could feel the beating of her heart.

"I'm sorry, Annie," he said, trying hard to control his shivering but failing. "There wasn't any harbor there, and now it's too dark to try again."

Just then, as if to demonstrate what lay ahead, they came over the top of another sea, not a big one, but it threw enough spray to instantly freeze over the windows again.

"David, look! There's something out there!" Annie's finger drilled into his heavy coat, and she pointed at the windows. Clearly visible through the only unfrozen section was a dim light of some sort, bobbing and dancing as if it were on a boat. As they watched, two more lights appeared near the first one. The three lights seemed to be angling away from the *Karen A*.

"David, maybe it's a boat, maybe somebody heard us! Turn on the spotlight so they can see us!"

"No, here, steer a minute. I'll use a flare. The lights are so iced-over, they'll never see them." Lars had showed them where the emergency equipment was, and David took the flare gun from under the chart table and stepped outside.

The wind was even stronger than just a few minutes before, but he could clearly see three boats spread out in a line, their spotlights sweeping across the wild expanse of flying snow and moving hills of water. As he watched, a big sea passed between them, and for a moment the whole top of it was shining transparent green from the three spotlights beaming into it. And then the other boats burst over the top, the spray flying high and wide. For a brief moment he could see the shapes of the boats clearly, and he was sure the middle one was their father's.

"Annie," he cried out, fumbling to put one of the big parachute flare cartridges into the gun. "It's Dad, it's Dad, it's the *Sea Bird*, I'm sure of it!"

Annie released the wheel and darted out the pilothouse door to get a better look. Already, in just the few minutes since they had first seen them, the lights of the boats were noticeably dimmer, and she knew it was the ice. The boats came over another sea as she watched, and the spotlight from one shone briefly on the boat in the middle, and she felt the thrill of recognition.

David got the gun loaded just then, unlocked the safety, raised it over his head, and pulled the trigger. The big gun recoiled heavily, but there was no bright flare light, and he thought it was a dud, soaked that night in the Queen's Pond. The three boats turned a little more to the east, and started to draw away, and he stood there in disbelief; they hadn't been seen, and in a moment the snow would hide them completely.

Then the night was suddenly turned to day as the flare went off high above them, illuminating a hundred acres of water with its brilliant red light.

The three boats turned as one toward the *Karen A*, and Annie darted inside to throttle back, so they were just jogging along easy into the seas.

The lead boat drew closer, into the bright circle of light, and the twins could see the ice had already started to accumulate on it, giving it that eerie, bearded look they had become so familiar with.

But even so, they were positive it was the *Sea Bird*. The old, familiar boat came closer and rounded up to them until it was traveling slowly parallel, perhaps fifteen yards off, so the two boats wouldn't be swept into each other by the seas.

A man came out on deck, and they recognized him at once as their dad, even in the wind, the flying spray, and the strange light. And his voice came across the water, strong and sure, "Annie, David, is it really you?"

"*Dad, Dad, Dad!*" they both cried, yelling and waving, and for a few hundred yards the two boats traveled side by side, as they all tried to talk over the wind and flying spray.

"Follow me," the powerful voice carried over on the wind. "The cove's up around the corner. Just follow me."

Peter Ross went inside the *Sea Bird*'s cabin and slowly throttled up, swinging around easy until the channel to the cove was clearly displayed on his radar screen.

He looked out back to be sure the *Karen A* was following. The flare was lower to the water, but he could still see the other two boats taking up station on either side of Lars's boat. He engaged his autopilot, and looked long and hard at the boat that carried his children.

The flare dropped into the water, and the night was again

very black. But the other boats kept their searchlights on the *Karen A* the whole time as they steamed slowly along downwind. The seas humped up as the invisible channel closed around them, and there was an anxious moment, but then they were all through the worst of it and the great high shoulder of the island began protecting them from the wind.

In the morning Peter Ross rose quietly, taking care not to wake the twins. He lit the Aladdin kerosene lamp, adjusted the height of the bright flame to dim, took it into the spare bedroom, and set it on the table by their beds. After all those weeks of sharing tight quarters on the *Karen A*, his children refused to be separated last night. They were even reluctant to be away from Lars and his familiar snore.

It was all so unreal. Wednesday's mailboat had brought a letter from his ex-wife. She hated to write with bad news, but the children had disappeared. She had notified the authorities, but so far, no word. He went wild, packing and making plans to take the *Sea Bird* to Sitka and catch the next available plane to the Lower 48. Then this rough weather started and he was a prisoner in his own cabin, aching with fear and worry. And now, here they were, so grown up since he'd last seen them.

His little girl was becoming a woman, and his boy so strong and tall. He studied the faces on the pillows, serene in sleep, wishing they would wake. Finally he took the lamp out and closed the door quietly.

Peter made coffee, sat by the woodstove, and marveled

once again at the events of the previous evening. He'd packed and repacked his bag several times during the day, praying for word that the weather was improving and he could get to Sitka without drowning himself in the process, when Millie knocked frantically at his door.

"Peter, it's your children!" She was out of breath and didn't even have a coat on. He pulled her inside, closed the door, and waited for her to be able to speak. Her story came out in gasps: "Sarah and I were yakking on the radio and someone broke in on our frequency. She said she was your girl, Annie, and that she and David were close by, in Lars Hansen's boat, that Lars was sick and they were trying to find the cove, but their radar was busted and . . . "

Peter flew to the CB radio and realized that he'd turned the volume down too far. He turned the knob and instantly recognized the voices of some of the other fishermen from the cove:

" . . . my engine's apart just now, so I'll go with Roger, he's got a bigger boat anyway. Anyone heard Peter on yet?"

"I saw Millie heading over there . . . "

Peter picked up the microphone and broke in, "Breaker, breaker, yeah, this is Peter. *Karen A, Karen A*, pick me up, *Karen A*, come in, please." But when he released the transmit switch on the microphone, there had been only the faraway static whine. He called again with only the same result. Finally a clipped tense voice came back to him.

"Peter. Roger here. We've been calling ever since we heard that call to Millie, but their radio must have died. I just got aboard, but I had my alternator belts off, so it'll be a couple of minutes before I can get underway. Jimmy was just going aboard his boat when I got here, and I think Kevin was coming down the dock. It's making up out there, dress warm . . . "

Peter clicked the transmit switch twice in the traditional radio shorthand for "Got it," dropped the microphone to dangle on its cord and was at the closet, pulling out a hat, parka, and gloves, all in the same motion.

As he did, the radio spoke again, "Everybody in the cove, let's go up one to leave this channel free." Then different voices chimed in, "Judy, going up," "Ron and Susie, going up," "Karen going up." For in a place like Hidden Cove with no regular telephones, the CB radio was like an old-fashioned party line, with an almost-constant stream of news and gossip for anyone who tuned in.

"Millie." Peter was at the door, boots on, ready to go. "I don't know what's going on. I know it'll be a bad night out there. Whoever we find will probably be really cold. Maybe you could start running a tub—here and maybe at your place, too. The hot water takes so long."

Then he was gone, out the door and running, sniffing the air, taking in the windy, snowy night. He had been watching his wind gauge when Roger was talking on the CB: fifteen miles per hour and ten degrees. Outside the harbor, it would be blowing even harder: perfect icing conditions.

As he ran he could hear generators starting up and see lights coming on around the cove. Shapes of other figures walked rapidly toward the dock, and he could see flash-lights across the cove as others got into their skiffs to motor across as the word of an emergency at sea quickly spread among the twenty or so houses that made up the small settlement. They knew, as he did, that it could be his missing children—or could it?

As he walked carefully down the icy ramp, the engine of his boat started up with a puff of smoke out the stack. A moment later the running lights came on and the radar antenna began to rotate: Kevin, his crewman, had made it there before him. The two young men who worked on Roger's and Jimmy's boats were standing on the dock by the tie-up lines.

"All ready to go, Peter," Kevin called down from the pilothouse.

"Let's just wait until this little squall passes so we can find our way out of here." As Peter spoke, a gust of wind and snow swept down from the hills, the air full of thick flakes that temporarily blinded them all. Then it was gone, and Peter could see the red flasher blinking in the harbor mouth. He untied the lines and stepped aboard, pushing off as he did.

Outside the harbor the visibility dropped almost to nothing, and the three boats spread out to cover as wide an area as possible. They called the *Karen A*, switching up and down the channels, called and called, but there was no answer. They all saw the pictures on their radars slowly dimming from the ice on the antennas, and felt their boats' motion change from the weight of it. No one voiced the concern aloud, but everyone knew that they would have to turn around soon to go back into the harbor and knock off the ice before they could go out again. The three boats had just come close together and were talking about going in, and Peter wondered if the whole thing wasn't some sort of cruel radio hoax.

Then in that wonderful instant, the night turned to day as the brilliant flare burst high over them, and there was the *Karen A*—ghostlike, iced-up, heavy—and there were his children.

It had been like a dream. They jogged side by side, waved at each other and tried to yell back and forth over the wind and the distance. Finally they headed in. As they made the last turn into the cove and the sea died away, he saw a procession of lights winding from the cabins down toward the dock. The whole community had been listening to the unfolding drama on the CB, and everybody was coming down to welcome Lars and the twins home.

He watched them dock, Annie out on deck with the stiff and frozen lines ready in her gloved hands. David carefully reversed just at the right moment at the float. Peter docked in front of them, left the tying up to Kevin, and ran down the slippery dock, jumped aboard and wrapped them both up in his arms until he thought he would burst. The tears ran down his cheeks and froze into his beard.

Then everyone in the cove was hurrying down the ramp onto the dock, calling out to the twins, talking, and trying to hug them all at the same time. Millie pushed down the wheelchair, and enlisted Peter and Kevin to wrap Lars in blankets, bring him up from the foc's'le, carry him off the boat and into the wheelchair on the dock.

The crowd hushed and stepped back to give them room.

"He's alive," Millie called out to the waiting faces. "He's breathing, but he's real cold. We need to get him up to my place and into the tub, get some fluids into him." Four men quickly stepped forward to maneuver Lars up the ramp and across the frozen ground, with Millie breathlessly following behind.

It had been a miracle. There was no other word for it.

Peter looked around his house, just one floor, with three bedrooms and a bath off one end and a big "everything" room on the other. It was Christmas Eve, but there was hardly a decoration in sight. When the twins had left, it had taken the heart out of Christmas for him.

He looked in on the twins again. They were still asleep. They would probably sleep half the day or more, after all they had been through. He wanted to wake them up, wanted to ask them a hundred things, but knew they needed to rest. When he had finally gotten them into the house, they had been too tired to do anything but tumble from the tub to their beds.

When Peter made his first pot of coffee, he discovered how empty the propane refrigerator was. He'd purposely eaten through everything in preparation for leaving. Quietly he closed the door to the twins' room and turned on the CB radio.

"I figured you'd be calling," answered Ronnie Davis, the owner of the settlement's store. "After seeing the twins and old Lars on the dock last night, I remembered you hadn't gotten any fresh food on the last mailboat on account of your hunting trip. Just that bad-news letter from your ex. Don't that take the cake? C'mon over, we can fix you up."

Peter wrote a quick note on the back of an envelope in case the twins woke while he was gone. He put on his cold-weather gear and quietly stepped outside. The wind had stopped in the night and the sun had just come over the mountain. From each cabin around the cove a plume of wood smoke rose straight into the stillness of the day.

Walking down to the dock, Peter felt very different than he had just the morning before. The way the sun slanted and played on the cabins and the boats at the dock, the way the spruce trees smelled, the way the sea out beyond the point sounded; somehow having the twins come home so unexpectedly made it all much richer. Then he realized: so much of him had been taken away when the twins had left, it was as if he'd been only half alive all the years since.

He brushed the new snow off the seat of his rowboat, shoved off from the float, and slowly stroked across the narrow harbor, glad that he didn't have to ruin the stillness of the morning with an outboard motor.

Hidden Cove, like many small communities in Southeast Alaska, was built around a long and narrow harbor. There were neither roads nor cars, and many residents used a small boat or skiff to get back and forth.

Ronnie Davis stepped out of the door of his floating business that served as Hidden Cove's store, bar, fish-buying station, and post office, and took Peter's bowline. In a place where the tide rises and falls twenty feet every six hours, having a store built on a big raft of floating logs made a lot of sense. Ronnie could carry the groceries from the mailboat right in the front door without having to lug everything up a ramp onto a dock, across the dock to shore, and so on. Many of the residents had their own docks, so it was very convenient to just row or motor over to the store.

"The wind came on harder after you guys got in last night," Ronnie said quietly. "I came down around three to check on things here. You'd never know it now, though." He nodded out at the still harbor.

"It was really bad out there," Peter answered. "They're lucky to be alive."

The two men stood on the float quietly for a long moment, looking across at Lars's boat at the town dock. The night before, Peter's eyes had been for his children, and getting them into the harbor. He hadn't looked at the boat that carefully. But now, in the clear light of day, the sobering dimension of the boat and their trip was plain. The *Karen A* lay listing slightly to one side from the weight of the accumulated ice. The radio antennas were both broken off, and the radar, raft, rigging, trolling gurdies, and anchor winch were all sheathed in thick ice. The three forward windows had been broken out and replaced by plexiglass. Except for the salt-covered exhaust pipe, there was hardly a place on the boat's exterior that wasn't thickened with a coat of ice.

Then Peter spoke, "Mind if I use your radio? I've gotta call the Coast Guard and tell them to take the kids off the 'missing children' list. Guess I better call their mother, too, if I can find her." And the two of them turned and went in.

Annie woke to the smell of bacon, wriggled up from the thick down comforter, and looked around. There were her dolls on the shelf in the corner, there were her old schoolbooks, there was the picture of the *Sea Bird* that she had painted in second grade. It was her room.

"It's not a dream."

Peter turned from his cooking to see Annie standing in front of the woodstove in a long bathrobe, slowly looking around. He went over and hugged her again for a long time. Neither wanted to let go. Finally he got his coffee, put the bacon on a used paper bag to drain, and they both sat down by the warm stove.

"On the boat, I used to dream I was here. I'd wake up and it would be dark and I'd be way under the covers. I didn't want to come out, because I knew that I'd be on the boat again. And it was so cold," Annie got up and stood as close as she could to the woodstove. "Dad, David and I, we dreamed about all this," she waved her arms around the room. "But the trip was so long and so hard, at the end we even stopped dreaming."

"Oh, honey, I can't believe you went through all that," Peter said, his voice catching in his throat, "to find me."

The bedroom door opened, and David burst in to run over and wrap his arms around Peter. Then David also stood as close to the woodstove as he could in his sweats.

Peter nodded toward a closed door. "Hey, David, I'm sorry about your room. I've been using it as a storeroom. We'll clean it out and get you back in there."

"Yeah, I want to get all my stuff spread out around me again," David said. "Oh, man, it's so great to be warm!" David put his hands out over the woodstove and rubbed them together as if over a fire. "It was like, after we got the windows busted out in the Queen's Pond, the stove in the boat could never really keep up with the cold."

Then he looked around, as if remembering something. "Lars," he said, suddenly anxious. "How is Lars?"

"He's going to be okay," said Peter. "Of course, he'll never have full use of that one arm again, but we can help out whenever he needs it, right? Millie says we can stop by and see him later on."

The twins looked immensely relieved. And then it all came tumbling out: coming home to no mom and no furniture, finding Lars, the pictures of themselves on the milk carton, Lars's spells, breaking down, the man that attacked Annie, the Native friends who helped them, and all the rest of their trip.

The twins talked as Peter set the table and laid the food out before them: eggs, bacon, pancakes, juice, and canned milk. They ate and talked, and ate some more.

"Well, you two don't have to worry about the milk cartons anymore," Peter said. "I called the Coast Guard from the store this morning. I told them you were in safe hands now, and that you were going to stay in safe hands.

"And . . . " The twins realized that their father was having a hard time talking about something else. "Well, it's your mom. I tried to call her this morning, too. They wouldn't let me talk to her, but at least I got to leave a message that you were okay and here. She does love you guys, you know? She's just . . . anyway, she's trying rehab again."

The twins exchanged glances, then looked directly at their dad.

"Maybe this time, huh, Dad?" David said. He rose, took his plate over to the sink, and stopped by a picture on the wall. It was the *Sea Bird,* tied to what looked like a new dock, with old cannery buildings in the background that someone was fixing up.

"Dad, is this the old cannery up the head of the bay?"

"Oh, yeah," Peter said, "we got some of that state oil money, you know, and we're fixing the place up to do something with all the fish around here."

There was a knock at the door, and David stepped over to open it.

A group of adults and kids stood outside in a little half circle around a perfectly shaped silver fir Christmas tree about seven feet high. "Merry Christmas!" they shouted, then laughed for a moment at the surprised look on the faces of Peter and the twins. Next they launched into a ragged rendition of "O Christmas Tree."

"Hey, Peter!" It was Kevin, the man who crewed on Peter's boat. "It's been five years since you've had a Christmas tree. We thought you'd want one, but might be a little pressed for time."

Peter stepped out to touch the tree with its erect, dark cones that mark a true fir.

"I . . . I . . . thank you," he could only stammer. Kevin's wife handed Annie a tin filled with Christmas cookies, then the group headed off down the path, and Kevin called back over his shoulder, "Remember, kids, if you're up for it, today's the day to catch your Christmas King, and there's the community dinner tonight."

"Dad, it's the *Christmas King,* it's *tradition*!" Annie and David chimed together. In the cove, it was custom for fathers to take their families out on the day before Christmas. They'd drag the hooks for a while outside the harbor, and the king salmon went to the children, who would sell them at the store and use the money for gifts.

The twins wrestled the tree through the door as Peter rummaged around until he found the stand and set it up in one corner of the cabin.

"Dad," Annie said, "we got some real ornaments. Just a few. We'll get them from the boat, and then we can put fishing ornaments on like always."

"I think most of the boat stuff's here." Peter waved at a collection of bags and boxes by the door. "Kevin brought it all up this morning already. He figured you might be needing your stuff . . . "

Peter put some logs into the woodstove, made himself a cup of coffee, and brought out the box of ornaments from the closet. Many were homemade—the angel carved from driftwood, with an aluminum foil crown, the hand-carved fishing lures, with tooth scratches in the paint—and each had a tale to be shared once again: a family tradition.

Annie unwrapped two small and old glass balls, and another tale was added to those already on the tree. She told Peter of the day she had spent with the kind Native woman on their floating house in the vast wilderness north of Johnstone Strait.

David added a carved fish he had made with the knife John had given him, on one of the first nights of their trip, and told about their stay with the friendly couple in the cabin near Turn Point while Lars recuperated from his stroke.

And the three of them sat with the sweet fragrance of the tree filling the room and talked of all that had passed since the last time they had been there together. Finally Peter got up to put the ornament box away, and when he turned back around there were two gifts under the tree, in newspaper wrap, but tied with bright ribbon.

Peter felt his eyes get hot and busied himself at the sink for a moment. When he turned around, he started to say something about not having any presents for them, but Annie cut him off.

"Dad, don't you see?" She waved her arm, taking in the tree, the room, and the whole cove and community outside. "This is our Christmas—it was our dream for years to come home again, to you and to all of this."

There was a toot of a boat horn just then and David got up to peer out the window. "Hey, Dad," he said excitedly, "The *Princess* and *Wanderer* are leaving the dock already. We better get going! It'll be dark soon and we want to catch our Christmas King. But first we want to go see Lars, okay?"

Millie's place was just a short hike away. Peter rapped on the door and led the way in without waiting for an answer. From the kitchen, Millie called, "Come on in! Lars will be so glad to see you!" The trio stepped out of their boots at the door, then filed into the back bedroom, where Lars was resting. Over the bed hung an IV bag with a tube that led to the old man's arm. But he was awake, and the color was back in his face. Peter went over and hugged him the best he could.

"Thank you, Lars. Thank you for bringing them home. You are an amazing man," he said. The twins smiled from the foot of his bed.

"It was them," Lars said to Peter in his hoarse, accented voice, as he nodded at David and Annie. "I never do it without them. After Butedale, I was sick, too sick to get up. They came all that way. They are the ones who are amazing."

Lars started to cough and Millie shooed everybody out

of the bedroom. She came out a minute later and closed the door behind her.

"He's tough," Millie said admiringly. "I gave him some fluids and started him on an antibiotic, and he perked right up by this morning. If he keeps it up like that, he'll be fishing again by spring."

"We want him to move in with us, when he's ready," Peter said. "It won't be any trouble. And give me the bill for any medical expenses, you hear me?"

Millie grinned and waved them off with an "Oh, you, get on with you now, and Merry Christmas, you Rosses!" and they headed down to the dock.

Peter started up the *Sea Bird*, Annie put away the tie-up lines as if she had been doing it for years, and David maneuvered the vessel away from the dock and into the channel. Peter's eyes fell on the *Karen A*, still iced over and low in the water. He thought about what Lars had said, and the distance from Butedale to the cove. He marveled again at his children, in the cold and snow of the last weeks, picking their way north, not knowing fully how to get to the cove, or even if he would be there if they made it. He remembered the recent nights when he had stopped at the door of his woodshed, looked out into the windy, bitter black, and wished for it to end so he could get out and make a run for Sitka. And his last memory of the twins again, caught off that bleak and unfriendly shore in the blackness, iced-up, with the radar out, trying to find the cove. He shivered at how close they'd come to being lost, on his very doorstep, after coming all that long way.

"Look, it's the *Wanderer* and the *Princess*, and they've got their fish already!" The bright voices of the twins brought him out of his trance. They were just approaching two other boats from the cove, headed in. As they passed close by, a child waving from the pilothouse of each boat made a "big fish" sign with their hands.

Peter lowered the trolling poles, threaded the leaders through the salted herring, and set the hooks, his hands working automatically, but his mind still full of all that had happened so recently.

The low, northern sun burned in the sky, the land and water shone, and Annie was the first to get her fish. A twenty-eight pounder the color of gunmetal rang the bells on the starboard pole when it struck at the smell of the herring in the dark water beneath them. Peter hauled the salmon in carefully, hand over gloved hand. Without a word, Annie handed him the gaff, and they watched the fish, waiting for the moment. It was strong, but Annie could tell that it was tired, and finally, in a long, fluid motion, Peter gaffed it neatly behind the eye, and hauled it up and over the bulwarks. The big fish landed aboard and thrashed on the white and snowy deck for a moment before falling still.

"All right, Annie!" David cheered. "Now it's my turn." They went inside the *Sea Bird*'s pilothouse, and Peter showed the twins how to line up two trees on shore just right so that the herring and the hooks passed through the dark water just above the bottom. An hour passed, the sun disappeared into thick clouds; Peter worried that there would be just one king today.

"Oh, yeah!" David finally sang out, seeing the pole move even before the bells jingled. "I got mine, Dad, I got one!" Peter had him work the gurdies, engaging the clutch, and watching as the stainless wire wound steadily onto the drum. He gave David the gaff, and pulled in the leader until the fish was in the water beneath them. David said nothing, waiting for his chance. When it came, he was ready, gaffing the salmon smoothly and bringing it aboard with only a little help at the very end.

Then a snow squall enveloped them and the twins snuggled into the pilothouse beside their dad. The spray flew as they crossed the channel, running down the windows in slush. Then at last they were across, and the snow let up suddenly as they came around the point and spied the cove before them.

Each cabin was cozily lit in the early dusk, and they saw a procession of little points of light moving slowly along the path from one cabin to another. One of the cove Christmas traditions was walking through the snow, torches in hand, caroling at each cabin in turn.

"Dad, it's the carolers!"

"Can we go, Dad? Could we clean up the boat later? Could we?"

Peter felt his eyes getting hot again. "Your ol' dad's voice isn't that great, but yeah, we can go up. Hold on, though, it'll just take a minute to sell and clean up the boat."

They stopped briefly at Ronnie Davis's dock and left the two salmon in the ice inside the building with a note. Then the twins stood on deck, tie-up lines in their hands, waiting for Peter to come in to the town dock.

The *Sea Bird* made her turn and reversed alongside the float, and the twins jumped down to tie her up.

And then they were gone, the three of them hooting and

running up the ramp together in the pink dusk to catch up with the carolers, to join them in singing the old, familiar songs as a light snow began to fall with the coming of the night.